**Matt McGuire** was born in Belfast and taught at the University of Glasgow before becoming an English lecturer at the University of Western Sydney, Australia. He has published widely on various aspects of contemporary literature and is the author of the first DS O'Neill novel, *Dark Dawn*.

# Also by Matt McGuire
*Dark Dawn*

# When Sorrows Come

## Matt McGuire

Constable & Robinson Ltd
55–56 Russell Square
London WC1B 4HP
www.constablerobinson.com

First published in the UK by C&R Crime,
an imprint of Constable & Robinson, 2014

A copy of the British Library Cataloguing in
Publication data is available from the British Library

ISBN 978-1-78033-832-3 (trade paperback)
ISBN 978-1-47210-611-7 (ebook)

1 3 5 7 9 10 8 6 4 2

Printed and bound in the UK

'When sorrows come they come not single spies but in battalions ...'

William Shakespeare, *Hamlet*

*For Claire*

# ACKNOWLEDGEMENTS

I would like to thank my agent, Peter Straus at RCW, for his support and enthusiasm. All the team at Constable & Robinson, but particularly James Gurbutt for his insightful editorial suggestions. I would also like to thank my colleagues at the University of Western Sydney, especially Peter Hutchings, Sara Knox, Gail Jones, Brian Stout, Anthony Ulhmann, Ivor Indyk, Hazel Smith, Chris Andrews and the members of the Writing and Society Research Group. The support of my family has been consistent throughout the writing of this book – Maree, Liam, Jack – and I cannot thank them enough.

# ONE

**Belfast, 2 a.m., Tomb Street**

A man, a boy really, beaten to a pulp. Cracked ribs, broken jaw, fractured skull. Kicked in the head, too many times to count. Around him a puddle, slowly expanding, a halo of blood and piss and rain. The air was damp, clouds gathering, more rain on the way.

Tomb Street runs through the docks, going nowhere, at least nowhere you'd want to be at two in the morning. At the far end, a young fella stumbled out of a nightclub with a skinful on him. He was thinking a slash, then a taxi up the road. He staggered a hundred yards, ducked into an alley, unzipped his fly. He squinted over his shoulder, into the dark, at a shape, motionless on the ground. Even in this light, in this state, he could tell.

The mobile came out – 'Ambulance ... Tomb Street ...'

Back at the club it was chucking-out time. Young ones poured out like the walking wounded. Wee girls in too much make-up and not enough skirt. In the middle of the road, a boy of seventeen put his hands on his knees and puked his ring. His mates stood watching, pissing themselves.

The ambulance arrived, parting the sea of bodies. It parked at the mouth of the alley and two paramedics stepped down. They moved slowly, in green overalls, like tired workmen. One of them crouched and put two fingers to the boy's

1

throat. He stared into space and waited – nothing.

He looked at his partner, face set, and slowly shook his head. The other man shrugged and headed back to the rig for the paperwork.

Five minutes later, a police Land Rover rumbled into Tomb Street. It parked up, the tape came out, the alley sealed – POLICE LINE DO NOT CROSS. No one noticed, no one cared. The stragglers had moved on, heading for town and the weekly shoving match over kebabs and taxis. The armoured wagon sat there, squat and scarred, like a front row forward. It gazed after them, its windscreen a blank pitiless stare.

O'Neill pulled into Tomb Street in an unmarked Mondeo, a pool car that smelled like stale sweat and cold coffee. The town had been jumping since he came on – Drunk and Disorderly, Aggravated Assault, the usual Saturday night.

O'Neill was a DS, mid-thirties but looking closer to forty; eight years of shift work will do that to you. His hair was cut close, going grey at the sides. Beneath his shirt he wore a medal, Saint Michael, the patron saint of peelers. O'Neill wasn't religious. His ex-wife had given it to him when he joined up and he figured, what the hell, might as well have someone watching your back. Catherine had jumped ship last year, taking their six year-old daughter with her. They were still in Belfast though, in the old house, and he saw Sarah on weekends, when the shifts allowed.

O'Neill sat in the Mondeo for a moment, staring at Tomb Street, at the warehouses and their walls that were black like a cancerous lung. This was old Belfast, the docks. Half a mile away were the shipyards, or what was left of them. The place was being redeveloped. The Titanic Quarter, all luxury flats and loft apartments, the new Northern Ireland, at least that's what the brochure said. O'Neill looked in his rear-view mirror. A teenager was pissing in the street while his mate lurched at the traffic, trying to flag a cab.

Tomb Street had come in just after two – Suspicious Death. O'Neill had grabbed a set of car keys, glad to get out of Musgrave Street and the pile of paperwork on his desk.

He opened the car door and approached the Land Rover, recognizing Terry Donnelly, a uniform with ten years on him. There was another cop there, young looking, like he was bunking off school.

'Who are you then?'

'Green, sir.'

O'Neill smiled, thinking 'No shit.'

'How old are you?'

'Twenty-one.'

'How long you in?'

'Three weeks.'

'You meet our friend then?' O'Neill thumbed at the alley.

The rookie nodded doing his best Clint Eastwood, like he saw bodies everyday, at Tesco or the youth club, or wherever it was his life had been before it stuck a uniform on him and brought him to Tomb Street. You could see it a mile away – the pretence, the bullshit, the fakery. They all did it, especially at the start. Don the mask, like you'd seen it all before, like nothing could surprise you. Then one day, without noticing, you turn round and realize it's true. O'Neill turned and nodded towards the young fella perched in the back of the wagon.

'Jerome Collins,' Donnelly said. 'Found the victim.'

O'Neill gave him the once-over – hands, face, shoes – no sign of a scrap.

'Where's he from?'

'Downview Avenue.'

It was Volvo country – doctors, lawyers, accountants.

'Said he was in the club, heading home, needed a piss. Dandered into the entry, found your man, called the ambulance.'

'Does he know him?'

'No.'

'Record?'

'Nah. I called it in and they put him through the PNC. Computer says he's clean.'

'If the computer says so ...' O'Neill said cynically. 'Right. Move the tape back, seal the street, start the log. Everyone that comes in or out.'

He stepped away, pulled out his mobile and called Ward. The DI answered first ring and said he was on his way.

O'Neill looked back down the alley. Tomb Street would bring the flies. There'd be journalists, newsmen, reporters – all looking for a story, a bit of excitement for the folks back home, munching on their Corn Flakes.

He looked towards town. They'd need to do a canvass. He called the duty sergeant and asked for more bodies. Robinson laughed – it was Saturday night, two in the morning, he could have three.

O'Neill walked to the back of the wagon and Jerome Collins. The kid was eighteen, nineteen tops. He was rat-arsed, the eyeballs rolling in his head. O'Neill shook his head and called Donnelly over.

'Take a statement, get a signature, send him home. Custody's full, he's no priors and we need him sober anyway.'

O'Neill turned back to the entry, smelling the vomit, the

4

piss, the stale beer. He crouched down, putting his torch on the body, trying not to think. Ward had taught him his first year in CID. You stayed stupid, just looked, allowed the scene to register.

The victim was an IC1 male, five foot ten, early twenties. He was in dark jeans, brown brogues and a pale-blue shirt. Well turned out, O'Neill thought, from a nice home. From the dirt it looked like he'd rolled a bit, probably covering up, trying to protect himself. At his head was a puddle, black and viscous, like a miniature oil spill. O'Neill looked at the face. It was swollen, distorted, like it had been used as a punch bag. It was starting to bruise. Right eye shut, lip split, forehead open. O'Neill sighed. Someone had hit this guy and kept on hitting him, long after it ceased to be a fight.

He thought about other Saturday nights, other assaults – the streaming blood, the broken noses, the missing teeth. He frowned, looking at his new friend.

Behind O'Neill a white van pulled up and two scenes of crime officers got out. They put on their white suits and took out a camera. Sporadic flashes lit the walls of the entry.

'Someone send for the cavalry?'

O'Neill turned to see Ward step out of the darkness. The DI was in his fifties with a full head of hair and a moustache he'd never thought to get rid of. He had bags under both eyes, like it was a long time since he'd seen a full night's sleep. Ward always looked tired, but O'Neill wondered if something was up, if the idea of his retirement next year wasn't starting to work him over.

He shone the torch on the corpse. 'Meet contestant number one.'

Ward crouched down. 'All right, son. What about you?'

5

The DI was twenty-eight years in, ex-RUC, one of the few that hadn't jumped ship after the Agreement. The prisoner release had done it for most of them. Watching the TV as five hundred men walked out of jail: gunmen, bombers, murderers, guys who had killed cops, shot them walking the dog, in front of their wives, in front of their kids. And now they were all out, back on the street, like butter wouldn't melt in their mouths. Half the force had walked away, going for early retirement; you couldn't blame them.

Ward stood next to O'Neill, two cops at opposite ends of their careers. O'Neill was in CID three years and still felt like the job was a privilege. Being paid to go out there, to be a witness, to see a world that folk never saw. He felt like he knew things, that he was privy to secrets, that he understood words like evil, violence, brutality. Ward, on the other hand, could smell retirement round the corner. He was tired, exhausted, done. Thirty years of wading through the shit. In quiet moments, over a smoke or in the car, it would dawn on him, what he'd learned after it all, the one thing he was sure of – there was only so much one man can shovel.

Ward turned to O'Neill. 'So talk then.'

'Saturday night special. Looked at the wrong bird, bumped the wrong guy, said the wrong thing. A lot of reasons to get your head kicked in out here.' O'Neill pointed to the club at the end of Tomb Street. 'Fiver says he was in there.'

Behind them two DCs, Kearney and Larkin, pulled up in a black Astra. They got out and Ward briefed them. 'Uniform are coming. Let them know. Then hit the taxi drivers, the kebab shops, the doormen. Anyone half sober.'

The two detectives stepped away. They knew they were

pissing in the wind, so did Ward, but there was procedure to follow, boxes to be ticked.

Ward looked at the body and shook his head. 'Used to be, a guy was on the ground not moving, you stopped pummelling him.'

'The good old days ...'

'I wouldn't go that far.'

'Detectives ...' A voice from behind the tape.

A SOCO floated out of the darkness, holding a wallet. O'Neill gloved up and took it. Inside were credit cards, a driving licence, till receipts. There were business cards – Jonathan McCarthy, Trainee Solicitor, Thompson and James. O'Neill showed Ward.

'A taxpayer.'

Ward smiled and shook his head. 'That's all we need. Wilson will love this.'

The Chief Inspector had a thing about PR. If it had been some wee hood, well then, that was no problem. So long as he didn't make a mess. Taxpayers though, taxpayers were a different matter. They had parents, parents with solicitors, parents that *were* solicitors. They asked questions and wanted answers. When you had citizens getting beat to death outside nightclubs, well, it didn't play too well.

O'Neill looked at the wallet. There were receipts from the club, rounds totalling forty, fifty quid. He showed Ward.

'Lets go then,' the DI said.

At the nightclub, O'Neill made a fist and pounded on the door. He looked up, noting the CCTV camera pointing at the entrance. After a minute a bouncer appeared – sixteen stone, shaved head, monkey brow. O'Neill pulled his warrant card, 'CID-ed' him and stepped in.

The club was industrial chic – leather sofas, exposed brickwork, low arches. The bouncer dragged his knuckles back to the bar and wrapped them round his post-work pint. Three bar staff sat in the corner, a fella and two girls, also having a drink. Behind the taps a figure in a white shirt and tie was emptying the tills. O'Neill noted two more CCTV cameras, one on the bar, one on the dance floor. He stepped up to the chrome counter.

'CID, Musgrave Street. We're here about an incident outside. One of your customers ...'

The man smiled. 'If it's outside then surely they're *a member of the public*?'

The accent was Dublin, smarmy. O'Neill stared at him and waited. Eventually he spoke. 'Who are you?'

'Martin Keenan. I'm the manager.'

Keenan was late thirties with a receding hairline and an expanding waistline. O'Neill could see he rated himself. He imagined sleazy comments directed at blonde girls half his age.

'What do you know about the incident?'

'Know nuttin abou' it.'

'You have any trouble tonight?'

'We don't let it in.'

'Throw anyone out?'

'Like I said. We don't let them in.'

The bouncer grunted, enjoying the show. O'Neill glanced at him, imagining the kid mouthing off, getting thrown out, the bouncer taking him round the back, giving him a hiding. It wouldn't be the first time. He looked round the nightclub. It was owned by Paul Lafferty, who had half the bars in Belfast.

'Nine o'clock,' O'Neill said. 'Monday morning. I want your CCTV, I want every card payment, I want your staff list, I want names, addresses, National Insurance numbers. I want your shift rota – the doormen, the glass collector, the wee African in the toilets ...'

'We don't have a *wee African* ...'

O'Neill glared.

Keenan tried to hold out, but couldn't. 'That'll all take time.'

Ward sighed and stepped forward.

'I'll tell you what'll take time. Explaining to Paul Lafferty why his club's been shut down for six months, why we're sifting through his accounts, why there's a police investigation into his business, why his name's in the paper every week, why no one comes here any more, why—'

Keating raised his hands. 'OK, OK, I get it.'

Ward turned and walked out the door, O'Neill following. On Tomb Street he signalled to Larkin.

'Get statements from everyone. Start with the bar staff, take your time, do the manager last. And check the bouncer for any kind of record.'

O'Neill stepped away and lit a cigarette. Ward drew level and got out his own.

'Wrong side of bed?' O'Neill asked.

'Something like that.'

O'Neill smiled, knowing how it felt. He'd been running uphill for a year, since Catherine left, since Laganview, since he ended up in hospital with a concussion and a dislocated shoulder. He thought about his ex. She said it was the shifts, the late nights, the last minute phone calls – 'A job's just come in ...' You got away with it once, maybe twice. Eventually it wore thin. His daughter Sarah would be seven next weekend. He was supposed to be seeing her tomorrow, a trip to the cinema. O'Neill looked at his phone, knowing he'd have to make another one of those calls.

A white television van pulled up at the end of the road. O'Neill watched as a reporter and a cameraman stepped down and started to set up.

'How'd the press get this?'

Ward rubbed his thumb against two fingers. 'Musgrave Street, leaks like the *Titanic*.'

O'Neill tried not to think about it. He shut the phone call to Sarah out of his head, staying with the job, the details, the facts. He walked down the road, notebook in hand, drawing a map of the street. He marked things out – the club, the alley, the position of the body. He noted the names of various businesses and watched as the SOCOs started to pick their way through the scene. The white suits and facemasks, like a nuclear clean up. In a doorway, he came across three empty cans, Tennent's Super. He picked one up with his pen, looking at it, thinking.

For half an hour he forgot about everything. Forgot about Sarah, about Catherine, about his empty flat in Stranmillis. He forgot about Wilson, the Chief Inspector, about the fact he hated him and wanted him out of CID. He forgot about the pain in his shoulder, the headaches he still got, the emptiness that never seemed to be far away.

At the top of Tomb Street he paused and took in the view. He looked back at the job, watching it unfold – the armoured Land Rover, the uniforms, the SOCOs. He was always taken by it – the story being written, right in front of you, the sudden burst of facts: names, addresses, times; witnesses, statements, phone numbers; photographs, reports, evidence.

O'Neill paused, put his notebook in his pocket and lit a cigarette. He took a drag and exhaled slowly, allowing himself to watch it all, just for a minute.

# TWO

**Sunday, 11.04 a.m.**

Martin Toner skidded the bike to a stop and lowered his hood. He looked back over his shoulder, breathing hard, waiting.

No one came.

High Street was quiet, the shops closed, the town still in its pit. In the distance the Black Mountain and the Cave Hill looked down on the city, a couple of disapproving parents. Pensioners trickled into St George's Church, heads lowered for last minute prayers, the reaper on his way.

Marty glanced at the mountain bike between his legs. It was fifteen speed, brand new, folk should take more care. The guy chased him a few streets, screamed 'You fuckin wee hood' and gave up.

Marty was seventeen and dressed in his usual – grey tracksuit, black trainers, grey top. He had his hood up, shielding his face from security cameras and CCTV that was dotted round the town. There were no bright colours – no logos, no swooshes, nothing you could pick out from a distance. He was bland, easily forgettable, better that way. You lay low, kept your mouth shut, your eyes open. Marty had seen other dealers, all decked out, head to toe in the latest Ted Baker, Nike Air Max and Stone Island. You could tell who was doing well, who was coming up, who to watch out for. It was frigging stupid, Marty thought, advertising yourself like that, attracting attention.

He looked around before stashing the bike behind the café. He still had the black eye from Thursday and looked like any other hood, the kind security guards followed round shops, the kind you saw on street corners, smoking fags and skulling cider. The kind that liked happy hardcore and cursed their heads off, that never had a job in their life. The kind that smoked blow and snorted speed, that sold gear and would fight you at the drop of a hat. The kind that would tell you to go fuck yourself and pull a knife on you as soon as look at you.

Inside the café was dead. There were two fat Americans in matching kagouls. On the back was a cartoon leprechaun, his dukes up – *'The fightin' Irish'*.

'Fucking Yanks,' Marty muttered, spotting Petesy sitting near the back.

The waitress dragged herself between the tables. She was sixteen with pale skin and that pained comedown expression. Marty smiled, recognizing the bloodshot eyes and the zombie walk. She stopped in front of the Americans, bracing herself for the friendliness.

'An Ulster Fry, ma'am,' the man said, like he'd invented it. 'And some of that hot tea.'

'I'll have the same,' the woman chirped.

The waitress groaned and shuffled off. The Americans leaned in, grumbling about the service.

Petesy was sitting down, his walking stick beneath the table. He was wearing glasses and a brown knitted sweater.

'Right, Specky,' Marty said, sitting with back to the wall, like always. 'Love the jumper. You going fishing?'

Petesy gave him the finger.

They'd been friends since they were ten, since Miss Delaney's class, when they sat up the back arguing about which of them she most wanted to ride. At fourteen, they ditched school and spent their days round the town, shoplifting, getting wasted, playing 'FIFA' on the PlayStation.

At sixteen, they'd started dealing, selling blow for Johnny Tierney who ran the Lower Ormeau. For every twelve quarters they shifted, they got one for themselves. After four weeks Marty had had enough.

'This is shite,' he said. 'Even in McDonalds they don't pay you in fucking hamburgers.'

It had been Marty's idea to go out on their own.

'*Dragons' Den*, Petesy son, that's us. Entrepre-fucking-neurs.'

They managed to score a nine bar from Petesy's cousin up the Ardoyne. They knew the risks, knew what would happen if Tierney caught wind of what they were doing.

Marty didn't give a shit. 'He who dares, Petesy son, he who dares.'

They were smart about it, avoided the lower Ormeau and the Markets. They stuck to the Holy Lands, the square mile of student digs around Queen's. It was full of culchies, all with student loans or still on the tit with Mummy and Daddy. They pocketed two hundred quid the first week, twice the week after.

'Businessmen,' Marty proclaimed. 'That's us, son. Businessmen.'

That weekend they celebrated, getting wasted on White Lightning and a load of speed. It was brilliant. Both puked their ring before crawling home at six in the morning.

It was three months before the wheels came off. Tierney had a search party out. Men in ski masks burst into Micky Trainer's party. There were knives, baseball bats, Marty and Petesy were mentioned by name.

Eventually the clock ran out. Marty remembered it like it was yesterday. They were caught, the two of them, and given a hiding. Tierney picked out Petesy and they did his knees. The others pinned Marty down, grinding his face into the concrete, making him watch. They set upon Petesy with hurley bats that had nails through them. It had been a year and still, when Marty closed his eyes, he could hear Petesy screaming, that primal sound, like an animal being tortured.

Afterwards, Petesy had lay sobbing, his legs twisted, his trousers wet from where he'd pissed himself.

When he finally came out of hospital Petesy had quit dealing, said he'd had enough. He went back to the Tech to try and get his exams, some GCSEs, maybe even A-levels. He said he wanted to go to Queens, or somewhere across the water. It was a mug's game, Marty reckoned, Petesy kidding himself. But who was he to say.

Marty was on his own now. He'd no choice and six weeks later started taking Tierney's gear into the Holy Lands, hitting up the same students that him and Petesy had sold to.

That was ten months ago. Now, he had his own crew – Lockesy and wee Anto. They were shifting Tierney's gear but Marty had another supplier as well. It was risky though, the guy lived in Ballybean and was UVF, all tattoos and steroid abuse. He only cared about money though and Marty figured he liked the idea of having his own wee Fenian, messing with Tierney's business. Marty kept the Ballybean gear quiet and didn't tell anyone, not Locksey, not Anto, not anyone.

15

He had three rules that he lived by – you trusted no one, you didn't use dope and you weren't greedy.

In the café, Marty's foot knocked Petesy's walking stick under the table. His mate still needed it – even after four surgeries, three plates and eight pins. He'd always need it and every time he walked into a room, heads would turn and he'd see folk whispering – 'Fucking wee hood... deserved what he got.'

In the café, Petesy ran his hand down his brown jumper.

'Smart, eh?'

'You look like a fruit.'

'Not what your ma said ...'

Marty smiled, realizing how much he missed his mate. Since Petesy went back to the Tech he hardly saw him. He'd stopped hanging out and barely left the house.

'Nice shiner by the way,' Petesy said.

'You should see the other guy.'

Petesy had already heard. The other guy was Dee McNally. He was in the Royal Victoria Hospital with a broken nose, a busted lip and a cracked skull. McNally was eighteen and had already done twelve months in Hydebank Young Offenders. Like Marty said – 'You'd have thought it counted for something.'

They opened their menus, Marty screwing his face up - Irish stew, wheaten bread, champ.

'What's this shit?'

'It's for the tourists,' Petesy said, nodding at Tweedledum and Tweedledee.

The waitress came over.

'Burger and fries, ma'am,' Marty said, in a loud American accent. 'You got any tomay-to sass?'

The girl tried to force a smile. As she walked away Marty studied her arse.

'Like a dog with two dicks,' Petesy said.

Marty took it as a compliment. 'Here,' he said. 'How's the fanny at the Tech anyway?'

'Wouldn't know. Too busy studying.'

'Away an' shite.'

Petesy looked sideways, 'Well, there is this one bird ...'

'Go on, Petesy my son.'

They sat back laughing.

'What about you anyway?'

Marty thrust his fingers under his mate's nose.

'Sinead Walters.'

Petesy pulled back. 'You dirty bastard,' he said, laughing again.

The waitress brought their drinks over. When she left, Marty asked about his knees.

'Right's OK, left's fucked. I should use both the sticks but I can't be arsed.'

Marty remembered visiting Petesy in the hospital after he'd been done. They'd him strung up, in hoists, both legs. His granny arrived, looked at Marty and told him to frig off. Petesy had lived with his granny for four years, since his ma ran off to Derry with some guy she met. The old girl was sharp and knew that whatever led to Petesy ending up in the hospital, you could be sure Martin Toner was involved.

The waitress dropped the plates in front of them and announced, 'Ten eighty.'

Marty produced a twenty-pound note and slapped it down.

'Don't worry,' he said to his mate. 'I've got you.'

Marty always paid.

'How are the books going anyway?' Marty asked. 'You had an exam or something.'

'An essay.' Petesy paused. 'I got a B.'

'What do you mean you got a B?' Marty was annoyed.

'It was a B plus.'

'Aye, plus what?'

'Away to fuck. If you care so much you write the next one.'

Marty was bankrolling Petesy, partly out of guilt, partly to see if he could actually pull it off. Books, A4 pads, pens. He sorted him out with a laptop a couple of months ago, for the assignments and everything. Petesy had phoned him the next day.

'Who's Price Waterhouse?'

'Why?'

''Cause half his shit's still on this computer.'

Marty laughed. 'Just delete it. I'm sure he won't mind.'

They ate their food, talking about birds, about Man U and how Liverpool were still shit. When Marty was finished he put his fork down, his face suddenly serious.

Petesy looked up, still chewing. 'What?'

Marty didn't speak.

'Listen, if you're going to propose you can fuck off.'

Marty smiled. 'I want to tell you something.'

'Look, I already know you're gay ...'

'Fuck up would ye.'

Petesy smiled, then sat quiet, listening.

'I'm gonna do something.'

Petesy waited.

Marty held back. He'd told no one. Petesy was the only one that mattered, the one person he could trust, the only one that needed to know.

'Tierney,' he said.

'Tierney what?'

Marty looked across the table, not speaking.

Petesy's eyes narrowed. 'You're full of shit.'

'I'm not.'

'Wise up.'

'It's them uns that need to wise up.'

'What are *you* gonna do to Johnny Tierney?'

Marty leaned forward, whispering. 'I'm gonna do him, that's what.'

Petesy laughed, his voice trailing off when he saw the serious expression on Marty's face. Tierney was older, in his late twenties. He ran with Sean Molloy, who was another psychopath.

'They'll kill you, you know. And that's if you're lucky.'

'Fuck 'em,' Marty said.

'What about McCann?'

Tierney answered to Gerry McCann who was older, in his fifties, an ex Provo. He ran everything – drugs, racketeering, robbery. Nothing happened within three miles of the Markets without McCann knowing.

'You don't think he'll come for you?' Petesy said.

'He'll need to know it was me first.'

Marty sighed and leaned back in his chair. He told himself he couldn't take it any more. The nightmares, lying in bed – Petesy screaming, pleading with them, begging them to stop. He told himself it was revenge. He remembered Tierney and the others, laughing as they walked away, fucking laughing.

Marty had told himself the same story, over and over – about getting his own back, about what they did to Petesy, about how it wasn't right. It got rid of the fear, helped him get angry, helped him believe in what he was about to do. In his head though, he knew it was about money, about getting rid of Tierney, about making a move.

'They're not getting away with it,' he said, his voice insistent, self-righteous.

'I've news for you,' Petesy said, tapping his leg. 'They already have.'

After a few seconds Petesy spoke again.

'Do you know what they did to wee Stevie?'

'I heard.'

'Aye, all he done was nick twenty quid. They stripped him bollock naked and locked him in a room with a pit bull.'

'Aye, wee Stevie got caught though.'

Petesy shook his head. 'And Skelters. He just disappeared. Jackie said they took him out into the country, to a disused abattoir or something. They hung him up on one of the hooks, left him there and went drinking. When they came back they got the knives out, the butchers' ones, like for gutting the pigs ...'

Marty didn't flinch. 'How does Jackie know what they did?'

'I dunno, but he does.' Petesy looked at his mate's face, realizing it was too late, that he'd already decided.

'What are you going to do?'

'None of your business. You won't be involved. Nobody will. Only me.'

'Who are you? The Lone Ranger?' Petesy lowered his voice. 'Even if you get Tierney, even if you get Molloy, McCann will send someone ...'

'They'll have to know it was me though.'

Petesy shook his head and looked away.

Marty's eyes narrowed, annoyed. He wanted something more, a fucking thank you at least. It was always the same – Petesy not backing him, too worried, too afraid. He was angry with him, angry about everything, for staying in and hiding, for going to the Tech, for not being around, for not running faster, for falling over, for getting caught ...

Marty pushed his plate aside and stood up. 'Gotta go, son. Things to do. People to see.' He pulled out forty quid and tossed it on the table. 'Here, buy yourself some more books.'

Marty took a step to the door. He turned, smiling.

'And no more Bs, you hear.'

# THREE

Ward sat at his desk in Musgrave Street and rubbed his eyes. It was Sunday, just after noon. He'd been on for fifteen hours and knew there was more to come.

They'd got in from Tomb Street at 5 a.m. O'Neill was still down the corridor, writing up statements, pulling a file on the victim. Ward liked the chip on his shoulder, that he took it personally, like every job was about him and whether he was good enough. He thought back, wondering if he'd been the same. He remembered the buzz, walking round a scene and that quiet thrill as someone's world suddenly opened up to you – all its embarrassments, its embellishments, its dirty secrets.

Tomb Street was ten hours old. They'd released a press statement and put a rush on the forensics. The post mortem was Monday and they had the victim's family that afternoon. The McCarthys lived outside Lisburn, the father a millionaire, some big deal in property. Ward had rolled his eyes when he heard, feeling the shit storm already start to gather.

Alone in his office, he took a sip of coffee and tried to ignore his desk drawer. He didn't want to open it, didn't want to take them out, to start looking at them again. It was weeks since Ward had had a proper night's sleep. It was always the same: waking after a few hours, unable to get back off. He'd end up at the kitchen table, with a cup of tea and yesterday's

*Belfast Telegraph*. He'd look through the window at the sky, bleeding from purple to grey.

Ward turned his head. There was laughing in the car park outside. He walked to the window and looked down on a couple of uniform, young guys, reliving a story. The station wall towered over them, twenty foot tall, three feet thick. Musgrave Street, still like a fortress, like the Troubles were over, but no one was taking any chances. Ward looked up at the bruised sky, there was more rain on the way. In the distance he heard the hum of machinery and the rattle of a pneumatic drill. It was the building site round the corner, Victoria Square, another cathedral to consumerism.

Musgrave Street was quiet. Sunday afternoon, Senior Management at the golf course, or the boat club, or wherever it was they spent their weekends. It didn't bother Ward. He liked it, just you and the job. You could forget the politics and all the posturing that went with Monday to Friday and the nine-to-five brigade.

The Chief Inspector, Charles Wilson, had already been on the phone to get his debrief on the nightshift. It was a weekly performance, a quick sniff, but nothing that might spoil your day. Ward told him about Tomb Street and the other two assaults. He was vague on details, knowing Wilson wouldn't care, not until the press got wind and started huffing and puffing. He pictured the headlines: *Tomb Street Tragedy*; *City Centre Chaos*; the usual guff.

Wilson was a new breed, a politician dressed as a peeler. Ward tried to remember when exactly it was that they handed the force over to the bean counters. These days it was all Excel spreadsheets and PowerPoint presentations. Maybe Wilson was right, maybe he was the dinosaur, a

23

relic from another era. The Chief didn't like that he was ex-Special Branch, the old anti-terrorism unit. The Branch had a reputation, a force within the force, a law unto themselves. They'd run informants, conducted interrogations, tried to stop the daily carnage that had ripped the North apart for thirty years. They may have bent the rules, but it saved lives so Ward was apologizing for none of it.

He remembered the Peace Agreement like it was yesterday. He'd been in Musgrave Street at the time of the prisoner release, standing in the canteen, watching the news. The whole room stopped, cops shaking their heads in utter disbelief. They watched as some of the most dangerous men in the country just walked out of jail. The TV showed a crowd, the pumping of fists, heads ducking into waiting cars. Ward knew all the faces, all the names. In the corner of the canteen someone in uniform puked in a bin.

The next thing, the politicians disbanded the force. *Sayonara* RUC. They took the name, the badge, the uniform. Ward had seen friends killed in that uniform and suddenly they had to give it up, like it was no big deal. Half the force walked away, men with fifteen years' service, some with more. They'd been sold out, stabbed in the back. Words like 'honour', 'loyalty' and 'service' seemed offensive, like someone taking the piss out of you.

Ward watched as Wilson and the bureaucrats took over. And now the new recruits, all wide eyed and bushy tailed. He didn't blame them, just young guys looking for jobs. He'd stayed on though, refusing early retirement and the golden handshake. It felt like blood money, like you were being bought off.

Ward put his hand on the desk drawer and hesitated.

He thought about Tomb Street, picturing the injuries, imagining what it must have taken to ruin someone's face like that. If the police had changed, so had the world. People were different, meaner, nastier, like they'd grown accustomed to the violence and there was no going back.

He'd been in custody before, checking the tail end of last night's carnage. They had a sixteen-year-old in on Attempted Murder, stabbed someone outside an off licence. The reason –

'Slagged my trainers, so he did.'

The week before it was sexual assault, victim in her seventies, a grandmother. On Thursday, it was a young fella on the Dublin Road, in a coma in the Royal, and all for his mobile phone.

In the corner of the office the portable TV was on with picture, but no sound. Ward had watched the news, wanting to see the press statement about Tomb Street and the appeal for information. An ad came on from the Northern Ireland tourist board. A young couple, blonde and beautiful, on the Giant's Causeway, smiling out to sea. It was all blue skies and sunshine, the whole nine yards. They twirled at a ceilidh, sipped Guinness in the Crown, played golf at Portrush. Ward reached for the remote and killed the clichés.

He sighed and pulled open the drawer. Inside were eight envelopes, pastel pink. He took the top one, holding it in his hands, like he was weighing it.

Detective Inspector Jack Ward
c/o Musgrave Police Station
60 Victoria Street
Belfast
BT1 3GL

They'd even put the postcode on. It was the same each week, every Friday there was another one. Ward reached inside, pulled out the card. Flowers adorned the front, a bunch of roses in faded pastel colours. 'With Deepest Sympathy' in looping, elegant lettering. He opened the card, examining the neat cursive handwriting:

In Loving Memory of Jack Ward. May He Rest in Peace.

The eighth one in as many weeks. Same card, same message, same implicit threat. He'd laughed it off at first, telling himself it was some arsehole, trying to be funny.

Then the second card arrived, and the third, and the fourth ...

Ward took a drink of coffee. Whoever it was, they were methodical – one a week, every week, and always Friday. They weren't in a hurry either. And then there was the handwriting. They could have typed it, written in bold, but it was like they were teasing him, egging him on, looking for a chase.

He hadn't told anyone, knowing he'd be mothballed if word got out. Wilson would jump all over it, chain him to a desk, any old excuse. Ward knew it would be a waste of time. If someone was going to come for him, the last place they'd do it would be at work. No, they'd get him at home, or driving somewhere. You'd be stopped at the lights. A car would pull up, the window down, the passenger leaning out.

Ward stood from his desk and walked to the filing cabinet. His old notebooks were locked in the bottom drawer. He took them out, setting the pile on his desk and started to read. The past came flooding back to him, the names, the jobs. He took his time and made a list.

An hour later and some cross checking, there were six contenders – Michael Hannah, Barry McKeown, Billy Reid, Sam McAttackney, Gerry McCann, Peter McGinn.

Ward knew them all, had sat in interview rooms feeling the hatred across the table. They'd all been involved, all killed people, all of them with reason to come after him.

The phone rang on his desk.

'DI Ward.'

'So you're not in church then?'

He recognized the voice instantly. Pat Kennedy, his old DI from Special Branch. Kennedy had been retired five years but still kept in touch. They met for lunch occasionally, the odd pint.

'Church?' Ward said. 'I think it's too late for me.'

'Don't sweat it, son. I spoke to God. Told him how it was. We're gonna work something out.'

Ward laughed.

'So tell me about Tomb Street?' Kennedy demanded.

'You joined up again?'

'Come on now. Don't have me to come down there.'

'Hang on a second,' Ward said, laughing, 'I'm about to go through a tunnel here …'

Kennedy sensed the brush off. 'All right then. I get it. Anyway, this lunch you owe me. It's my birthday tomorrow. We're going somewhere classy.'

'I can't,' Ward said. 'I'm taking my other boyfriend out.'

Kennedy snorted.

It was the same every month. They went for lunch, somewhere quiet and out of the way. Ward spoke, Kennedy listened. You could see he missed it – the people, the peelers, the whole shouting match.

'Pick me up at noon then,' Ward said.

'Dead on. And you better have some good chat. I don't want no shoplifters you hear, no bag snatching.'

Ward laughed. 'I'll see what I can do.'

He hung up and turned back to the cards, wondering what Pat would say. There was a knock at the door. He put the cards away and closed the drawer.

'Come in.'

O'Neill appeared, a folder under his arm.

'Sit down,' Ward ordered. 'Tomb Street … talk.'

'Victim's Jonathan McCarthy. Twenty-five years old. Trainee solicitor at a firm in town.'

'Where did he live?'

'Bell Towers, the new apartment complex at the top of the Ormeau Road.'

'Home address?'

'Outside Lisburn.'

'Family?'

O'Neill looked at his notes. 'Parents Richard and Ann. Father's an ex-rugby international, played for Ireland, in the property business now. Worth serious dough, owns a string of mortgage shops, the housing boom.'

He passed an article from a Sunday supplement he'd pulled off the internet. The photos showed the McCarthys' house, a six-bed mansion complete with stables and four acres. The father spoke about the property market.

'"… the North's destiny",' Ward read aloud, '"payback for all those years of hardship."'

He smiled at the middle-class propaganda. 'How's the property market up the Falls these days? Or the Shankill? Any millionaires there?' He handed the article back to O'Neill. 'You speak to the parents?'

'Uniform woke them, four in the morning, a hat-in-hand job.'

Ward looked at his watch. 'Let's go then.'

'I need to step out for half an hour.'

'Right. Get me when you're ready.'

O'Neill nodded and left the office.

When he was gone Ward opened the drawer and took out the cards, tossing them on the desk.

# FOUR

O'Neill left Musgrave Street, heading for Tivoli Gardens, the place he'd bought with Catherine the year Sarah was born. He must have driven the Cave Hill Road a thousand times and watched as familiar objects rolled by – the Water Works, Westland fire station, the old dentist's. For a moment he forgot the last year, everything that had happened, and felt like he was driving home at the end of a shift.

At the house he knocked and waited, feeling unwelcome, like a Mormon minus the name badge and the boyish good looks. He heard Sarah bounding down the hall. The door opened and she leaped into him.

'Daddy, Daddy, you're early!'

O'Neill lifted her, feeling her arms wrap round his neck.

Sarah was breathless. 'The film's at three so before that we could go to the park or maybe bowling or maybe swimming or maybe—'

'Wow wow. Hold up there.' O'Neill set his daughter down and took a knee, brushing her hair out of her eyes. 'Listen, love, I'm really sorry.'

Her eyes, confused.

'Something bad happened last night. Daddy has to go to back to work. We're going to have to go to the pictures another day.'

He watched her face fall and the lower lip tremble. Her eyes started to fill. O'Neill waited, putting a hand on her shoulder.

'I promise, next time, you can have the biggest carton of popcorn they sell *and* an ice cream *and* a Coke.' He leaned in, voice lowered. 'Just don't tell your mummy, all right? We'll even sit in the front row. How's that sound?'

Sarah nodded slowly. 'What happened?'

O'Neill pictured Tomb Street, the young fella, his head caved in. He took a breath.

'Is there a bad man?'

'That's right, darling.'

'Did he hurt someone?'

'Aye.'

'Are you going to get him?'

'That's right, love,' he said, liking the child's logic and how straightforward it made the world.

'OK,' Sarah said, wiping her eye with a small, bunched fist.

O'Neill heard footsteps on the stairs and saw legs, torso then a face. Catherine still had that swimmer's build, the long limbs, the square shoulders. O'Neill looked at her, feeling something stir in him, remembering when they first went out and couldn't sleep in the same bed without first having sex. It was like an addiction or something, an itch that they both had to scratch.

Catherine took one look at O'Neill's suit and guessed the rest.

'Inside,' she snapped at Sarah.

'Its OK, Mummy. There's a bad man ... Daddy ...'

'I said inside.'

Sarah knew the tone. O'Neill let her go, watching her walk away, her head lowered. He stood up and took a stance, waiting. Catherine gathered herself, pausing until Sarah was out of earshot.

31

'Listen,' O'Neill said. 'I didn't want to just phone her. Something's happened all right. There's nothing I can do about it. This young fella—'

The door slammed, six inches from his face.

O'Neill closed his eyes, pressing his teeth together, feeling the rage rise. Catherine could go fuck herself. Who did she think she was? Where did she think the maintenance came from every month? Did it grow on a tree, fall from the sky, come down the river in a frigging bubble? Or maybe someone was out there, busting his balls every day, wading through all the shit the city had to offer. Taking every bit of overtime that was going, all so she could live the suburban dream, with her Volkswagen Golf, her Marks & Spencer, her trips to Euro-fucking-Disney.

O'Neill turned his back on the house and marched towards the car.

On the drive back to Musgrave Street he pointed his anger at Tomb Street, running over the scene, planning what he would ask the victim's parents. He knew what he was doing – the distraction, the avoidance, the burying yourself in someone else's misery. It was a habit, but it worked, so what could you do?

It was getting on for two and he hadn't eaten. He pulled into the Esso at Fortwilliam, bought a sandwich and grabbed a *Sunday Life*. In the car, he scanned the newspaper. Front page was a footballer who had slept with his teammate's wife. Page two was a bikini-clad blonde and some crap about *Big Brother*. Page three carried a picture of an armoured Land Rover, officers in riot gear, a crowd hurling missiles. The paramilitaries had gone underground it said. They were running counterfeit goods, the drugs trade, sex trafficking. There was armed robbery, tiger kidnapping, targeted car thefts. The strapline read 'NORTHERN IRELAND: GONE TO THE DOGS'.

'Tell us something we don't know.'

The story finished on the Northern Bank robbery. Masked men had held the manager's family hostage, while he went to work and emptied the vault. They got £25 million, the largest bank job in British history. So far the police had nothing.

O'Neill took a bite of the sandwich, tomato and cheese, soggy and tasteless. He tossed it on the passenger seat and lit a cigarette, before starting the engine and heading back to Musgrave Street.

In the car park O'Neill rang Ward, told him he was downstairs. They were heading out to talk to the McCarthy parents.

He got out and leaned against the car, watching a Land Rover rumble through the armoured gates and park up. The back doors opened and a female peeler dropped down. O'Neill saw the blonde hair and the one-inch ponytail and instinctively straightened up.

He'd been at police college with Sam Jennings in the nineties. They'd become mates, or more than that, mates with potential. They'd got together a couple of times last year, right after Catherine left. He had thought things were going well. Two weeks in, she'd stopped returning his calls. There was silence, then a text message – 'I can't. I'm sorry.' O'Neill had left a message, then another, then given up. He figured she'd had her reasons.

They'd dodged each other for months, barely speaking

and then only work chat and always with others around.

He watched her cross the car park, talking to her partner Brian Stout.

Sam looked up and saw him as they approached. 'You go on, Brian. I'll catch up.'

Stout kept walking, sliding his key card and disappearing through the heavy station door.

Sam turned to him. 'How's it going?'

'Fine. You?'

'Fine. I heard about Tomb Street.'

'Yeah. We're going to see the parents.'

She nodded and a silence fell between them.

'Listen, John ... I need to apologize ... about last ...'

He shook his head. 'It's fine.'

'No, it's not. Look I want to ...'

'Doesn't matter.'

She paused, realizing it was no use, not here anyway. 'How have you been anyway?' she asked.

'Fine,' he said. 'Busy.'

'Yeah.'

O'Neill looked at her, fighting the urge to ask what had happened, where she went, what she'd been playing at. He held back, worried about giving her the leftovers from the door slamming an hour earlier.

Behind them the station door opened. Ward came out, looking haggard and browbeaten. He squinted at the light, walking towards O'Neill.

Sam put her head down. 'I've gotta go,' she said, 'Sir-ing' Ward as she passed.

The DI opened the car door and lowered himself in. O'Neill got in, expecting a comment, a raised eyebrow, a knowing nod. The DI slumped into the seat and looked straight ahead.

'Let's go.'

They drove out the M1, tracking Milltown Cemetery which ran parallel to the motorway. It skirted the Falls Road and Andy-Town, what the cops called 'Comanche country'.

The rain had started to thin, weakening to a drizzle. In the car neither man spoke. O'Neill thought about Tomb Street, forming questions, angles, hypotheses. Ward was thinking about the sympathy cards, going over names, remembering faces. There were men out there, men he'd locked up, men with memories. He gazed across the traffic to the headstones of Milltown. There were neat rows of polished granite, mostly black, a few greys, the occasional white. Ward's eyes narrowed. Half the Belfast Brigade were in there, hardened Provos – Joe Hughes, Michael Tomalty, all the boys. Killed on active duty, fighting for the cause, Ireland's heroes. Ward snorted, remembering the poem from school. It was Sassoon or Owen, one of them – *'Dulce et Decorum est'*. He thought about the dead men, about their families and old comrades. Were they still out there, nursing old wounds, brooding over scores that needed settled?

After ten minutes O'Neill signalled and turned off the motorway. He drove through Lisburn, following the one-way system. On the far side, the houses thinned and after a while they were in rolling farmland.

O'Neill slowed when he saw the house number and turned up a long drive. The road wound through an acre of neatly mown grass, dotted with saplings. He parked before a large villa with steps to the door, a wraparound porch, mock Doric columns.

'How the other half live,' Ward said, pulling the door handle.

To the right of the house was a paddock where a woman in her fifties was trotting astride a tall brown mare. She kept her head down, concentrating, like she was shutting out the world.

O'Neill figured it was the mother.

After another lap she sat up and the horse slowed. She got out of the saddle and made her way to the fence and the two cops. She was ageing well and wearing a dark green Barbour jacket and tanned jodhpurs. The horse followed her over, staring at them, its black eyes like snooker balls. The woman looked exhausted, like the lights were on, but nobody was home.

'Mrs McCarthy. I'm DS O'Neill; this is DI Ward. We're from Musgrave Street.'

She gave a nod. 'Richard's in the house, I'll take you in.'

The kitchen was a large open space, floor-to-ceiling glass, views across fields. On the dining table were photographs, taken from a shoebox, pawed over then abandoned. O'Neill glanced as they passed – a teenage boy, good-looking, in school uniform. He did a double take, barely recognizing the victim's face.

At the end of the hall she took them into an office. Richard McCarthy was behind a polished oak desk, looking at a newspaper. He stood as they entered, clocking the haircuts and the suits.

'Would you look at this,' he said, holding the paper. 'My son's been killed and all these ones care about is some footballer shagging his mate's wife. It's a disgrace.'

McCarthy was sixteen stone, with no neck – the classic prop's build. Along the wall were framed press cuttings, photographs, an Irish rugby jersey. The man had the same bloodshot eyes as his wife.

When they were arranged round a coffee table O'Neill spoke.

'We need to ask about your son.'

He took his notepad out and began asking questions. O'Neill jotted down answers, slowing the conversation to a deliberate, forensic pace. Ward listened, watching the mother and father, how they spoke, their gestures, the way they looked at each other.

'When was the last time you heard from your son?' O'Neill said.

'His mother talked to him Thursday.'

'And what about you?'

'I wasn't home.'

'So when was the last time *you* spoke to him?'

'He talks to her more than he talks to me.'

'Are you saying you can't remember?'

McCarthy sat forward. 'I'm saying what's this got to do with anything?'

'We're just trying to get some background, Mr McCarthy.'

'We don't speak much. I mean we didn't,' he said, realizing the wrong tense. 'I was here though, he knew that, knew where to find me if he needed me.'

The mother sat quietly, the husband holding court. McCarthy demanded to know about the scene, where they found the body, who was there. O'Neill sidestepped but the father kept coming, like he was back in the front row, like he wanted answers, like he was entitled to know. What lines of inquiry did they have? What suspects? When would they know who did it?

O'Neill allowed him to vent. Eventually he'd had enough.

37

'Mr McCarthy, this investigation is fourteen hours old. At this stage we have questions, we don't have answers.'

He paused, letting the father settle.

'Do you have any idea who might have wanted to do something like this to your son?'

'No.'

'What do you think happened to him?'

'I've no idea.'

O'Neill heard a note of embarrassment, a faint humiliation that someone had beaten up his boy, that he hadn't been able to defend himself.

'Who was Jonathan out with on Saturday?'

'Peter Craig, his flatmate. I called him this morning. He'd no idea what happened. Some mate, eh? He said he thought Jonathan had got together with someone, taken her home.'

'Is that par for the course?'

'They're young guys, you know.'

O'Neill felt Ward beside him, watching, quiet.

'Do you know if Jonathan was involved in anything he shouldn't have been?'

'No.'

'Drugs?'

'No.'

'Are you sure?'

'Listen,' the father said, indignant. 'He graduated top of his class at Queen's, got a traineeship with Thompson and James, bought his own flat by the time he was twenty-three. The boy was going somewhere, you know, his life ...' McCarthy's voice trailed off.

O'Neill waited.

'Mr McCarthy, do you know if he had a girlfriend?'

'Don't ask me. His mother could tell you.'

O'Neill looked, the mother shook her head. He turned back to the father, trying to figure out what he was so angry about. Someone had beaten up his son, killed him, but there was more. Like he was embarrassed, or blamed himself, or something else.

On the way out to the car, Ward asked the wife to show him the horse again. She walked off and the DI followed, flicking O'Neill off.

Ward and the woman approached the fence as the pony trotted over. The animal put his face down, inviting her to stroke him.

'Smart creature,' Ward said. 'It's like he knows something's wrong.'

'He does,' she said, running her hand along the animal's face. Ward stayed silent. After a few seconds she looked up, eyes to the distance.

'They keep phoning the house,' she said. 'Journalists. Our number's not even listed. Every time the phone rings ... I keep thinking it's our Jonathan ... and it's all been a mistake ... that yous are gonna ...'

A tear ran down her cheek.

'They're resourceful,' Ward said. 'Don't answer the phone. It'll calm down. We'll put a car at the bottom of the drive in case any of them call.'

She nodded. 'Our Karen's in London. Jonathan's sister. She's flying home tonight. That'll help.'

Ward waited before speaking.

'What's the story with your husband?'

'How do you mean?'

'Was there something going on between him and your son?'

The woman shook her head. 'They're just men.'

Ward nodded but didn't press. 'We'll need one of you to come and identify the body for us. He's at the pathologist's at the moment, at the Royal. We'll call you, probably tomorrow.'

'OK.'

The roads were quiet as the detectives made their way back to Belfast. It had just gone five and the daylight was already fading. The Mondeo summited a hill and the lights of the city swung into view, shimmering in the dusk.

'So what are you thinking?' Ward asked.

'I'm thinking they're holding out, not telling us everything.'

'Who does?'

O'Neill thought about the father, wondering how he would feel if something happened to Sarah. He pictured his daughter's face that morning, the smile, the tears.

'How'd you go with the mother?' he asked.

Ward nodded. 'She'll open up next time.'

'The father's a piece of work,' O'Neill said. He paused, thinking about his own da. 'Mine never came you know.'

Ward knew what he was talking about, but waited.

'When I was in hospital, last year, after Laganview, with the shoulder and the concussion.'

'When they were checking for brain damage,' Ward said, looking sideways.

'Aye. Something like that.' O'Neill hesitated, not finished. 'My ma came you know. But not him, not the old boy.'

His voice was flat, unemotional, stating the facts.

40

'My passing out was the same. They give you two tickets. My ma brought her sister. He refused.'

'The police thing?'

'I guess so. Then he goes and dies. Before I could talk to him, have it out, ask him what he was playing at. It was just like him. Auld bastard, always had to have the last word.'

'Hard to have a conversation with a ghost.'

'Aye. I remember standing in the church, listening to the priest – "a good man, a family man, well respected" – he hadn't a clue, never met my da in his life. Didn't mention the drinking, the nights at the bar, the lost weekends. Didn't mention the opinions, the judgements, the way he always knew better. She was about to leave him you know. I overheard her, talking to my aunt. Then he got the diagnosis, liver cancer, six months to live.'

O'Neill remembered Roselawn Cemetery, his mum there, his two brothers, watching the earth being shovelled into the hole. They turned to go but he hesitated, wanting to stay to the end, to make sure they filled the whole thing in.

'Come on you,' his brother called, and O'Neill fell in behind.

The car pulled into Musgrave Street. Ward paused before getting out, like he was going to say something but had second thoughts.

'See you tomorrow,' he said, pulling the handle.

O'Neill watched the DI get into his car and drive out of the station. He thought about doing the same, before picturing the empty flat, the Chinese takeaway, the cold six-pack. They could all wait, none of them were going anywhere.

He got out of the car, swiped his card and disappeared into the station.

# FIVE

Marty Toner jerked awake.

In the dream he'd been standing over Tierney, knife in hand. The older man was asleep, snoring quietly, dead to the world. Marty looked at his throat, watching the soft skin as it rose and fell. He took a breath, steadying himself. Suddenly a hand snapped up, grabbing hold of his wrist. On the bed Tierney opened his eyes, looked at Marty and slowly shook his head.

Marty lay there with his eyes open, his heart pounding, his palms sweaty. He looked around. It was a girl's bedroom, a mess of make-up on the dresser – foundation, eyeliner, lipgloss. There were posters on the wall, boy bands he'd never heard of. The room smelled sweet, a mix of perfume, cigarettes and blow. Next to him Sinead Donnelly was curled in her trackies and a T-shirt, still asleep. The night started to come back to him. He'd texted her at one in the morning and she'd sneaked downstairs to let him in. Sinead was sixteen and game for anything, especially after a few spliffs.

Marty pulled back the duvet, careful not to wake her. He looked at the ring of love bites round her neck. They weren't his, probably Micky Lapin or Dee McLaughlin. He didn't know and didn't care. It would be the last time, with Sinead at least. Wee girls were all the same, talked too much. There were a hundred Sineads. All it took was some chat and a bit of blow.

Marty looked at his mobile. It was almost nine, time to be moving.

He slid out of bed, hearing breakfast TV burble up through the floorboards. Sinead lived with her ma who spent her life watching talk shows, collecting the dole and smoking John Player Specials.

Marty had slept in his tracksuit bottoms, in case he had to bolt. He checked his pocket for the roll of notes, which was still there. On the bedside table lay the remains of the quarter he'd watched Sinead smoke. He left it for her, calling it a going away present, as he backed out of the bedroom, careful not to wake her.

On the landing he sat down to put his feet in his trainers. Through a slit in a doorway, a pair of five-year-old eyes stared out at him. Kevin was Sinead's wee brother, the youngest of four kids, all to different dads. Marty smiled and put a finger to his lips. The boy slowly came out of the bedroom. Marty stayed on his knees, putting his fists up like a boxer. Wee Kevin did likewise, edging forward, throwing baby punches. Marty ducked and feinted, giving him a few taps before tickling him into submission.

Behind him he heard Sinead stir.

'Time to go, son.'

Marty took a tenner from his pocket and gave it to the kid, watching the boy's eyes suddenly widen. He ruffled his hair before disappearing into the bathroom and closing the door behind him. Marty climbed on to the sink and opened the window, edging himself out. He grabbed the drainpipe and shimmied down to the yard. The wall was topped with a cemented line of broken glass. Through the living room window he saw Sinead's ma, in her dressing gown, fag in one hand, tea in the other.

She didn't see him lower himself off the wall, drop silently into the alley and steal away into the morning.

It was Monday and the Markets were quiet. The oldies weren't out yet and the young ones were still in their beds. Marty crossed the Albert Bridge, heading for the Short Strand and his ma's place. He walked with his hood up and his head down, eyes peeled. The morning traffic had started to thin out, the worker bees, buzzing at their desks. Overhead the sky was grey and the light flat. It wasn't raining but it was in the post. From the crest of the Albert Bridge, Marty looked at Laganview Apartments. They'd been completed a month ago. You could see in the windows – the flat screen TVs, the leather sofas, the big stereos. It was Yuppieville. Outside was a line of cars – an Audi A3, an RX8, a Golf GTI.

Marty felt his mood darken, like he'd been taken to a sweet shop and told he wasn't allowed anything. He wondered if he'd ever have a car like that. It wasn't the money; he'd no licence. It would attract attention, plus where would he keep it? Still, he thought, there might be some good customers down there. They'd be mostly looking for coke, maybe some blow. He'd have Locksey go down next Friday, hang about, talk to folk as they got in from work.

Half a mile away stood the Short Strand, a dozen streets of red-brick terraces. Marty swung off the main road, taking a detour through the back entries where folk kept their bins and young ones rode their bikes. It was safer, he figured, fewer windows, fewer eyes. When he got to the door he climbed a bin and pulled himself over. The key was under the flowerpot, where it always was. It was his ma's precaution, for when she had blackouts or got so blocked she'd leave her handbag in the back of a taxi or at some random guy's flat.

Marty turned the key and quietly stepped in. He hadn't slept at the house in over a year. The kitchen was a mess, the fridge bare except for some out-of-date milk and an empty bottle of Smirnoff. Vodka was his ma's poison – vodka and coke, vodka and soda, vodka and white, she wasn't fussy. 'From Russia with love,' she'd say, one of her favourite lines.

Yesterday was Sunday. She'd have started early and finished late. Marty stood still for a second, listening for sounds, trying to tell if she was home. Half the time she had company. You would hear snoring and peek into the bedroom to see some guy lying there, his gut hanging over his boxers. She would run out of money and let men buy her drink. Half of them passed out, trying to keep up.

In the living room the TV was still on, the volume on mute. Marty imagined her steaming, thinking it was broken, not realizing. Out of habit, he checked the cigarette packet next to the ashtray. It was empty – again, no surprise. He crept up the stairs, taking them slow, stepping over the top two which always creaked. To the right was his old bedroom. It was empty, the toys gone, his PlayStation sold to one of the neighbours.

He put his eye to his ma's door. She was on the bed, comatose, fully dressed. He stepped in, knocking over an empty wine bottle. It thudded loudly but she didn't stir. He shook his head – you could set a bomb off and she'd be none the wiser. He looked at her face, the smudged lipstick, the Alice Cooper eyes, like she'd been crying in her sleep. Folk said she was a looker, back in the day. Marty couldn't remember. All he could picture were the bruises and her cowering beneath his da. He remembered her limping round the house, groaning as she lowered herself into a chair. Standing over her, he closed his eyes, hearing the thud-thud-thud, from the time she 'fell' down the stairs. It got so as he could read the signs, like a storm warning. His da at the kitchen table, eyes black and empty. He'd sit chain-smoking, getting torn into the whiskey, waiting for his excuse. He'd goad her, push her, wanting her to answer back, to ask who the frig he thought he was. She never disappointed. That was one thing about his ma, she rarely let you down.

When he was eight, Marty walked into the kitchen and found them. His da had her by the throat, choking the life out of her, her eyes bulging. He called her a hoor, told her he was going to fucking kill her. Marty had grabbed a fork from the sideboard and stabbed him in the thigh. It was as far up as he could reach. His da screamed and chased him up the stairs, cornering him on the landing. There were fists, feet, the belt came off. Marty was off school for a fortnight. His ma phoned in and told them he'd tonsillitis and had to get them out.

Six months later a car hit his da. He'd been drunk and walked into oncoming traffic on the Ravenhill Road. Marty wished he'd been there to see it. He pictured himself kicking his da's lifeless body, putting the boot into him.

There was a honeymoon period after that, six months, a year maybe. Him and his ma got on grand, just the two of them, the best of mates. Then she started on the bottle and everything became Marty's fault. He was a waste of space, a useless wee bastard, just like his da. The more she drank, the worse she got.

Marty would go to Petesy's granny's. He'd ping the

windows and his mate would let him sleep on the floor in his bedroom.

Petesy was the only one that ever stuck up for him. When three older lads started on him, calling his ma a hoor, Petesy had piled in. He didn't care that there was three of them, that they were older, that he couldn't punch his way out of a wet paper bag. Afterwards, the two of them had sat round the back of the Spar, sharing a smoke and nursing their injuries.

Standing in the bedroom, Marty watched his mother quietly snoring. He stepped on to the landing and closed the door behind him. He went into the bathroom and put the snib on. From the ledge of the bath he reached up, dislodging the trapdoor into the roof space. Marty stretched into the dark, groping round, feeling for the handle. He pulled down a black Adidas bag and set it on the floor.

Kneeling before the bag, he unzipped it, his eyes wide.

Fourteen grand, used notes. Counted, wrapped, tied.

Marty fought the urge to pour it out, to hold it, to start playing with it. He reached underneath the cash, felt the handle and pulled out the Browning pistol. He'd found it a year ago when he was burgling a house off the Ormeau Road. The pistol was black and slender, the handgrip cold. He slid the chamber back and allowed it to snap forward, checking the safety before putting it in his pocket.

Marty left the money in the bag, putting it above the ceiling and sliding the trap door back. He stood for a second, still, listening. There was no sound.

He slipped the snib off the door and moved quietly to the landing then back to his ma's bedroom. She looked peaceful, a half-smile across her face. Marty wondered if all her dreams were set in pubs and involved a generous bartender and a bottomless glass. He reached down and lifted her purse from the floor. It was light, empty, a mere fashion accessory. He had a flashback of being ten, all the times he'd gone into her purse to steal from her. Mondays were the best, when the dole was in and the family allowance, before she'd been to the off licence.

He prised open the purse, looking at the 50p and the couple of coppers. He pictured her at the bar, counting it, sighing when it wasn't enough. He reached into his pocket and took out a roll of notes, then peeled off two twenties and put them in her purse. It would keep her oiled for a day or two. She wouldn't know who, wouldn't know when, wouldn't know why. It didn't matter though. Money was money and the guy at the offy didn't care where it came from.

Marty slipped down the stairs. At the back door he paused, looking round the mess in the kitchen. He felt like he'd lost something and instinctively tapped his pockets – mobile, money, gun. It was all there. He shrugged the feeling off and locked the back door, climbing the wall and dropping down on the other side.

# SIX

It was half eleven in Musgrave Street. Ward was at his desk, reading over the interview notes from the McCarthy family, thinking about the mother and father. He pictured the dinner table, the da holding court, the kids sitting there. No interest in rugby, your da a millionaire, how did you measure up? Phrases floated round his head – 'off the rails', 'proving yourself', 'fathers and sons'. The family seemed strange when he called with O'Neill. Then again, most folk didn't rehearse being woken in the dead of night by a peeler with his hat in his hands.

The Chief Inspector had come looking for Ward that morning. Wilson was flustered and annoyed. The *Belfast Telegraph* had been on the phone first thing, wanting a comment. McCarthy would make front page, unless they got something better, of course. Ward wondered what something better might look like.

He set the interview notes aside, thinking about the stabbing and the kid they'd arrested on Saturday night. Ward shook his head. *Slagged my trainers.* It was like there was something out there, like the whole city had been let off the leash, everyone feeling entitled, like they were owed something and had nothing to lose.

Keenan, the manager of the club, had slid into Musgrave Street at five to nine. He'd brought the CCTV, the staff list and the till roll from Saturday night. O'Neill was in CID, working his way through it now, looking for names, for connections, trying to piece together a story.

Ward's mobile trembled in his pocket. Pat Kennedy.

'I'm outside.'

'Gimme two minutes.'

On the stairs Ward passed Wilson. He wondered what the Chief Inspector would say if he knew he was having lunch with one of his old mates from Special Branch. Kennedy was in his sixties now, retired five years. His kids were grown up and across the water. He lived up the coast with his missus, Eileen. When Ward's own wife had died, Pat and Eileen had adopted him. Sunday lunches, Christmas Day. Afterwards, him and Pat would slink off to the bar while the kids argued over their new toys.

Outside, Kennedy was parked on Victoria Street in a brand new Saab.

'Nice wheels,' Ward said, lowering himself in.

Kennedy had driven rally cars, back in his twenties.

'You getting the itch again?'

'You kidding. She'd kill me.'

Pat Kennedy had deep-set eyes, dark brown, almost black. They stared at the world – unmoved, unconvinced, unimpressed. Pat had spent half his life in interview rooms with men who wanted to kill him. It changed how you saw things. He'd put half the Belfast Brigade behind bars: Michael Hannah, Barry McKeown, you name it. That was before the Peace Process, before the politicians started handing out 'Get Out of Jail Free' cards.

In the passenger seat, Ward rubbed his eyes and tried to smother a yawn. He'd been up till two in the morning, thinking about the sympathy cards, about the threats, about who it might be and how they'd come at him.

Kennedy slipped the car into gear and pulled away from the kerb.

'You look like shit,' he said.

'Says George Clooney there.'

Kennedy smiled, waiting for Ward to speak.

Nothing.

'So what's up?' he asked.

'I'm hungry,' Ward said.

'Aye,' he said sarcastically. 'What else?'

Silence.

'Cancer?'

'For lunch?' Ward said, still dodging.

'The ticker?'

'That too.'

Kennedy smiled, realizing the blinds were down. 'What happened, your boyfriend break up with you?'

'You know there's only you.'

'You say that to all the fellas.'

Both men laughed. Ward enjoyed it with Kennedy, like old times, like it was the two of them again, driving to some job, taking on the world.

'Speaking of cancer,' Ward said, 'you seen Davy?'

David Price was another former Branch man. He was Pat Kennedy's best mate, since they'd grown up together on the Newtownards Road. Davy was diagnosed with testicular cancer eight years ago, but he went under the knife and beat it.

In the car Kennedy indicated and changed lanes.

'He's in Iraq now, doing security work. He's still mustard.'

The Saab rounded the gothic tower of the Albert clock, skirting Customs House, running parallel to the Lagan before crossing Queen's Bridge. Ward looked up at a crane as it swung its arm over another building site. More development – Obel Tower, like a giant shard, stabbed into the city.

'How's Tomb Street?' Kennedy asked. He'd seen the appeal for information on the TV the day before.

'Early days.'

Kennedy smiled, knowing what that meant. 'Some wee hood?'

'Nah. This one's a citizen.'

'Didn't think there were any of them left. Who's up front?'

'O'Neill.'

'How's he doing?'

'He's working it.'

Kennedy nodded.

'We had this kid on Saturday,' Ward said. 'Sixteen, stabbed someone. You know why? Guy slagged off his trainers.'

Kennedy shrugged, like nothing could surprise him.

'I mean seriously. At least there used to be reasons. The Brits and the Provos, the Prods and the Taigs. These days it's a free-for-all. And the kids out there ... they're off their nut.'

'Tell me about it,' Kennedy said. 'Why you think I moved to the middle of nowhere?'

The Saab drove into east Belfast, skirting Ballymacarret and the Union Jacks that still fluttered from lamp posts. Two guys were painting a mural across the gable end of a house, a two-storey *Titanic* sailing up Belfast Lough. The next house featured the Somme, with a ten-foot picture of the Queen smiling from across the road.

'So Tomb Street,' Kennedy said.

'The kid is called McCarthy. Early twenties, took a hiding, guy jumped on his head.'

52

Kennedy listened, nodding.

'You know the McCarthy Mortgage Shops?' Ward said.

'Aye.'

'That's the da.'

Raised eyebrows. 'Wilson'll be wetting his knickers.'

'He was in my office this morning, twice.'

'Is the son into anything?'

'Doesn't look like it.'

'I've heard that before.'

On the Newtownards Road the car passed Stormont. Ward looked up the long straight drive to the white columned building, nestled amid manicured lawns. Kennedy caught the glance.

'You know the problem with parliaments, Jack? Full of politicians.'

'Aye. Like the man says, no matter who you vote for, the government always gets in.'

The Saab pulled into the car park of Stormont Hotel. The bar was empty and they sat at the back out of habit. The barman dragged himself from the television screen to take their order. Ward went for the stew, Kennedy the chilli. They waited until he was gone before speaking again.

'So how's retirement?' Ward said.

Kennedy shrugged. 'The garden centre, the golf course. What can you say?'

Ward sensed the boredom and the dullness, ordinary life not measuring up. It was ironic; peelers spent years working nightshift, working weekends, dreaming about some normal life that the rest of the world got to live.

'The missus is doing her nut. Says I'm under her feet, keeps sending out me for milk. The security guard at Tesco thinks I'm a shoplifter.'

Ward laughed.

'She wants to go on holiday again. Some cruise round the Holy Land, the pyramids, Jerusalem. I'm trying to get her to take her sister.'

Kennedy had been pining for months. He missed the job, missed the lads, missed the banter. He missed the scumbags, lying through their teeth, trying to keep themselves out of the clinker. He even missed the bosses, sniffing round, looking out for their careers and the next photo opportunity. He wanted nothing more than to suit up and get after someone.

'Would you look at that?' Kennedy said, nodding at the TV.

It was the lunchtime news. A man in an Armani suit walked round a boxing gym accompanied by a reporter. In the background were scrawny kids skipping, thwacking punchbags, trying to ignore the cameras. The two men watched, shaking their heads.

'Gerry McCann,' Ward said.

McCann had been involved during the Troubles, a Provo from South Belfast. When the Peace Process broke out he'd gone legit, setting up businesses – hairdressers, car washes, tanning salons. He'd eight on the go and was turning a good profit. The police had questioned him last year in connection with the murder of Joe Lynch, a former volunteer they found in an alley with a bullet in his head. McCann had smiled knowingly as he declared himself a legitimate businessman.

'That the same thing as a legitimate target?' Ward had said.

On TV, McCann strutted round the gym in his Armani suit. He tried to look humble as he handed over a cheque for ten grand.

'Used to box here when I was a wee lad,' he told the reporter, 'and it's good to be able to give something back. This'll get the gym some pads, new gloves, a lick of paint.'

Ward shook his head. 'Gerry McCann, the great philanthropist.'

'How did we never manage to put him away?'

'He'd a good lawyer.'

'The brother?'

McCann's brother, Michael, had been a solicitor. He was a diehard Republican, the whole family were. Michael knew every loophole, every technicality, every way to beat the system. Even the peelers were unanimous – if you ever got arrested for something, then you wanted Michael McCann defending you.

'The Loyalists did the world a favour when they stiffed him,' Kennedy said quietly.

Michael McCann had been murdered outside his home in Belfast. Two men had watched him pull into his drive, approached the car and opened fire. Sixteen bullets, point-blank range. There'd been an investigation and allegations of collusion, Special Branch feeding intelligence to the gunmen. Kennedy was in charge at the time but nothing was ever proved.

On the TV, McCann shared a joke with the reporter. In the background was another face Ward recognized – Johnny Tierney. He was younger, late twenties, one of McCann's boys. He'd been the number one ranked amateur in his day, a lefty with a vicious jab. The Boxing Board banned him after he was caught bare knuckle fighting and almost killed a guy.

Ward and Kennedy turned from the TV as their food arrived.

'Honestly,' Kennedy said, the waiter gone. 'This place is going to the dogs. I was walking through the town the other day and you know who I saw? Peter McGinn.'

McGinn was a Provo who had killed two cops. He'd been sent down for twenty years and served four, let out through the Peace Process.

'Bastard's sitting there, in Bewley's, a cup of tea and a cream bun. Fucker looks at me and nods, like butter wouldn't melt in his mouth.'

Ward listened as Kennedy spoke, like it was some sick joke.

'You see them about the town, just watching, waiting. I'm telling you, leopards don't change their spots. Trust me on that. And justice? Don't start me. There's no such thing. I mean look at the state of us. You hold the line for thirty years, get threatened, shot at, blown up. Think of the guys we lost – Tom O'Loan, Peter Downey, Terry Hughes, Paul Briggs, Phil McNamara ... Gone, all them. And what was it for? So the government could waltz along and let these guys out. And what do they do to us? Throw us a few bob, thanks, lads, take it easy, mind how you go. Justice? Don't make me laugh. The Provies were right you know. The only justice worth speaking about comes from the barrel of a gun.'

'Come on. You don't really—'

'Don't really believe it? Try me. You talk to some of the boys, ask them what they think. Ask if they reckon they've been sold out. You see what they say.' Kennedy shook his head. 'Twenty-five years, you thought you'd seen everything.'

A silence fell between them. Ward lifted his glass and took a drink.

'Anyway,' Kennedy said, the sting out of him, 'tell me about this cancer then. Where is it? Your balls?'

Ward smiled faintly and shook his head.

'Come on, you look like death warmed up, son. Tell Uncle Pat.'

Ward shrugged. 'It's nothing.'

'So tell me then.'

'I'm getting death threats.'

'Means you're doing the job right.'

Ward shook his head. Kennedy waited.

'This is different.'

He explained about the sympathy cards, the messages, the regularity. Kennedy nodded, the face deadpan.

'Any thoughts?'

Ward shook his head. 'It's nothing. I mean, how many times in your career did someone threaten to do you?'

'I stopped counting.'

'Me too. And it's like you said, they're out walking the streets, bored, looking for things to do, ways to occupy themselves.'

'What have you got at the house?' Kennedy asked.

'Glock. Shotgun. Dog.'

'Good. 'Cause you know if anything's going to happen, that's where they'll come.'

'A nice thought.'

'It's probably some arsehole messing about.'

'Sure,' Ward said, both men smelling the lie.

After a few minutes, they pushed their plates aside, Kennedy's clean, Ward's full.

In the car on the way back they didn't speak. Kennedy talked about how shit Liverpool were, trying to smooth the cracks with something vaguely normal.

'So what *do* you do all day then?' Ward asked.

'Read. Sort the car. Try not to drink.' Kennedy reached into the glove box 'Here, try this.'

He tossed a book on Ward's lap. Ernest Hemingway, *The Old Man and the Sea*. The cover showed waves rising like cliffs, beneath them a tiny row boat and a lone sailor.

'You calling me an old man?' Ward said.

Kennedy smiled. 'If the shoe fits ...'

Back at Musgrave Street, Ward got out of the car. 'Give Eileen my best, will you.'

'Sure. And here, if you fancy a jaunt round the Med ...?'

Ward smiled. 'Seasick, mate. Send me a postcard.'

He closed the door and watched Kennedy drive off, turning the corner into Victoria Street. Ward glanced up at the lookout post embedded in the station wall. He nodded at the small window of bulletproof glass. A few seconds later, the buzzer sounded and he disappeared through the armoured steel door.

# SEVEN

O'Neill was in the CCTV cupboard at Musgrave Street, reviewing the footage from the nightclub. The room was dark and functional, a long desk, a bank of screens. It smelled like stale crisps and Old Spice.

There was a knock and the door opened, the corridor strip lights suddenly blinding. A silhouette appeared, a voice, DC Kearney.

'Chief Inspector wants to see you.'

O'Neill waited.

'He was looking for Ward. Said you'd do.'

'Story of my life.'

O'Neill stopped the tape and headed upstairs. The third floor was Senior Management, the Monday-to-Friday crew, the nine-to-fivers. He stood outside the Chief Inspector's door and knocked. There was the usual pause, Wilson reminding you of his rank.

Finally a voice. 'Come in.'

The office was oak panelled, large, the same size as CID, which housed six desks. Floor-to-ceiling bookshelves covered the back wall. There was a university degree, framed photographs – Wilson with Bill Clinton, Wilson with Tony Blair, all smiles and handshakes.

The Chief Inspector was writing something and didn't look up. He was in full uniform – white shirt, dark tie, shoulder boards with three silver diamonds. He had a side parting and clear skin, like a teenager with grey hair.

Wilson signed his name with a flourish and looked up.

'Where are we with Tomb Street? The murder?'

O'Neill liked the 'we', as if the Chief was involved, as if he hadn't spent the weekend at the golf course or whatever it was he did while the rest of them were on nightshift.

'Not a murder yet, sir. Suspicious Dea—'

'Don't start me, O'Neill, I'm not in the mood. I've got the *Belfast Telegraph*, Radio Ulster and *UTV Live* all breathing down my neck. The Chief Constable's been on the phone twice this morning and I've got the son of an important local businessman lying on a slab in the city coroner's. Realize, O'Neill, Richard McCarthy's got profile. You know what that means? CID needs to make sure they get it right, that this gets one hundred per cent of our effort. Do you understand?'

'Everyone gets one hundred per cent of our—'

'Save it for the promotion boards.' Wilson looked out the window, ignoring O'Neill for a moment.

'I suppose you saw the *Sunday Life* yesterday.'

'No, sir,' O'Neill lied, wanting the Chief to relive his lousy report card.

'Organized crime, ex-paramilitaries, streets not safe. Listen, the McCarthy kid's going to be a story. You need to make sure it's the right story. Quick turn around, someone in cuffs, someone to charge.'

'With all due respect—'

'I don't want to hear it, O'Neill. I don't want an excuse, I want a suspect, you hear me?'

O'Neill wondered who was writing Wilson's lines for him. He felt like telling him offenders didn't walk into the nick, clutching a knife shouting, 'I killed the bitch.'

Wilson wouldn't care though. Like he said, he didn't want explanations, didn't want excuses. He wanted his good news story, his clearance rate, his crime stats. Get a charge, that was all, the conviction was someone else's problem. Find a suspect and convince the Public Prosecutor to saddle up. Job done, box ticked, move on.

'Go fast, Sergeant,' Wilson warned. 'But go careful. Anything comes up ... anything embarrassing ...'

'We follow the evidence, sir.'

'Save me the Ward impression, would you?'

O'Neill shut down, donning his street face, waiting to be dismissed.

'You need to understand something, O'Neill. So far, you've led a pretty charmed life round here. The Laganview collar, Sergeant's promotion, Ward watching your back. Well, the DI's retiring next year and if I were you, I'd think about who my friends are going to be when he's gone.'

O'Neill, stone-faced.

'Transfers happen all the time, you know. A cop could easily find himself in Bally-go-backwards – chasing sheep rustlers, refereeing farmers who have fallen out with one another. Real high-end stuff.'

A silence fell between them, Wilson watching to see if he'd made a dent.

'Has a bit of a following does the old DI among the younger lads. The mystique of Special Branch. Well, you take it from me, Ward's no altar boy. Nobody came out of that unit without some dirt on them.'

O'Neill listened, his expression blank. Wilson watched him for a moment before going back to the paperwork on his desk.

61

'You can go,' he said finally, without looking up.

Ward was in CID waiting for O'Neill. There were going to interview McCarthy's flatmate Peter Craig. He lived in Bell Towers, a new development at the top of the Ormeau Road. The DI let go of a yawn.

'Partying on a school night?' O'Neill said.

'I wish.'

O'Neill thought about Wilson's speech, trying to guess what he'd been insinuating, wondering if he should tell Ward.

'Right,' the DI said. 'Let's go.'

On the way to the car park, O'Neill dialled Tivoli Gardens. Catherine answered on the third ring. He could hear Sarah in the background.

'It's me.'

'What do you want?'

'Can I talk to Sarah?'

'She has her swimming lesson. We're halfway out the door.' Catherine put her hand over the receiver and shouted, 'Not that one, the other one.'

'Look, I just wanted to talk to her.'

'We're already late ... Coat now, come on.'

'I'm her father you know.'

'Listen, you were her father yesterday, remember, when you stood her up. And last weekend, when you bailed on the movies. And the time before that—'

'Look, that's not—'

'We've gotta go, John.'

The line went dead. O'Neill stared at the handset, Ward looking at him across the roof of the car.

62

'Happy families?'

'Yeah. Something like that.'

It was half one and the Ormeau Road was busy. Office girls hurried back to their desks, mobile in one hand, latte in the other. Yummy mummies pushed £500 prams around the old Romanian woman, crouched on the pavement, selling the *Big Issue*.

O'Neill caught sight of a blonde ponytail disappearing into the Spar. He thought about Sam, the way she'd lingered in the car park the day before. She didn't have to and could have easily kept her head down and walked into the nick. He allowed himself to think back to the night he knocked on her door, after eleven, her raised eyebrow, like she'd always known he was coming. He thought about the Saturday mornings at St Clement's on Botanic Avenue. They'd drunk coffee and read the papers, their bodies still tingling from the sex an hour earlier. He thought about phoning her now, asking to meet up, somewhere outside work, away from the job, somewhere they could talk.

The address was coming up on the left and O'Neill turned his mind back to Tomb Street. The victim had lived in Bell Towers, a new development, in what used to be the Good Shepherd Convent. The car slowed at the gated entrance.

'Property,' Ward said cynically, 'the new religion.'

Above them the building reached for the sky, five floors of red brick crowned with a pitched slate roof. O'Neill located McCarthy's name on the intercom.

'Hello.'

'Peter Craig.'

'Yes.'

'CID.'

There was a pause before the gate slowly swung open.

Craig stood in the corridor, waiting for them. He was dressed for work – dark suit, hair slicked, eyes puffy.

Inside, the apartment smelled of fresh paint and newly laid carpet. The walls were white, with large abstract paintings dotted around. It reminded O'Neill of one of Sarah's early efforts, only worse. An open staircase led up to the mezzanine and the bedrooms. The place was neat, tidy, like it had just been cleaned.

O'Neill walked in, looking around him.

'Some place you have,' he said, all matey.

'Yeah, thanks.'

'How long you guys been in here?'

'Just six months.'

'Wow. This is great. How much were these going for again?'

'They started at one thirty, ours was one fifty, because of the finishings and all.'

'Worth it though, eh?' O'Neill said, playing along.

'Yeah, we thought so.'

O'Neill sat on the sofa, Craig opposite.

'So how are you doing then?' he said, keeping up the old pals routine.

'Pretty shit.'

'Yeah, I can imagine.'

'Feel like it's my fault. Like I'm his mate, you know. You're supposed to keep an eye on your friends, look out for them.'

'Things happen. You can't always be there.'

Craig turned his mouth down, like it was little consolation.

'The best thing you can do is help us catch who did this.'

Craig nodded.

'Let's start with Saturday then, talk us through the night, as much detail as you can remember.'

'We started off here about seven, got a carryout, had that girl from Johnny's work over and her flatmate. We were just drinking, listening to music, having a laugh. Then we headed into town. Got a taxi.'

'What time do you think that was?'

'About ten, half ten. We were pretty blocked.'

'We were just at Milk, you know, the club, having a good time. We were dancing, drinking, doing a few shots. Johnny has had a thing about Sally Curran for a while, the girl he works with. I'm riding shotgun, looking after her mate. She's a bit of a sourpuss, some postgrad from Queen's, all hairy legs and principles. Anyway, it must have been almost two and I turned around and looked for Johnny but he wasn't there. I thought he was in a corner somewhere, off with Sally or something. Then she came back from the toilets. I thought he'd had a whitey or something, gone outside, or just bailed and headed home.'

'Is that normal?'

'Look, if you'd been drinking what we'd been drinking ...'

O'Neil raised his eyebrows, interested, impressed. 'Pretty wrecked then?'

'Beer, flaming sambucas, Jäger Bombs. We were off our faces. I got a taxi up the road and crashed out. His bedroom door was closed so I figured Johnny was in his bed. Never thought to check.'

Craig paused, staring into space.

'Some frigging mate, eh?'

O'Neill sat silently, waiting to see where he would go. Craig just shook his head.

'Was there any trouble at the club?' Ward said, taking over.

'Not that I know of.'

'Were yous talking to anyone you didn't know?'

'Nah.'

'Would anyone might have wanted to hurt Jonathan?'

'Nah. Johnny was a good guy. Knew everybody. I'm telling you, you'd walk into a bar and folk would be all *Johnny, what about you?*'

'What about the girls?'

'Johnny's had a thing about your woman Sally. They started their traineeships at the same time. She's from up the Falls originally. Her fella's from the Springfield Road, Milo or Mullo or something. He works on that building site, Victoria Square. Johnny reckoned he was a bad lad from some of the stories she'd told him.'

'What do you mean?'

'I don't know. Maybe the crowd he runs with ...'

'And what about drugs?' O'Neill said, stepping in again.

'I honestly don't know the guy.'

'And you boys?'

'What?'

'Look, we're not daft. These days, everyone's doing a bit of something.' O'Neill said it casually, like he was chatting about the weather. 'We really don't care. We just want to get who did this.'

'Seriously, nah, not us. The drink's enough. At least the way we do it. Johnny was the same.'

O'Neill nodded and watched.

'Listen, we need to have a look around. Go into Jonathan's room. We might need to take a few things back to the station with us.'

'Sure, go on ahead.'

O'Neill went to the car to get evidence bags, leaving Ward to chat. When he came back the DI was in the bedroom, already gloved. A king-size bed owned the middle of the room. There was an en suite bathroom, walk-in wardrobes, a desk with a laptop and a stack of magazines – GQ, *Esquire*, *Men's Health*. O'Neill bagged the computer and set it on the bed. He took his notepad out and moved to the cupboards. There were jeans and shirts and sweaters, all on hangers. O'Neill looked at the labels – Calvin Klein, Diesel, G-Star. It was like a department store. He counted the clothes, taking note of brands and how many of each there were.

'Hundred pound a pair,' he told Ward, pointing at a pair of jeans.

On the desk were photos – the two flatmates, partying in the tropics. There was sunshine, cocktails, palm trees. Girls in bikinis, lads in board shorts.

'Portstewart?' Ward said sarcastically.

'Donegal surely.'

In the desk drawers was a car key for an Audi A3. O'Neill lifted it. There was McCarthy's old post, a couple of bills, some bank statements. He scanned the columns before putting them in the evidence bag.

Downstairs Craig was on the sofa.

'Some good photos up there.'

'Yeah, last summer, we went to Miami Beach.'

'I might have to start saving. Listen, we're gonna take a few things with us here. And we'll need to talk to you again, probably this week.'

The two detectives walked back to the car in silence. O'Neill put the evidence bag in the boot before climbing behind the wheel and slamming the door shut. Ward was in the passenger seat, staring out at the grey afternoon.

'What do you reckon?' O'Neill said.

'He's full of shit.'

O'Neill nodded in agreement. 'Yip. Full of shit.'

He started the car and pulled on to the Ormeau Road, heading back to the station.

At Musgrave Street the Press Briefing Room was packed. Reporters were squashed into rows of plastic chairs, pens hovering, Dictaphones at the ready. There were TV cameras at the back, local news only, the big boys not interested. Wilson stood at the podium, like a headmaster addressing an assembly. Behind his head, the new badge of the PSNI.

O'Neill and Ward slipped into the back row to watch the performance.

The Chief Inspector cleared his throat, calling the room to attention. He was stately, polished, reassuring. The death of Jonathan McCarthy was a tragedy. No stone would be left unturned. Perpetrators would be brought to justice. It was calm, assertive, what people liked to hear. Wilson affected a serious concern, like he didn't want to be standing there, having to talk about something like Tomb Street. It was an unsavoury job, that's right, but someone had to do it. O'Neill saw the confidence and the command of the room. He felt like he was watching an actor.

He closed his eyes and was back at the McCarthy house, in the father's study, talking to the parents. He looked round the room with its collection of trophies, the rugby caps, the framed shirts. He watched the da again, his clothes struggling to cover his prop's build. He listened to him, the anger, the disappointment, the sense that the son didn't measure up.

O'Neill opened his eyes and pictured his own da, rolling in from the Chester with a skin full on him. He'd inherited a building company and taken ten years to piss it away. It was someone else's fault, always was – the customers, the suppliers, the bank manager. O'Neill would hear him rattling round the kitchen, looking for more drink. He would creep down the stairs and stand by the door.

'The O'Neills, son,' his da slurring. 'We were the Kings of Ulster. That was us. We were something, a big noise ... all those red hands (hiccup) ... on the walls like...'

His father would sway, pointing the finger, turning nasty.

'I see yous looking at me, you and your ma. We'll let me ask you something – what are you gonna amount to, eh, son? Nothing. Wait till you see. Sweet fuck all.'

O'Neill would slide upstairs to bed, leaving the auld boy nursing his wounds.

In Musgrave Street Wilson called the press conference to a close, throwing out another sound bite about police commitment, the new Northern Ireland and the bright tomorrow they were all working towards together.

Walking out, O'Neill turned to the DI. 'What do you reckon?'

Ward smiled wryly. 'Full of shit.'

O'Neill snorted quietly, and followed the DI upstairs.

# EIGHT

It was dark out, almost eight and the streets were dead.

Marty Toner crouched in the shadow of the alley, staying back, out of the glare of the street lights. He'd been there an hour, staring at 46 Rutland Street, Tierney's ma's place.

That afternoon he'd done the circuit, using a BMX nicked from a garden off the Ravenhill Road. Tierney slept in three different spots – Stewart Street, Cooke Street, Rutland Street. The girlfriend, the bit on the side, the mother. He was smart and trusted no one, constantly changing it up, never the same house two nights on the trot. Marty spent the day weighing each location up, thinking about hiding places, escape routes, the potential for witnesses.

He needed to do Tierney and slip away without anyone seeing him. He'd thought about a silencer for the Browning, like something off James Bond, but knew he was dreaming. Marty had stashed the gun round the back of the Maxol, worried about the peelers doing a random stop and search and finding it.

Behind the wheelie bin in the entry, he made a decision – Rutland Street.

Once a week, sometimes twice, Tierney stayed with his ma. He used it as a stash house for whatever gear or money he happened to be holding that week. Marty considered stealing it, making the whole thing look like robbery. It was stupid though; too risky, too greedy, too much arsing about.

No, it had to be simple – come from nowhere, put a bullet in him, then vamoose.

Rutland Street wasn't perfect but it was the best of the bunch. He could lie out of sight, wait for Tierney to show. The front door was twenty yards. Marty would come out of the dark, be there in seconds, gun at his side. He thought about what he'd say – 'This is for Petesy', 'Your turn dickhead', something like that. He shook his head, reminding himself this wasn't Hollywood and he wasn't Bruce Willis or one of them other clowns. Plus what if Tierney didn't die, or at least lived long enough to speak to someone, to finger him for it. Like everything else, Marty thought, the best idea was to keep your mouth shut and your head down.

He looked at his phone. It was getting on for nine, time to go. Marty jogged to the far end of the entry where it led into Balfour Avenue. He lifted the BMX from between two bins, pulled up his hood and headed out into the night.

'This is a load of balls.'

Locksey stared at the scratch card, coin in hand, shaking his head. Marty sat opposite on an upturned milk crate, smoking a fag. They were round the back of the Maxol, waiting. Every two minutes Marty looked at his watch and shook his head.

'Three cherries, fuck sake, never four.' Locksey said, tossing the card. 'It's like they dangle the carrot, just so they can snatch it away.'

Marty was half listening, his mind back at Rutland Street, rehearsing things, running over options.

Locksey looked towards the main road, his head swivelling.

'Where the fuck are they?'

They'd been there twenty minutes and there was no sign of the gear. No girl pushing a pram, no kid on his bike, no taxi slowing, waving them over. Marty took a deep draw against the cold and looked at his phone – 9.22.

'It's bad business,' Locksey said. 'Folk are waiting to score, get their night going. We don't show they'll just go somewhere else.'

'Calm down and shut up,' Marty said.

He'd had the crew eight months – him, Locksey and Wee Anto. Locksey was on the money, Wee Anto the gear. Marty touched nothing, something he'd learned from watching Tierney. You sat back and watched, let others take the risk.

'Here,' he said, flicking the lit cigarette at Locksey.

'And where the fuck's Wee Anto? He some kind of part-timer?'

Anto was at the same place he always was – the Golden Fry, feeding the puggie.

'It's ball freezing out here,' Locksey said, eyes narrow, teeth gritted. 'Bet Tierney's not out in this. Probably at home, sipping a beer, getting his knob sucked.'

Anto rounded the corner. Fourteen years old and full of swagger.

'A'right, dickheads.'

Marty watched the two of them every weekend, blowing everything they made. With Locksey it was clothes – Diesel, Firetrap, Lacoste. You never saw him without a label. What Wee Anto didn't gamble he spent on his Xbox. 'Call of Duty', 'Grand Theft Auto', 'Gears of War' – the more violence, the better.

The three heads turned as a black Porsche purred into the garage and sidled up to a petrol pump. A young guy in his twenties got out and started filling up. In the passenger seat was a girl with long blonde hair and high cheekbones, pouting as she applied lipgloss in the mirror.

Anto whistled to himself. 'Would you look at that?'

'Aye, car's not bad and all,' Locksey said.

'Right, darling,' Anto called, the girl not hearing him. Her fella had gone into the shop. 'I'm going to talk to her,' Anto chimed, making to stand.

Marty glared, suddenly angry. 'Sit yourself down and shut the fuck up.'

Anto made to answer but saw Marty's face.

'We're working here.'

'All right, dead on,' Anto said, 'take a chill pill, would ye?'

Marty looked away and lit another fag. Anto looked down, spying the scratch card at Locksey's feet.

'Still a loser eh?'

'Not what your ma reckons.'

Marty watched the two of them go back and forth, each less original than the other. He thought about Petesy, wondering where he was, what he was doing. He pictured him with his face in a book, the eyebrows furrowed, the desk lamp casting a halo of light. It had been good seeing him yesterday. He knew he left it too long and made a promise to ping Petesy's windows once it was all over, once the Tierney business had been sorted.

For six months the three of them had been selling Tierney's gear round the Holy Lands. It was Belfast's student ghetto. Landlords squashed as many twenty-year-olds into damp houses as they could legally get away with. They were good customers, all with part-time jobs, student loans and rich daddies. Marty had mixed his own gear in with Tierney's, not telling Locksey or Anto. They were pulling in two grand a week, half of which was Marty's.

He looked at his mobile – 9.32 p.m., the drop-off was half an hour late. Tierney never used a phone, too paranoid, too worried about the peelers.

Marty thought about his own money, the fourteen grand at his ma's. No one knew about it, not Locksey, not Anto, not even Petesy. What was he going to do with it? He thought about a car, but there was the licence issue. A plane ticket, but he'd no passport and besides, where would he go?

'Here,' he said, curious. 'What would you do if you won fourteen grand on that scratch card?'

'What?' Locksey said.

'Fourteen grand. What would you do?'

'Why fourteen?'

'It doesn't matter how much. What would you do?'

'I'm just saying like, fourteen's—'

'Easy-peasy,' Anto interrupted. 'New TV, flat screen, new PlayStation, load of games, load of Es.'

'Nah,' Locksey said, getting into it. 'You'd get decked out. Ralph Lauren. Tommy Hilfiger. Giorgio Armani. The fanny'd be hanging off you.'

Marty listened. They were like everyone he knew – couldn't see past the next weekend, the next bit of cash, the next chance to get off your face. For some folk it was drugs, for some it was cars, for some it was girls. Nothing was ever more than seven days away.

The three lads stopped talking as an armoured Land Rover pulled into the petrol station. Their eyes narrowed, each of them putting on their game face.

The doors creaked open and two peelers stepped down.

They walked to the back of the station to the three hoods. Marty recognized one of the peelers. Donnelly was in his thirties, six foot two, sixteen stone. The other one was younger and brand new; you could tell by the uniform, and the startled eyes he was doing everything to hide.

'What are yous doing?' Donnelly demanded.

The hoods stared up, none of them talking.

'Up,' the peeler signalled, gesturing them to their feet. He came round and squared up to Marty. 'I said what the fuck are yous doing.'

Donnelly moved closer, getting into his face. Marty let his eyes go soft, focusing on the cop's chest, refusing to eyeball him. He knew the game – let them have their fun, talk some shit, run their mouths off. Eventually they'd get bored and go try their luck with some other poor bastard.

'I know you, you wee shit,' the older cop said, searching his memories. 'Toner, right? Marty Toner.'

Marty didn't acknowledge it.

'The Markets. Your ma's an alkie, bit of a hoor too.'

Marty gazed through the peeler, allowing the words to float past his ears.

'Empty your pockets,' he said, gesturing to the wheelie bin.

Marty turned them out. A tenner, a fag packet with two singles and a lighter. Always the same.

The cop shook his head, disappointed, but still gloating. He turned to his mate.

'Fucking Al Capone, eh? A tenner? Who says crime doesn't pay?' The cop shook his head. 'That's the problem with you wee hoods. No ambition, no imagination, no brains. A year's time, we'll roll by this garage and you wee dicks will still be sitting here, still shoplifting Mars bars, still pulling your wires. I mean is this it do you reckon? Is this life for yous? Is this what it's going to be?'

Locksey and Anto kept their heads down. Marty fixed his eyes on Donnelly's chest. He wanted to answer, to tell the peeler that in a year he'd still be in his Land Rover, still giving shit to sixteen-year-olds, still acting the big lad. Who was the sadder bastard? Marty wasn't sure.

'This is the last time I want to see yous anywhere near this garage, you hear? There's normal people use this place. Go and be fucking hoods somewhere else.'

The three lads sloped off, walking as slow as possible.

Marty sent Anto to the George to get word to Tierney. Half an hour later he got a phone call with details of a new drop-off.

They walked through the Markets, stopping at the bank of Lagan. Broken glass shimmered on the asphalt. Marty looked around. It was the spot where Petesy had been done. He chose it deliberately, wanting to go there, wanting to remind himself.

Anto and Locksey threw stones into the black water of the river. Marty stood for a second, closing his eyes, allowing the memories to come back to him – the screaming, the pleading, the sound of bones breaking. He lifted his hand to his face, feeling his cheek where they'd ground it into the gravel, making him watch.

He opened his eyes, thinking about Rutland Street, the alleyway and Tierney.

# NINE

Ward was asleep in his bed.

He dreamt he was twenty-two again, walking the waterfront at Bangor, holding Maureen's hand. It was before they were married, before the cancer, before the chemo, before everything. It was balmy, late August and their shadows stretched out in front of them. The promenade was crowded so they walked a while, wanting to be alone, away from the world. Ward pulled Maureen close and looked at the ocean. Somewhere in the distance a dog was barking.

When they'd left everyone behind he steered her towards a bench.

'You getting tired,' she teased.

They sat there, neither of them talking. A serious expression fell over Ward's face, like he was mulling something over, something he was afraid of.

'You know ... I've been thinking.'

'Careful now.'

He laughed. It was vintage Maureen, couldn't be serious if you paid her. He heard the dog again, closer now.

'I'm serious. I'm mean about me and you.'

'Oh aye?' she said, pressing herself under his arm.

Ward closed his eyes, smelling her perfume, the L'Air du Temps she saved for and bought from Anderson MacAulay's.

'I think we should go ahead, you know, go ahead and get ...'

The barking closer now, more urgent, threatening. Ward

looked over his shoulder but there was no dog. He turned back to Maureen, trying to remember where he'd left off.

Again the dog, panicked, insistent ...

Ward snapped awake, his hand reaching for the bedside cabinet and his Glock. Outside the bungalow the dog was barking urgently. He'd had the Alsatian four years, an ex-police canine. It was part company, part security. He looked at the alarm clock – 4.15. Ward got out of bed, staying low, sliding to the wall. He peered through the side of the curtain. It was pitch black out, the light flat, the moon hidden. He couldn't see the hedge, two hundred metres away, at the bottom of the garden.

The dog barked again, harder this time, more insistent.

This is it, Ward thought, his mouth dry, his heart pounding. He gripped the gun in two hands and released the safety. He thought about the sympathy cards in the drawer back at Musgrave Street. He remembered Pat Kennedy's words – 'if anything's going to happen, that's where they'll come.' A thought started to play inside his head – Bastards ... bastards ...

Ward padded through the house in bare feet, boxers and a vest. He suddenly pictured himself, discovered by uniform, lying on his front lawn in his underwear. He shut the thought out and moved through the house, checking out through each window. The light at the bottom of the drive was on, the sensor tripped. There was at least one then, coming up through the garden.

Ward rubbed his palms against his vest, trying to dry the sweat. He adjusted his grip on the gun and looked at the back door, not wanting to go out.

Again the dog – aggressive, determined, convinced.

Ward lowered his head, telling himself he wasn't going to be gunned down in his own home.

'Bastards,' he said, stepping forward and sliding the deadbolt back on the door.

The dog stopped barking as soon as the door opened and Ward stepped into the yard. It came to heel, ears up, eyes open.

'Good boy,' he whispered, reaching down, stroking him.

Beyond the house the wind blew across the fields, buffeting the grass, making the sycamores move. The bungalow was hidden amid rolling farmland, outside Belfast, a coupe of miles from Carryduff. The road was at the bottom of a long garden, the length of a football pitch, dotted with large shrubs. The trees writhed in the wind, threatening him, goading him on.

The dog let out a low growl.

'Easy fella,' Ward said, as much for himself.

The street lights were out on the Carryduff Road, putting the lane in total darkness. Ward forced himself forward, close to the house, gun in both hands. At the corner he stopped and peered into the utter darkness.

He sniffed and rubbed his cheek with his shoulder. He'd a sudden déjà vu, like he'd been here before, like his whole life had been leading to this moment. He shrugged it off and opened the gate, letting himself out and leaving the dog behind. Ward took a breath and went forward, moving quickly, towards the cover of two ferns at the top of the lawn.

He buried himself in their soft branches and looked out, catching sight of something to his right.

Ward rounded, levelling the pistol.

Nothing.

He held his breath, listening.

Nothing.

He exhaled slowly, hands trembling.

Ward swallowed and began to edge his way down the drive. The security light flicked off. He tensed, then remembered it was on a timer.

To his left a shadow moved. It was distant, low down, nestled against the hedge at the edge of his property. Ward squinted and backed his way to the fern again. He half raised the gun, readying himself, peering through the dark. He scanned the hedgerow.

Nothing.

Then it moved, again, the shadow. It was crawling along the ground.

He tightened his grip on the gun and levelled it. There was someone there, along the hedge.

Ward looked back to the house; it was too far. He watched the shadow work its way along the hedgerow. It stayed close in, low down, well hidden. He tried to steady his breathing. The shadow paused, listening, looking. Ward imagined a gunman, lying down, his gun trained on him. He thought about the Glock, cursing himself for leaving his shotgun in the house.

The shadow moved again, making its way slowly towards the house. Ward moved back against the fern, pressing himself into the branches. He panicked. There'd be others, the back of the house, behind him. They never send one guy; there'd be a team. He swung his head round, unable to see. He turned back to the figure advancing, lying in the lee of the hedge, willing him into range.

Behind the gate the dog let out a quiet whimper. Ward looked. The Alsatian was staring straight at him, giving away his position.

'Shit,' he whispered, pressing himself back into the bush.

The shadow had seen it too and began to move towards him. Ward watched the dark shape advance, staying low. Thirty feet away the shape stopped. Ward pointed his gun and exhaled, ready.

The shadow darted forward, suddenly turning into a fox as it cleared the overhang of the hedge. Ward heard the dog bark behind him. He felt his bowels loosen and had to hold on.

In the middle of the lawn the fox stopped and started, its eyes blank.

Ward let out a sigh and put his hands on his knees, suddenly exhausted. He felt the tension drain out of his body.

The dog barked again at the fox as it scarpered, its sleek body disappearing through the darkness of the hedge.

Ward shook his head and straightened, heading back towards the house.

'Come on in you,' he said to the dog, holding the kitchen door open.

Inside he boiled the kettle and put a glug of Black Bush in the bottom of a mug.

He gave the dog a biscuit and sat at the table, allowing the whiskey to do its work. It was almost five now and there was no use going back to bed.

Ward stood up, bolted the door and poured himself another Bush. He sat there, slowly sipping the whiskey, feeling it burn him inside. He looked at the Glock, lying on the kitchen table in front of him.

Eventually, he went back into the bedroom where he lay down, watching black turn to purple and the room slowly lighten. He tried to think about the promenade at Bangor, about that summer evening and the walk with Maureen.

After ten minutes he gave up, sighing as he rolled out of bed. In the living room the dog raised its head from its paws and looked at him. He poured out a bowl of dog food before making his way to the bathroom, for a shower and a shave, and the start of another day.

# TEN

O'Neill was in the car, heading to the State Pathologist where he was to meet the McCarthys for the official ID.

It was almost lunchtime, as he pulled out of Musgrave Street. He'd seen Ward on his way out of the station, the DI looking like death warmed up.

'Where are we?' Ward had said.

'Meeting the McCarthys at the Royal. Then seeing the two girls he was with on Saturday.'

'Keep me posted.'

O'Neill had looked at the DI, the bags beneath the eyes, the heavy gait. He wanted to ask, but knew it was a waste of time. Ward could have cancer, be on death's door and he'd never let on.

O'Neill had taken one of the pool cars and pulled out into Victoria Street, rubbing his eyes in an effort to clear the fog from last night. He'd got home late and spent two hours on the sofa, consoling himself with a six-pack and some lower league football. By the third beer he was thinking about Catherine, wondering how she was spending her Monday night. He imagined her online, some dating website, fielding enquiries. He wondered how long it would take before she moved on, before she was back in the game. He pictured Sarah – 'Mummy's got a new boyfriend. We're going to the zoo next week.' It would be the zoo, the pictures, the swimmers. Then he'd be there in the evenings, at the table, playing happy families. Malcolm or Tom or Glen; something reliable, something dependable, the Volkswagen of boyfriends. O'Neill pictured himself being slowly sidelined. It would be a weekend away, then a holiday, next thing Tom or Glen or Malcolm would be moving in ...

In his head he heard a voice, telling him he'd no one to blame but himself. He'd fucked it up, the whole thing. Night after night, week after week, month after month. Like being in the driver's seat of your own, slow-motion car crash. What was he supposed to do though? Just look at his watch, walk away from the job – 'I'm sorry, love, I know you've just been raped, but it's half six, you see, and my dinner's on the table.'

The justifications were easy. It was the consequences that were hard to swallow.

O'Neill had sat on the sofa, thinking about Sam Jennings, wondering what she was up to, whether she was working. He remembered Sunday morning, the lingering in the car park, like there was something she wanted to say. By the sixth beer he had his phone out and was scrolling through numbers. He found her and was about to call when he looked at his watch. It was two in the morning. He'd tossed the phone aside and gone to bed, before he did something he might regret.

The McCarthys were already at the pathologist's when O'Neill arrived. They were parked up in the black Range Rover, outside a nondescript office building round the back of the Royal. On her plinth, a cast iron Queen Victoria stared across the car park, looking unimpressed and unamused.

As O'Neill parked the car he began to detach, deliberately distancing himself from the McCarthys and what he was about to do. Richard McCarthy saw him and stepped out of the car, offering a curt nod. The mother, Ann, got out of the passenger side, looking pale and drawn.

'Receptionist needs to work on her people skills,' the father said. 'Gave us a lecture about smoking near the building. I nearly throttled her.'

O'Neill opened the door for the McCarthys. Inside, he stepped up to the counter and produced his warrant card. The room was classic Civil Service – pastel colours, plastic chairs, an aroma of disinfectant. There was the impression of procedures and protocols, of abstract and deadening bureaucracy. From behind the counter the receptionist looked up, barely interested. She was in her fifties, overweight, a sullen expression. She let out a sigh as she ran her finger down the list, looking for Jonathan McCarthy. O'Neill wondered whether it was some kind of act, an attempt to protect herself from the people that came here and the reason they did so.

'I'll call down,' she said. 'You know your way?'

O'Neill nodded and led the McCarthys through a set of double doors. They walked down a long corridor lined with offices, the doors closed, like folk didn't want to know. Ann McCarthy shuffled along, looking lost, confused, uncertain how she'd got here, how her life had brought her to this place and this particular moment. O'Neill knew the look. Next to her, the husband stared straight ahead, the jaw set, the eyes focused, like he was about to scrum down.

At the end of the corridor they went down a staircase into the bowels of the building. There was the familiar smell of embalming fluids, growing stronger, more intense. The walls were solid concrete, grey and nondescript. O'Neill had heard they were soundproof, because of the screams. He never thought to doubt it.

At the end of the corridor were more doors, solid wood, no windows. There was a row of chairs and O'Neill asked the McCarthys to sit. He knocked and entered, disappearing behind the closed door.

A minute later he came out and invited them in.

The room was small, twelve feet square, with another set of doors at the far end. There were no furnishings, nothing except for the wheeled stretcher, parked in the middle with a white cloth draped over. At the head of the stretcher stood a man holding a clipboard. He was dressed in a lab coat but had the face of a mechanic, someone who worked with his hands. Ann McCarthy stepped forward, her husband behind. The pathologist hovered at the head of the table, looking at the detective. O'Neill nodded and he folded back the white cloth, revealing the head and shoulders of a young man in his early twenties.

They'd used make-up to hide most of the discolouration. The swelling was all there though, the right eye still closed. Despite their best efforts, you could see the hiding that had been doled out.

Ann McCarthy stepped forward, shaking her head.

'No,' she said, matter of fact.

O'Neill's eyes narrowed.

'It's not him,' she said. 'No.'

Her face fell.

'No,' she said. 'No, no, no ...'

Her words went from sob to scream to howl. She turned to her husband, burying herself against him, her shoulders shuddering.

Richard McCarthy put a large hand to the back of her head, stroking her hair. He held on to her, pressing her against him.

He looked at O'Neill, his face plain, his eyes empty. Quietly, without speaking, he gave a single nod of his head.

In the car park, O'Neill told them he had some more questions and suggested the hospital canteen. The McCarthys looked out of place as they threaded their way along corridors, past visitors with their stoicism, their steadied concern, their sense that things would get better.

In the canteen, O'Neill directed them to a table and bought three teas. Ann McCarthy wrapped her hands round the polystyrene cup, as if prayer was all she had left. O'Neill looked at the father.

'What can you tell me about Jonathan's flatmate?'

'Peter Craig?'

'Yes.'

'What do you want to know?'

'How long have they known each other?'

'Since university.'

'What's he like?'

'All right,' the father said, non-committally. 'The two of them bought that place together. Our company did the mortgage for them. They were lining up somewhere in the Holy Lands next, a buy-to-let, they were going to get students in. He's all big ideas, Craig, you know.'

'How do you mean?'

'The flats, the mortgages. That holiday to Miami. It was all him. What I want to know is where was he when our Jonathan was getting the crap kicked out of him outside that club? I mean, what kind of a mate's that, eh? Wait, is he a suspect in this?'

'Mr McCarthy, we're looking at every possible angle. I can't tell you much at this stage. But I've looked at the CCTV from the club and Craig's inside the whole time.'

McCarthy paused, allowing his suspicions to ebb.

'What do you know about Sally Curran?'

'Who's she?'

O'Neill turned to Ann McCarthy who looked up and shook her head.

'Did Jonathan ever mention a girlfriend? Someone from work? Was he involved with anyone that you know of?'

The father shook his head. 'His last girlfriend was that ... what was her name?'

'Paula McCusker,' the mother added. 'They did law together at Queen's.'

'Is she around?'

'No. They broke up twelve months ago. She moved to London and got work with a firm over there.'

'And there's been no one since?'

'Not that we know of,' the mother said. 'Do you think—'

O'Neill put his hand up, stopping her gently. 'Mrs McCarthy, at this stage we're not thinking anything. We're asking questions. But I'll tell you something, we're going to keep asking them. We're not going anywhere, you hear, not until we figure out what happened to your son.'

O'Neill held her eyes until she nodded and looked away. He excused himself, said he had to get back to work, that he'd be in touch. He stood up, leaving the McCarthys with their grief, trying to remember what ordinary life looked like and whether they'd ever see it again.

On his way back through the hospital O'Neill paused and looked through the glass into one of the wards. Visitors gathered round beds while children ate sweets, doing their best to sit still. A boy pressed buttons, lowering and raising the bed, while his da made faces. He noticed an old man at the far end, the only person without visitors. He sat in a chair with his back to the ward, gazing out the window.

An hour later, O'Neill pulled up at the house where Sally Curran and Lauren Matthews lived. Vauxhall Park was at the top of the Stranmillis Road, not far from his own place. It was close to the university and close to town and, unlike O'Neill's street, dear enough to keep the students out.

Sally Curran opened the door and he showed his warrant card. She was pretty, mid-twenties, with shoulder-length blonde hair and an athletic figure. He imagined her walking through a bar, fellas nudging each other, pointing her out. He followed her into the living room, noticing a walk that said she was used to the attention.

The flatmate, Lauren Matthews, was sitting on the sofa. She had bobbed brown hair, black frame glasses and wore a polo shirt with 'Ulster Rugby' across the back.

'I'm going to have to talk to you one at a time,' O'Neill said. 'It's just how we do it. Lauren, can you step out while I speak to Sally?'

'Sure, no worries,' the girl said, closing the door behind her.

On the opposite sofa, Sally Curran flicked her hair back and leaned forward.

'Shouldn't you be working today?'

'I went in yesterday,' she said, 'but they sent me home.'

'How long have you known Jonathan McCarthy?'

'A year and a bit,' she said. 'We started our traineeships together.'

'How would you describe your relationship?'

'Relationship?' she said, pulling back. 'We're friends.'

'Had you been out before? On the town I mean?'

'Only once. A few weeks ago. We mostly got lunch together.'

'And did Jonathan have any feelings for you?'

O'Neill watched the girl flick her hair.

'I've got a boyfriend. Johnny and I are—' she paused, her face falling '—*were*, I mean, just mates.'

'What happened on Saturday?'

'We went round to the flat for a few drinks, with him and Peter.'

'And then?'

'We got a taxi into town, went to Milk.'

'What time did you arrive?'

'Just after ten, I think.'

'And when did you leave?'

'Two maybe.' The girl screwed up her face. 'We were all pretty steaming.'

'Did you think it strange he just disappeared like that?'

'I guess. I dunno. Peter just reckoned he had been sick and done a Houdini.'

'A Houdini?'

'When someone vanishes like that, goes home without telling their mates.'

O'Neill noticed how collected she was, like she'd thought about him coming to ask her questions.

'What about your boyfriend?'

'What about him?' she said defensively.

'Where was he on Saturday?'

'I dunno. Out with his mates somewhere.'

'What did he say about you going to Milk with two other guys?'

'Didn't say anything.'

'Did he know?'

'He goes out with his mates. I go out with mine. He's not my keeper, you know.'

O'Neill's eyes narrowed. He rubbed his face, feeling tired. He'd had enough lies, enough of listening to folk look after number one.

'So tell me about the drugs,' he said, assumptively.

'What drugs?'

'Wise up,' he said, underselling it.

'I don't know what you're talking about.'

O'Neill stared at her.

'I don't do any of that,' the girl said, filling the silence.

'Listen,' he said, trying to appeal. 'I know you want to be a solicitor. You got to understand, anything you say to us is in confidence. We're not going to ruin anyone's career over this. But we need to know everything that happened.'

He spoke plainly. Not a threat, not at this stage anyway. It was merely an idea, a suggestion. If she wanted to mess him around then it could get ugly for her.

Sally Curran flicked her hair, holding her ground. 'Look, I've told you everything. I'm really upset about this. I've lost a really good mate.'

O'Neill watched the performance, wondering if this girl had a sincere bone in her body. He looked at her, thinking about McCarthy, wondering how much he would have fancied her.

'What's your boyfriend's name?'

'Ronan.'

O'Neill waited.

'Mullan. Ronan Mullan.'

'Where does he live?' he said, pretending he didn't know.

She gave an address.

'Has Ronan ever been in trouble with the police?'

O'Neill had already run a background check. He'd been arrested for assault two years ago.

'No,' she said, her face giving nothing away.

O'Neill found the flatmate in the kitchen, making a cup of tea.

'You want one?' she said.

'No. I'm fine thanks.'

He closed the door and took a seat. The girl had her back to him, putting the tea bag in the sink. 'Just so you know,' she said. 'I've only lived here six months. There was an ad in the paper for a female flatmate. I didn't know Sally before.'

O'Neill watched her, already distancing herself.

'You don't seem as upset as your friend?'

She shrugged. 'I hardly knew that guy. Jonathan McCarthy.'

'Had you met him before?'

'No.'

'What about his flatmate, Peter Craig?'

'No.'

'You don't seem sold on them?'

She shook her head. 'No, not really.'

O'Neill waited while the girl sat down. 'So what do you think happened?'

She paused, thinking.

'You ever meet someone you just know is trouble.'

'In my line of work?'

A small smile. 'I mean, it wasn't anything I saw, or anything he did. Him and his flatmate, they were just guys but they were real cocky, real arrogant. Going on about money all the time. If I have to hear the words "Miami Beach" one more time I'll kill myself.'

O'Neill smiled, encouraging her.

'Talk about fancying yourself.'

'What else did they talk about?'

'How they were buying flats together. They'd got that place in Bell Towers and were looking at somewhere down the Holy Lands, planning to rent it out to students, start making their millions.'

'Did they talk to anyone in the club?'

'It was like they knew everyone in the place. You know, when you're talking to someone and the whole time they're looking over your shoulder, like there's someone they'd rather be talking to. In the flat they pulled out these bottles of champagne, showing off like. I don't know, it just seemed a bit weird.'

O'Neill looked at the girl, how relaxed she was, unafraid. His eyes narrowed.

'Your da a peeler?'

She shook her head. 'Brother.'

'Where?'

'Omagh.'

O'Neill smiled. 'You talk to him?'

'Yeah.'

'What'd he say?'

'Said tell you everything.'

'What about drugs then?'

'Not me.'

'The others.'

'Not that I saw. But they were charging pretty hard. If you asked me to put money on it ...'

'And what about Sally's boyfriend?'

'Mullo?'

'Yeah.'

'He's all right. Only met him the once. Bit of a boy, but sure that's half the fellas out there.'

When they finished O'Neill gave her a card and told her to call if she thought of anything.

He headed back to Musgrave Street to type up the interviews. He tried Ward on his mobile, but couldn't get him.

Driving down the Stranmillis Road he thought about the McCarthys, about what it would be like to stand there, over the body of your own child. He remembered the hospital ward on his way out – the man and his wee boy, messing about together. He pictured the old guy sitting alone, staring out the window, his back to the world. Passing his flat O'Neill thought about the rest of his day – the empty flat, a Chinese takeaway, some crap TV.

He pulled the car over opposite the walls of Friar's Bush and took out his phone. He dialled Sam Jennings, listening to it ring, wondering if she was there, watching his name flash on her phone but not answering. It went through to voicemail. He thought about leaving a message but hung up.

O'Neill put the car in gear and turned away from the city centre, heading north, towards Tivoli Gardens. Ten minutes later he was outside the house. He stepped out of the car rehearsing his lines – just passing, wanted to say hello, ask Sarah about a birthday present for next week.

He saw his daughter down the side of the house. She had two balls out and was throwing them off the wall, singing to herself. O'Neill hung back, looking at how tall she'd got, trying to figure out when she'd changed into a proper little girl.

'Hey you,' he said, mock gruffness.

Sarah dropped the balls and came running.

'Daddy, Daddy,' she exclaimed, leaping up into his arms. He shushed her quiet, not wanting Catherine to come out.

He sat on the ground, his back to the wall.

'Keep juggling then.'

The girl resumed the steady rhythm, keen to show off.

'So tell me about school, love?'

Sarah juggled, rattling off the life of a six-year-old – her teacher Miss Cunningham, her new best friend, the dog she was getting for her birthday. O'Neill sat quiet, allowing her voice to spill over him, letting it wash everything away, Ann McCarthy's 'no', Sally Curran's lies, everything.

Eventually the front door opened and Catherine appeared. She looked at him, sitting there, her face unimpressed. O'Neill looked up and smiled.

'A dog, eh?'

Catherine frowned, preparing to have a go. He wasn't supposed to turn up unannounced. He felt her pause and for a split second imagined her asking him in for a cup of coffee. He would say 'yes' and they would talk, Sarah would like it, buzzing round the kitchen, pretending not to listen. It would be awkward at first but Catherine would warm to him, like when he first asked her out ...

He snapped back to her face, to the irritation, the disbelief, the disapproval. Who was he kidding?

'Party's this Saturday right?' O'Neill asked, all innocent.

Sarah's seventh birthday. He already knew the answer.

'That's right.'

'Cool. Just checking.' O'Neill stood and started to walk towards the car. 'See yous then.'

Catherine stood on the porch, her arms folded. O'Neill lowered himself into the car and drove back to Musgrave Street, feeling slightly better, wondering how long it would last.

# ELEVEN

Marty Toner stood at the top of May Street, waiting on Tierney coming out of the George. It was after two and a trickle of lunchtime drinkers filed out of the pub, heading back to their desks. Behind him the towering white facade of the Waterfront Hall reached up towards the cloud. To his right stood the Laganside Courts, three floors of reinforced stone and bomb-proof windows.

Marty saw Tierney come out of the pub and made eye contact. He fell in behind, walking at a distance as they cut beneath the Albert Bridge. Tierney stopped at a spot out of sight.

'What the fuck do you want?' he said.

'What happened last night?'

'What?'

'With the drop-off. We lost half our customers. By the time we did our round, they'd scored somewhere else.' Marty sensed Tierney rising up. He made to change tack. 'It's not good for business, you know. Takings go down, the boys get pissed off, everyone makes less.'

Tierney glared, then spat on the ground.

'I'm just saying,' Marty said.

Tierney spoke slowly, emphasizing each word. 'Who the fuck do you think you're talking to?'

Marty looked at him, wanting to tell him he was talking to a dead man. To a man that would soon be lying in a gutter, bleeding to death, begging for his life. A man whose last words would be, 'Please, wise up, don't ...'

Marty didn't speak. He knew that kind of crap was for the cinema, for Van Damme and Arnie and the rest of them. This was Belfast. Mouth shut, head down.

'Listen, dickhead,' Tierney said, breaking the silence. 'If you don't like the way we do things, you know what you can do.'

Marty clenched his jaw, his face giving nothing away.

'Now fuck off outta my sight.' Tierney stared at him, waiting for Marty to walk away.

At the bus stop on Cromac Street, Marty looked at his phone. He'd said four and it was already ten past. He replayed the conversation with Tierney, knowing he'd done the right thing, knowing he'd get his chance to answer back, all he had to do was wait.

An old lady stood at the bus stop, clutching her handbag, trying not to look at him. Marty watched the traffic, scanning for faces, wondering where Eddie was. He'd no idea what the car would be. He'd said low-key, a Corsa or an Astra, but with Eddie you never knew.

'A granny wagon,' his mate had said. 'Come on, wise up.'

'You want the money or not?'

'All right,' he'd said, sighing. 'Gimme half an hour.'

Marty lit a cigarette and looked at his mobile – quarter past.

Twenty yards away a black Golf rounded the corner, accelerating hard before stamping on the brakes. The old dear pulled her bag close as a laugh echoed from the car. Marty stepped forward and jumped in.

Behind the wheel Eddie stared straight ahead.

'Taxi?' he said, his voice all sing-song.

'Just go, would you.'

Eddie revved the engine and lifted the clutch, peeling away.

'Slow down,' Marty ordered. 'And quit fucking about. If we get stopped you don't get paid.'

'You're worse than my ma.'

Eddie slid down in his seat, collar up, cap low. He'd been joyriding since he was fourteen, nicking cars, goading the peelers into a chase. Last year the Ra caught up him and gave him a Padre Pio. It was a stigmata, a bullet through each hand. Eddie had screamed, begged them, said he'd never do it again. Two months later, hands still in bandages, he was back at it.

'Where we going?' he said as the car started up the Ormeau Road.

'Ballybean,' Marty replied.

'Same as last time?'

'Yeah.'

'Dead on.'

Marty had known Eddie for years, since primary school. He'd been getting him to drive the last three months. For a hundred quid, Eddie rocked up with a motor and took you where you needed to go. He would wait round the corner and if the shit hit the fan, could punch you out of any trouble. The peelers? The Provos? Not a bother.

In the car Eddie turned on the CD player, making a face at the classical music. He hit eject and tossed the CD out the window.

'Away to fuck Mozart.'

'Calm down,' Marty said.

They drove in silence, cutting through Rosetta, past the Cregagh estate, towards Ballybean. Marty found himself glancing at Eddie's hands, at the gold sovereign rings, the two white scars. They'd grabbed him one night, four guys, all wearing masks. They'd laughed as they beat the shit out of him, enjoying it. They'd held him down, standing on his forearms, gun to the back of the hand. Said he should be grateful this was all he was getting.

In ten minutes the Golf pulled into Ballybean, weaving its way along narrow streets of pebble-dashed houses. There were Union Jacks on lamp posts, painted kerbstones, murals leering down at them. FOR GOD AND ULSTER.

Eddie parked up, shaking his head. 'Gives me the heebie-jeebies this place.'

'Just sit tight. I'll be two minutes.'

Marty walked round the corner, out of sight, and knocked on a door. A guy with a shaved head and a bodybuilder's physique opened it, ushering him in without speaking. He had tattoos on both forearms – the Northern Ireland flag, the Glasgow Rangers badge. Marty handed over five hundred quid and picked up the gear, same as usual.

'I'll need more next week,' he said. 'Three times this.'

The man raised his eyebrows. 'You planning a party?'

Marty didn't speak.

'Triple's no problem,' he said, laughing quietly. 'My own wee Fenian. What does Tierney say about all this?'

Marty shrugged.

'No. That's what I thought.' The man shook his head. 'It's all money to me, kid.'

Afterwards, Marty walked to the car, fighting the voice inside him that screamed 'run!' He felt the eyes on him, the

100

large figure filling the door frame of the house behind him, watching as he walked away. He lowered himself into the car.

'Let's get the fuck outta here,' Eddie said.

'OK,' Marty said. 'But go slow.'

Marty stashed the gear and got Eddie to drop him off at the Tech so that he could see Petesy. It was after four and he should have been out by now. He noticed Mackers coming out the door, sporting his usual Man U top.

'Marty, big lad. What are you doing here? Signing up for a course?'

'Aye, likely story. I'm looking for Petesy.'

'Haven't seen him.'

'Thought he was in your class.'

'He was. Hasn't been about for weeks.'

Marty screwed up his face. 'What do you mean?'

'Hey, don't ask me.'

'Right. I'll see you later,' he said, storming off.

Twenty minutes later, he was at Petesy's granny's, lobbing stones at the window. After three hits a shadow appeared behind a net curtain. A few seconds later, Petesy came to the door, leaning on his stick.

'Get in would you.'

Marty went inside. He'd been barred since last year, the old girl blaming him for what had happened to her grandson.

'Boss out?' he asked.

'At the bingo.'

Marty stood in the living room, surrounded by miniature ornaments, sagging furniture and patterned carpet. The place smelled musty, like it was trapped in the seventies.

'I waited for you today.'

'What?'

'At the Tech.'

'I was sick.'

'And yesterday?'

Petesy looked away.

'You're not my da you know.'

'I saw Mackers. Said he hadn't seen you in weeks.'

Petesy's face fell.

'What's going on?'

'What do you mean?'

'Have you jacked it?'

'Fuck off would you.'

'Really? Fuck off? That's what you've got. The man with all the brains, Mr IQ, and the best you can manage is "fuck off".'

Petesy sat down on the sofa and let his shoulders sink. 'There's no point,' he said.

'What do you mean, there's no point?'

'I mean there's no point. I mean, look at me.' Petesy threw his stick across the room. 'I can get all the exams I want, but I'll still be limping round like a cripple.'

'What are you talking about?'

Petesy hesitated before speaking. 'I never told you.'

'Told me what?'

'It was a fortnight ago. Coming down the Ormeau Road. I was with Seaneen Quinn, you know, her with the tits ... anyway she's in my class. We're walking past the Hatfield and three guys come out, all shit-faced. One of them sees the stick and starts slabbering – wee fucking hood, slap it up ye, not so hard now ... We just kept walking, not letting on. Next thing he fucking swipes the stick out from under me. I'm

102

down like a ton of shit. And they're walking away, laughing. And you know what, it was the same voices.'

'What do you mean?'

'It was the same fuckers that did it. Not Tierney, but the other one, Molloy. I'd know his laugh anywhere. Spat on me and walked away.'

Marty felt his jaw tighten. 'So what are you saying? You just give up on the Tech then? 'Cause these dicks give you a hard time.'

'Look at this shit.' He gestured to his legs. 'This is how it works round here.'

Marty shook his head and stood up, turning towards the door. He put his hand on the latch.

'Hey,' he said, pausing before he left, the anger gone from his voice. 'You know how to get into my ma's house right?'

'What?'

'My ma's house. You can get in like?'

'You mean the flowerpot and the key and all. Sure. Why?'

Marty shook his head.

'No reason. Checking. Just in case.'

Marty opened the door and stepped out into the evening.

'Here, wait,' Petesy called after him.

Marty looked both ways before putting his hood up and walking off, his shoulders rocking from side to side.

# TWELVE

Ward lay for three hours, trying to get to sleep. Every sound had him on edge, every twig snapping, every branch in the breeze. He watched the time on the clock, expecting the dog to start up, to have him out of the house, in the garden again, pointing his gun into the dark. At half two he kicked the covers back and rolled out of bed. He thought about a cup of tea and last night's *Telegraph*. Instead he got dressed and grabbed his car keys. On the table was a black notebook, an old one from the early nineties. He'd brought it home from work, knowing what was inside, but wanting to check. He put it in his pocket and left the house.

The clock in the car read 02.56. On the passenger seat was the book Pat Kennedy had given him – Hemingway, *The Old Man and the Sea*. He set his old notebook on top of it and started the car.

The roads were dead as he crested the Castlereagh Hills and began the descent into Belfast. Traffic lights changed colour, signalling to empty streets. Ward headed through the east of the city, crossing the Lagan before skirting the Markets. He approached Musgrave Street, wondering who was on and whether he should call in. He put the thought away and kept driving. The car rose as he headed north, climbing the Crumlin Road to the Ballysillan and the Horse Shoe Bend. He parked up and looked down on the lights of the city, shimmering beneath him. He knew the clichés – the misty-eyed copper, soon to be retired, reminiscing over his beat. He looked down, picking out main roads, housing estates, the peripheral spaces he'd spent two decades wandering. He searched for some affection, an affinity with the place, a lingering sense of loss. There was nothing there. All he had was a feeling, a reminder, a warning – believe nothing, trust no one.

Ward picked up the Hemingway from the passenger seat and read the last three pages. The back cover showed the author, white and bearded, like some grizzly Santa Claus. Hemingway was an alcoholic, killed himself in the end. Ward had laughed at first, wondering if Pat Kennedy was taking the piss. He remembered him tucking into the chilli, the bowl spotless when he'd finished. That was Pat for you. Always ate like it was his last meal. Ward thought about all the jobs they'd worked together, the hours spent alone, side by side in a car. Kennedy probably knew more about him than Maureen did.

He'd read the Hemingway earlier that evening. It was about some old guy hooking a big fish. For days the thing tows him out to sea, struggling, fighting, following its instincts. Eventually he reels it in, only it's as big as the boat, so he has to tie it to the side. It takes days to row back to land and then the sharks come, in the middle of the night, taking bites, one after the other. By the time he gets home there's nothing left, only a carcass, a few bones and a memory of some struggle, him and the fish, alone in the darkness.

Ward lifted the notebook from the passenger seat, balancing it on the steering wheel, not opening it. He felt tired and thought about O'Neill and the hunger he still had for the job. He was on the McCarthy kid like he was family, like he was his own brother. They both agreed the boy was dodgy, neither of them believing the bullshit they'd been fed by the parents or the flatmate or the girl. Everyone lied, like it was basic human nature. Ward told them all, first day in CID, question everything – that was the job.

McCarthy was no choirboy, he figured, but it didn't mean he deserved Tomb Street. Ward heard himself warning the rookies about the big questions, about what people deserved, about what was right and what was wrong. He told them to stick to the basics – the who, the where, the when. That why stuff would ruin you.

After a while of looking at lights, Ward started the car and drove across town, heading towards Bangor. He passed the new IKEA, the twenty-four-hour Tesco, looming over the Knocknagoney junction. Belfast's facelift had left it looking like everywhere else. You couldn't blame folk, he thought. Round here they'd had enough of being different.

In Bangor, Ward parked near the seafront, ignoring the meters and the threats of parking fines. He lifted the old notebook from the passenger seat, buttoned his jacket and headed along the promenade. The wind was cold coming in off the Lough, the waves striking the seawall sending spray skywards. The sky was starting to soften as the purple pre-dawn bled in from the west. Ward figured the birds wouldn't be long.

Eventually, he stopped at a bench, unsure whether it was the same spot where he proposed to Maureen. Without thinking, Ward listened to see if he could hear a dog barking. He caught himself doing it and shook his head.

Maureen would be dead fifteen years in June. They'd never had kids. Every month was the same, the crying behind the bathroom door. She said she was sorry, it was her fault. He told her to wise up, that it would be fine, that it would happen. Then she got breast cancer. He could see it in her eyes, like it was God's way of punishing her. There was the chemo, the hair loss, the ulcers.

Three months later she was gone.

On the bench Ward thought about the sympathy cards, wondering what would happen if they killed him. There'd been a programme on the TV earlier about Shakespeare and *Hamlet*. It was about the son, learning his da had been murdered, vowing revenge. Ward thought about O'Neill. He was the closest thing he had, but still, probably not close enough. There was a tattered copy of the play in the house. It had been Maureen's, from when she took that night class in English.

Sitting on the Bangor seafront he took the old notebook out of his pocket. It was a year until he retired. He wondered if he would spend the whole of it lying awake, staring at the ceiling. And what about after that? When he'd downed tools and walked away. Would the sympathy cards follow him, the implicit threats, the unfinished business?

The notebook was 1991, 9 September to 14 November. Ward had been with Pat Kennedy, in Special Branch, working out of Tenant Street. He opened the book, flicked through the pages until he found the date, 5 October, the day of Michael McCann's murder. Ward remembered the scene.

The solicitor had been returning from work, pulling into the driveway when two masked men approached his car. They fired a total of sixteen shots, all from close range. At the autopsy the coroner took twelve bullets out of Michael McCann's body. His wife had heard the noise and come running out of the house. The gunmen were gone; all that was left was her husband, behind the wheel, seat belt still on. Gerry McCann had arrived at the house half an hour later and had to be restrained by six peelers. It was a crime scene. He couldn't go in. They didn't care who the fuck he was.

Later there had been talk of collusion – how had the gunmen got the address? How had they known the solicitor's movements? The make of the car? The registration? People pointed the finger at the police, at the Branch, said they'd been sharing intelligence with Loyalist paramilitaries. It was all hearsay and nothing was ever proved.

In the back of the notebook Ward had the sympathy card from last week. He opened it again, looking at the words, the curve of the letters, the care and attention. From the notebook he took a copy of a signed interview statement. It was Gerry McCann, the week after the murder. Ward compared the two pieces of handwriting – the jagged 'r', the looping 'p', the curly 's'. They were identical.

Watching the TV the day before, McCann at the boxing club, it all came back – the face, the eyes, the utter hatred for the police. Looking at the two pieces of writing, Ward was in no doubt now about who was sending the cards.

McCann wasn't stupid either. He'd sent them knowing full well that Ward would figure it out.

The DI sighed and stood up, made his way back to the car. He drove back along the empty carriageway, back to the house, for a shower and a shave before work. He thought about McCann on the TV, that knowing grin, the self-satisfaction. Ward watched the day break through the car windscreen, feeling his eyes slowly settle, his face start to harden.

# THIRTEEN

O'Neill arrived at Musgrave Street just after seven. He grabbed some coffee and sat rereading interviews – Sally Curran, Lauren Matthews, Peter Craig. Middle-class kids, their nice families, their grammar schools, their university degrees. They were liars, Craig and Curran at least. All playing the old game. Cover your back, keep your head down, look out for number one.

O'Neill pulled up Ronan Mullan on the police computer, wondering what Sally Curran knew about him and what she was so keen to protect. He imagined a good-looking guy with a silver tongue, someone who could charm the birds from the trees. Mullan's uncle had done time in the Maze – membership of a paramilitary organization, possession of a firearm. The cops had lifted Ronan last year for affray, a drunken brawl outside The M Club, him and five others. They each got a night in the cells and a two hundred pound fine. O'Neill pictured them the next day, bragging about it, the story alone worth the two hundred quid.

He looked up from the desk as DC Kearney walked in. He was carrying a folder in his hand, smiling like it was his birthday. Kearney was young, late twenties and had a criminology degree from some former polytechnic across the water.

'You gotta love the science,' he announced.

O'Neill frowned and waited.

'Forensics came back. The boyfriend, Ronan Mullan, we've got a DNA match. On the victim's clothing. It looks like Mullan's our man.'

'Aye, dead on,' O'Neill said sceptically.

'I'm serious, look at this.'

Kearney passed the folder.

'That's the lab report. They took swabs, cross-matched them with the DNA database. RO-NAN MULLAN,' Kearney said, like a game show host, 'come on down.'

O'Neill's brow creased as he read the report.

DNA was the new science, like fingerprinting on steroids. Management loved it. It was clean, scientific, efficient, or so they reckoned. For the last ten years the police swabbed everyone that came into the nick – every assault, every theft, every burglary. The guilty, the accused, the merely passing through. DNA was the perfect witness – it didn't lie, it didn't forget, it couldn't be intimidated.

O'Neill sighed, knowing that answers rarely fell from the sky. He looked at Kearney. 'Does Wilson know yet?'

Kearney shook his head.

'Make sure it stays that way. I'll go and get our boy Mullan, bring him in, you look at the CCTV, see if you can find him on Tomb Street, if he's anywhere near McCarthy. Brief me when I get back.'

At the building site for Victoria Square the foreman led O'Neill to an enormous crater – thirty feet deep, the length of a football pitch. It reminded O'Neill of a mass grave, like Auschwitz, Cambodia, one of them places. It was like they were trying to bury the Troubles, entomb it all under some giant shopping centre.

'Some size,' the foreman said, joining O'Neill.

Victoria Square was costing £400 million. The big brands were coming, it was a headline news – Ted Baker, Calvin Klein, Tommy Hilfiger. O'Neill pictured the gangs of hoods, the shoplifting bonanza. The billboard declared 'the biggest property development ever in Northern Ireland'. It was a 'cathedral to consumerism' complete with its own glass dome. He wondered if anyone saw the irony.

'That's him there,' the foreman said, pointing to a red hard hat and yellow safety vest. 'Ronan Mullan.'

O'Neill stood for a moment, watching the man in his twenties, busy splitting breeze blocks with a sledgehammer. He was five foot ten, well built, a tattoo crawling up the side of his neck.

'What's he done now?' the foreman asked, mildly interested.

'Have a guess?' O'Neill said, fishing.

'I wouldn't know. Drinking? Drugs? Fighting? These guys are all the same, all balloon heads.'

'You had problems with him before?'

'No. He reckons he's a hard lad though. Then again, they all do.'

O'Neill weaved through the site, feeling the eyes on him, the staring. Folk recognized the suit, the haircut, the walk. He liked the attention, liked that they were looking, that they saw he was on deck.

Mullan straightened as he approached and looked at him, face serious. He was covered in dust and had a black eye that was purple going yellow.

'Ronan Mullan?'

O'Neill got a blank stare, like he didn't recognize his own name. He showed his warrant card.

'I need to talk to you.'

Mullan stood his ground, performing for the onlookers. 'I'm working here.'

'Not any more.'

Back at Musgrave Street, O'Neill put him in an interview room. He left him to stew for an hour while he sat with Kearney, looking through the CCTV.

They had shots of Mullan entering the club, at the cloakroom, at the bar. He talked to Sally Curran at one stage, standing beside her, shouting over the music. She made aggressive hand gestures. Mullan tried to hold her arm, but she snapped it away and strode off.

'Doesn't look good,' Kearney said, enjoying it.

O'Neill's eyes narrowed. 'Any sign of him near McCarthy?'

'No. Not that I can see.'

'Is he off camera any length of time?'

'Drifts in and out. There are blind spots all over the place.'

O'Neill walked to the interview room, put his hand on the door, then pulled back; he'd give him another hour.

It was eleven by the time he walked through and sat down. He'd brought Ward, knowing the DI liked to see things for himself.

The interview room was plain, a two-way mirror down one side, a tape recorder and video camera set up in the corner. Mullan was sitting on a hard plastic chair, arms on the table. Ward hovered in the background, allowing O'Neill to make the running.

'You never asked.'

'Huh?' Mullan said.

'The whole way, on the site, in the car, back to the station – you never asked.'

'Asked what?'

'No, Ronan, asked *why*,' O'Neill said. '*Why* are we bringing you in? *Why* do we want to talk to you? *Why* do we want you? Normally, guys are curious, but not you. It's like you already know, like this isn't a surprise. You've been picturing in in your head.'

Mullan stared, feigning boredom.

'Sorry?' O'Neill said.

A glare.

'Nothing you want to ask us?' O'Neill said.

Silence.

'OK. I'll ask you a question, just to get us going. Where were you Saturday night?'

'Why you wanna know?'

'Where were you?'

'Why?'

O'Neill stared at him and waited.

'I was out.'

'Where?'

'In the town.'

'Where?'

'Robinsons, McHugh's, Milk.'

O'Neill didn't like that he'd volunteered to being in the club. 'Who were you with?'

'Mates.'

'Who?'

'Devils, Hound Dog.'

'Who?'

'Paddy Devlin and Micky Hind.'

'And what time did you get to Milk?'

'Dunno.'

'What time did you leave?'

'Dunno.'

Mullan smiled. O'Neill glared.

'We were on it all day. We were blocked.'

'Did you leave on your own?'

'Dunno.'

O'Neill's eyes narrowed. 'What happened to your eye?'

'Walked into a door.'

'Really?'

'Aye.'

'When was that?'

'Dunno.'

'Tell me about Sally Curran.'

'What about her?'

'You still seeing her?'

'Might be.'

'You know where she was Saturday?'

'No,' he said, lying.

O'Neill stared.

'Out somewhere.'

More staring.

'I'm not her keeper.'

'What do you know about Jonathan McCarthy?'

Mullan paused, looked away. 'He's dead.'

'How'd you know?'

'I saw the news.'

'You know him and Sally were friends?'

A shrug.

'Listen,' O'Neill said, raising his voice. 'A guy's dead, he was a friend of your girlfriend, at the same club as you Saturday, and you're not in the least bit interested.'

'He was a wanker. What do you want me to say? Now he's a dead wanker.'

'A wanker how?'

'Kind of guy who goes round trying to nick people's birds. Talking all sorts of shit. How he wants to go on holiday with them, Miami Beach, Las Vegas, crap like that.'

'So he was hitting on your bird then?'

'Never said that.'

Mullan's eyes shifted, the pieces falling into place.

'Am I under arrest here?'

'We haven't decided.'

'Lawyer,' he said, folding his arms.

O'Neill looked up at Ward who was standing behind Mullan, leaning on the wall. The DI looked at the back of the suspect's head. O'Neill tried to make out his expression, to read his thoughts, but couldn't.

Afterwards, Wilson was waiting for them in CID. He'd been watching the interview from the next room.

'Well?'

O'Neill broke it down for him: the DNA match on the victim's clothing, the flatmate's statement, the connection with the girlfriend. Then there was the argument with her in the club, plus Mullan's previous and his family background. Wilson didn't need any more.

'Get the Public Prosecutor round. We've enough to charge him.'

O'Neill could see the Chief Inspector's mind whirling – the good PR, the quick result, the speedy justice. He let out a sigh.

'Problem, detective?'

O'Neill looked round the room. Kearney, Larkin, Ward; all there, all listening. The Chief Inspector had given him a direct order. O'Neill took a breath.

'We don't have—'

'We've a few loose ends,' Ward said, interrupting. 'Be good to tie them up first.'

Wilson looked at the DI.

'It's a day's work. We want to check the footage, make sure we have it watertight before we send it up the line. Mullan's not going anywhere.'

Wilson looked at O'Neill, then at Ward, knowing he'd nowhere to go. 'Twenty-four hours. Then I want to see a charge. You understand?'

The two detectives nodded and Wilson left, heading back the third floor.

O'Neill sent Kearney and Larkin to Mullan's home to conduct a search. They were to recover the clothes he was wearing on Saturday night. He sat at his desk for the rest of the afternoon, typing up the interview, pulling files on both of Mullan's alibis, Patrick Devlin and Michael Hind. He wasn't surprised to see they'd been arrested for the fight outside The M Club earlier in the year. Devlin was the class act: charges for possession, assault, criminal damage. In May, he had put a brick through a pub window after being chucked out, steaming.

After six, Kearney and Larkin returned with an evidence bag of Mullan's clothes.

'How'd you go?' O'Neill asked.

'That was a barrel of laughs.'

'You get a cup of tea?'

'Not exactly.'

O'Neill gloved up and went through the bag. There was a pair of jeans, a pink Lacoste shirt and a black leather jacket. In the jeans pocket was an empty fag packet and an old raffle ticket. O'Neill looked at the number – 162.

'Don't think he won anything,' Kearney said. 'Maybe a stretch in Maghaberry.'

O'Neill didn't say anything as he put the clothes back and sealed the bag.

'I'm away to feed my rabbit,' he said, heading outside.

In the car park he lit up, watching the nightshift about to roll out. They congregated at the back of wagons, sharing jokes, ribbing one another. Behind him the station door opened and Sam Jennings stepped out into the orange floodlights. O'Neill looked up, making eye contact. Sam smiled. He wanted to know if she'd seen his call, if she was working next weekend, if she fancied …

'Oi, Jennings,' her partner, Brian Stout shouted, across the car park. 'Let's go.'

Sam raised her eyebrows as she hurried past. He watched her lithe runner's body, saw her adjust her gear before stepping up into the Land Rover. The armoured door shut behind her. As the wagon pulled out through the gates, O'Neill stubbed his cigarette against the wall and headed back into the nick.

He passed Wilson on the stairs, coat on, heading for home. He thought about a comment – What's for tea? Taking the wife out? – but held back and offered the customary 'Sir'.

Ward came looking for him and found him in CID.

'Twenty-four hours then,' O'Neill said, tossing Mullan's folder on the desk.

'Yeah,' Ward said. 'I know. Here, listen, are you in tomorrow morning?'

'Sure.'

'I need you for a job. Ten o'clock.'

O'Neill waited, expecting more. Ward didn't speak.

'Why the mystery?'

'It's nothing. I'll come find you.'

O'Neill nodded and headed back to the CCTV cupboard.

The footage from the club was still loaded up when he sat down. He had a lingering feeling. It was too easy, too obvious, the whole thing.

After two hours he looked at his watch. Eight o'clock – Sarah's bedtime. He thought about his daughter, the way she used to lie in bed, begging for one more story. He wondered what Catherine had read tonight. When she was three, it was *The Gruffalo*, always *The Gruffalo*. She would laugh and ask him if he had purple prickles all over his back.

In the darkness of the cupboard, O'Neill allowed himself a faint smile before turning back to the screen. He pressed play on the control panel and tried to tune in. After ten minutes, he sat back and put his pen down. It was no use; he'd been at it three hours and his eyes were burning. He reached forward and paused the tape, thinking about what he'd get from the Chinese on the way home. He reached for the power button to switch off the monitors but paused, his hand mid-air.

O'Neill stared at the screen. In the corner of the shot was a mirror, which allowed you to see a blind spot near the dance floor. A figure stood next to a pillar, hidden from the camera, but visible in the mirror. It was a boy, late teens, shaved head, hoop earring. He was watching someone, pretending not to, but glancing every few seconds.

O'Neill moved the mouse zooming in, cleaning the image. The picture sharpened and he sat back in his chair allowing himself a wry smile.

'Marty Toner,' he said. 'Well, well.'

He knew Toner from Laganview last year. He was a small-time dealer from the Markets whose mate had been kneecapped. O'Neill closed his eyes, waiting for it to come back – Kenneally ... Kirwin ... Kennedy, that was it, Peter Kennedy. O'Neill had tracked Marty Toner down and questioned him about both his mate and the kneecapped corpse they found on Laganview the week before. There was no joy. Marty Toner knew what was good for him and had kept his mouth shut.

O'Neill stood and stretched.

'Marty Toner,' he said. 'Long time no see.'

CID was empty when he stepped out of the CCTV cupboard. The shift had turned and Kearney and Larkin had gone home. He was still buzzing after recognizing and remembering Toner. It felt like a compliment, a reminder that he knew the street, that he had a handle on names and faces.

O'Neill sat at his chair. The radio buzzed in the background, control calling out jobs, uniform responding. He sighed, thinking back over the interview with Ronan Mullan. He was casual, cocky even, arrogant. It wasn't how you did it, not if you were involved. You kept quiet and watched, waiting to see what the police had. If you opened your mouth at all it was to say two words – 'No comment'. That was the game and everyone knew it.

The evidence bag with Mullan's clothes was still in the corner, waiting to be sent to the lab. O'Neill put it on the desk, gloved up and took out the jacket. The raffle ticket was sealed in its own bag. Number 162. He shook his head; Kearney had been wrong. It wasn't a raffle ticket, it was from a cloakroom.

O'Neill went back into the CCTV and rewound the footage. He watched Jonathan McCarthy enter the club, hand his jacket to Lauren Matthews who was lining up at the cloakroom. She handed over the two coats, taking a pair of tickets in return. She walked off in the direction of the bar. O'Neill sat back, allowing the tape to run. It was seven minutes before another person came to check their coat in. He gave a small grunt of satisfaction as the figure of Ronan Mullan appeared and passed a brown leather jacket to the attendant.

'That's your DNA transfer.'

Mullan's barrister would go look for it and, when he found it, he'd blow the charge out of the water. O'Neill's face softened. Wilson would have to wait for his headline and his quick clearance. He was looking forward to telling him in the morning and thought about quoting Ward, about following the evidence. It might be pushing it.

CID was still deserted when O'Neill returned for his coat. It was after eleven and he had his hand on the light switch. Suddenly the radio in the corner emitted the distress signal.

A voice came through, female, panicked.

'This is 32-88, officer down, Madrid Street. Repeat officer down.'

O'Neill recognized Sam's voice and felt the ground fall from beneath him.

He ran.

People burst from offices, joining the stampede. Tyres peeled in the car park, the station emptying. O'Neill took the stairs, three at a time. He was in the Mondeo and out the gate. Lights flashing, siren wailing. On the radio he heard Sam.

'Get back,' she shouted. 'Get back.'

O'Neill crossed Queen's Bridge doing sixty. Traffic swerved, diving for cover. He tore through the gears, engine roaring. He skidded into Madrid Street. A sea of peelers poured from Land Rovers, batons drawn. At the far end, a crowd had gathered. Teenagers, hoods up, scarves over faces. The debris was flying – stones, coins, golf balls.

O'Neill scanned faces, desperate to see Sam. He ducked between vehicles, ignoring the clatter of stones, the duty Sergeant ordering the troops. A bottle exploded ten feet away and he suddenly realized he was wearing his suit. He took cover behind a wagon, looked for Sam, needing to see her, to know she was OK.

On the footpath, two officers dragged a limp uniform back from the line. Shouts of 'Make a space', 'coming through', 'Officer injured'. O'Neill saw the blonde ponytail, the dark blood seeping from underneath her cap.

He ducked and ran towards them, then took hold of Sam's uniform, helping pull her to safety. Her eyes swirled, her face afraid. She looked up, recognizing his face. There was a faint smile, then a wince.

'She was hit on the head,' someone said. 'They got Brian Stout and all.'

Round the corner, they lay Sam in the back of a Land Rover. O'Neill stepped away, pacing as they examined her. Slowly, Sam gathered herself. After a few minutes she sat up, holding a compress to the cut on her head. Her first words were 'Where's Brian?'

'It's all right. We got him out of there.'

'Is he OK?'

'They're looking at him now.'

'Bastards jumped us. Four on two. Some bogus call to get us down here. It was just an excuse.'

O'Neill stood back, feeling the adrenaline begin to dissipate. He walked to the corner of Madrid Street and watched as the battle lines were drawn for another night. There were a dozen Land Rovers across the street, cops donning riot gear, ritualized confrontation. He turned back and watched Sam regain her composure. She wouldn't want to seem soft in front of the lads. He wanted to go over, put his arm round her, take her home. Sam resumed her street face, the eyes fixed, the jaw set. O'Neill felt something he'd not felt before, not for Catherine, not for anyone he'd ever been with. He didn't know what it was, but couldn't stop staring. Sam looked out from the back of the wagon, the blood drying at her temple.

'Where's my riot gear?' she said.

The duty Sergeant, John Robinson, approached the back of the wagon.

'How you doing, Jennings?'

'Fine, sir. Just a scratch. Ready to go.'

'Aye. To hospital.'

Sam shook her head. 'I'm fine, sir.'

'I know you are. Now take yourself off.'

Sam made to speak.

'That's an order.'

She backed down, offering a 'sir'.

The two officers started packing up the wagon. Sam looked at O'Neill. He thought about smiling but it didn't seem nearly enough. The two of them locked eyes, O'Neill nodding as the doors closed and the Land Rover rumbled off, turned the corner and disappeared.

# FOURTEEN

Marty crouched in the alley, between a pair of wheelie bins. He'd been there two hours, watching 46 Rutland Street, Tierney's ma's house. It was cold out, his breath visible, his feet like ice blocks. Marty had his hood up and a scarf round his face. It was pitch black but he was taking no chances.

He looked at his mobile – 01.25.

'Come on,' he whispered.

He'd felt sick at the start and after twenty minutes put his fingers down his throat and puked, trying to be quiet. He leaned against the wall, hands in pockets. In his right he held the Browning, fidgeting with the safety, flicking it back and forth.

He'd watched Tierney walk into the George just after eleven. He knew it was on. Tierney slept at his ma's after a few pints. Marty pictured the breakfast table, the old girl fussing over him – 'You want a fry, son? Help steady the ship.'

The image of food sent another wave of nausea through him.

He tried to ignore the voice in his head, the one telling him to wise up, to catch himself on. He thought about what Tierney had said the day before – 'Who the fuck do you think you are?' He thought about all the smart replies he never said. This was gonna be his reply, this would shut Tierney up, this would tell him exactly who he was.

Marty spat on the ground, still tasting the vomit. He thought about the peelers at the garage a couple of nights ago, Donnelly and the new guy – *yous are wee hoods ... never amount to nothing ... no imagination.* He tightened his grip on the gun, flicking the safety again. He heard his ma's voice – *a useless wee bastard ... a waste of space ... just like your da.*

Marty looked at his mobile – 01.27.

He felt his chest tighten. He couldn't do it. What was he thinking? He'd get caught. Someone would see and that would be it. Even with Tierney dead. He'd get nabbed some-where. A car would pull up, four guys, grab him. They'd take him somewhere, to the middle of nowhere in the middle of the night. He'd be let out, told 'Start walking, don't look back.'

Marty looked round the alley, suddenly seeing himself, on his own, on his hunkers, shivering in the dark. He thought about Petesy, wishing he was there. They'd share a joke, have a laugh about something. It would help, make him feel stronger, able to go through with it.

A panic started to rise in him. No, it was no good.

Marty stood up and walked down the alley, away from Rutland Street.

He'd had gone three steps when the sound of a car made him pause. He cocked his head and listened as it slowed near the mouth of the entry.

Without thinking, he took the gun out of his pocket and held it by his side. He pressed himself against the wall, feeling the cold brick against his back.

Marty watched as a man stumbled out of a taxi followed by his wife. He was short, in his fifties, half cut.

'Right,' he slurred to the driver. 'See you later.' Marty watched him search his pockets for his keys. He opened number forty-eight and disappeared inside, the woman following.

Marty shook his head. It's no good, he thought, he's not coming.

Another car, top of the street, headlights brightening as it got closer to the mouth of the entry. Marty listened as it slowed, hearing a door open and a voice.

'Right big lad ...'

It was Tierney.

His stomach lurched.

'... see you in the morning.'

The car dropped into gear and slowly pulled away.

In the alley, Marty stood motionless with the gun at his side. He watched Tierney walk to his door.

Marty stepped forward, the autopilot kicking in. He kept his head down and moved quickly. Out of the entry, into the glare of orange sodium. He was in the middle of the road, Tierney at the door. Marty stepped to the kerb, fifteen feet away, ten, six.

Tierney turned and saw the hood, the scarf, the gun. His eyes went wide.

'Wise up. Don't—'

Marty pulled the trigger.

A click – nothing.

Tierney blinked.

He squeezed again. Click. Nothing.

'Fuck.'

Tierney hurled a pot plant. It missed, breaking the window of a parked car.

Marty took off, his heart racing, his legs pumping. Behind him, he heard Tierney coming.

'You wee bastard.'

Everything was a blur. At the top of the street, someone rounded the corner.

'Here,' Tierney yelled. 'Stop that wee cunt.'

The guy sprang to life, lunging at Marty. He darted sidewise, dodging between parked cars. The guy was fat and middle-aged but he kept coming, trying to cut him off. Marty sidestepped as the guy dived and tried to grab him. His hood came down, exposing his head from the nose up. He didn't stop, bursting across the Ormeau Road. A Volvo skidded and almost hit him. Marty never stopped. He kept his head down and pulled his hood up as he ran. His lungs burned. He cut across two streets, made a right and kept going. He made another right, then a left, then a right. At the end of the road, he ducked down an alley, climbed a wall and dropped into the yard on the other side.

The house was in darkness. Marty stood, his back to the bricks, sucking in air. He forced his breathing to slow down, listening. It was quiet out. After a minute, he took off the grey hoody and silently dumped it in the wheelie bin. Beneath the top, he wore a red sweater with 'Kangol' printed in large black letters. Marty pulled a matching cap from his pocket and put in on his head, pulling it low. He shimmied up the wall and looked out. Coast clear. He threw his leg over and dropped down into the entry.

On Botanic Avenue, Wednesday night was starting to wrap up. Bouncers stood at doorways watching students stumble out of bars. Folk queued for kebabs and McDonald's. Stoned crusties hit the twenty-four-hour Spar, looking for boxes of cereal and cigarette papers. Marty glanced round casually before putting his head down and walking on.

***

Half an hour later he was back in the Markets. He decided to stay in Stewart Street, in the boarded-up house he sometimes crashed in. He'd discovered it two months ago and managed to prise one of the boards off the front window at three in the morning. Upstairs there was a mattress and some candles. He sat with his back to the wall, his knees pulled up, the Browning in his hand. He stared at the gun, shaking his head.

'Piece of shit,' he said, tossing it aside.

He looked round the room, at the old football magazine and empty Chinese cartons. He thought back over the night, wondering if the guy had seen his face. Did he know him? Could he recognize him? Was Tierney out there now, driving round, looking for him?

Images flashed through Marty's mind. The field again, the middle of nowhere. They'd march him across it, a gun in his back. He pictured an aluminium shed, a table with tools – hacksaws, pliers, a blowtorch. He saw himself tied to a chair, a spotlight, the sound of laughter.

He sighed and shook his head, the words coming out on their own.

'I'm fucked.'

# FIFTEEN

O'Neill was at his desk, burying himself in Tomb Street. He tried not to think about Sam, about Madrid Street, about what almost happened last night. He'd texted her when she was in the hospital and got a reply – 'Five stitches, hell of a sore head ... and thanks xx.'

He'd reread the message when he woke up, then tried to call. Sam's mobile was off. O'Neill had driven past her flat on his way in to Musgrave Street. The curtains were drawn and the lights off. He didn't stop.

In CID he reached for the notes from the Mullan interview, focusing on the job, on something more tangible. He didn't like Mullan. Too neat – the DNA, the motive, the MO. They'd get a charge and it would go to trial, but no further. Wilson wouldn't complain. He would have his clearance, the conviction would be someone else's problem.

Ward put his head round the door. 'You ready?'

'Sure,' O'Neill said, still wondering what he was ready for.

In the car park Ward walked to an unmarked Mondeo. 'I'll drive.'

'So what are we doing?' O'Neill said, lowering into the passenger seat.

'You'll see.'

Ward steered the car towards the station gates. O'Neill heard Wilson's words, the warning about Ward, about Special Branch and how they couldn't be trusted. He thought about the DI's retirement, how he'd be on his own when Ward left, no one watching his back.

They drove three blocks before pulling up outside the George. O'Neill knew the bar, by name and reputation. A year ago a man had been stabbed inside. It was Saturday night and the place had been packed but not a single witness came forward. Ward parked behind an S-Class Mercedes, black, with tinted windows. O'Neill looked at the car.

'Gerry McCann,' he said.

'That's right.'

Ward opened the car door and marched towards the bar. O'Neill quickened his pace trying to keep up.

The bar chat paused as the peelers stepped through the doors. An oak counter stretched down one side, behind it a row of optics with upturned bottles of various colours. Men sat in threes and fours; a few old-timers bent over newspapers, studying the form. The barman watched but didn't move, knowing they weren't customers. O'Neill swept the room, taking in the drinkers, clocking faces. He saw Mark McGinn, Jimmy Taylor and Neil Gillespie. Serious men, serious reputations. O'Neill felt eyes on him, the silent threat that they weren't supposed to be there.

Ward paused for a second, scanning the bar, staring folk down. He moved through the bar, walking slowly, as if he owned the place. O'Neill followed, feeling the room change as they moved through.

At the back of the bar McCann was in his usual spot, conducting business. Across from him sat Johnny Tierney, looking pissed off, like he wanted to kill someone. The word on the street was that someone had tried to do him the night before. O'Neill had shaken his head when he heard, wondering why it was the scumbags that always had nine lives.

McCann sat back when he saw Ward, adjusting the cuffs of his Armani suit. He silenced Tierney with a nod as the DI approached. Ward stood over them, close to Tierney, too close.

'Heard someone tried to do you.'

Tierney bristled but knew better.

'Better luck next time, eh?'

Ward stepped back. McCann flicked his head, sending Tierney to the bar. He slouched off and perched on a stool facing the room.

O'Neill hung back, one eye on the table, the other on the room.

Ward sat down slowly, like he'd all the time in the world. He looked at McCann, neither of them speaking. McCann sat still, putting on a show for the room.

After thirty seconds he broke the silence.

'Detective Inspector Jack Ward. You're looking a bit rough there. What's the matter, trouble sleeping?'

McCann smiled, warming up.

'You want a wee drink, Inspector? Sorry, my mistake. I forgot you're not so good on the drink these days. Went off the rails there for a while there, eh? Best to stay clear altogether.'

Ward stared at McCann, his face blank.

'I liked the entrance though. John Wayne and all. Reminded me of the good old days. The RUC. Before they took your name, of course, and your uniform, and your badge. You know, I always wonder which you miss the most?'

Silence from Ward. McCann chuckled to himself.

'The Royal Ulster Constabulary. Twenty-five years and hung out to dry. A police *service* now; not a *force*. Yous have gone soft, a castration really, like having your balls cut off. Or so they tell me.'

Nothing from Ward.

'Bet you miss it. Special Branch, you and the lads, the wee gang. All for one and one for all. How is Pat Kennedy by the way? Still up the coast with the missus, what was her name again, Eileen, that's it. How are they doing? I heard he went for the pension, the golden handshake, took the money and ran. Do you blame him? And what about Davy Price? He still in Iraq? Still training the Muslims? Showing them how to be peelers. You gotta wonder what he's telling them, eh? I'll tell you one thing, it won't be human rights. It'll be the good stuff – stop and search, seven-day detention, shoot first ask questions later.'

McCann allowed himself another laugh. Relaxed, confident.

'So what is it then, Inspector? You bored or something? You come down here to reminisce?'

McCann was fatter than Ward remembered, but still had the smugness and self-assurance. Ward could still see him the night his brother was shot. He turned up at the scene, pacing the street like he could kill someone. It was a crime scene and there were cops all over the house. Gerry McCann stood over the car that his dead brother had just been lifted from and wailed. Ward remembered the sound, an unconscious, primal roar.

'Tell me, Inspector,' McCann continued, 'how come you never went for the pension, early retirement? You could be sitting in Marbella now, sipping sangria, dreaming about the glory days.' McCann cocked his head and lowered his voice. 'Could you not walk away? Was that it? Do you miss the Troubles? You want your war back?'

McCann leaned forward.

'All that chasing about, the bombings and the shootings. Not the same, eh? Helping pensioners across the road, the tombola at the church fair ... You miss it, don't you? Them and us, the Provos and the peelers – folk knew where they stood, knew who their friends were, who they could trust.'

Ward sat listening, allowing McCann his performance. He thought about the designer suit, the black Merc, the charitable donations. The packaging might have improved but the contents were still rotten.

He was sure now, sure it was McCann that had sent the cards.

It was there in the attitude, the grandstanding. The whole thing rehearsed, thought out, like he'd been waiting for his moment.

Ward waited until McCann had blown himself out. He leaned forward, his voice low. 'You tell me about how it feels?'

McCann didn't respond.

'To be shut out by your old comrades. To have them turn their back on you.'

McCann's pupils dilated.

'The Northern Bank. I mean the boys pull off the biggest bank job in British history, twenty-five million, and you're not invited to the party. Because if anyone should be in Marbella right now it should be you, don't you think?'

Ward raised his eyebrows.

'So I'm wondering what you are doing here? Pedalling dope, running hookers, selling dodgy TVs. Pretty glamorous, eh?'

Ward shook his head. McCann looked over the table, feigning disinterest.

'I mean the suits are nice and all, the car out there, those businesses. Remind me again … tanning salons, nail parlours, car washes. Tell us this, Gerry, do you wash the cars yourself, or is there a guy does it for you?'

Ward paused, giving his words time to work. McCann looked impervious.

'And you never got anyone back, not for your Michael, eh, not for what happened to him. You can still see it, can't you? That night at the house, the car shot up, the plastic sheet, the blood on the ground. He was your wee brother. Supposed to look out for him, that's how it goes, isn't it? Must be rough carrying it, all these years. The guilt, the anger, the blame.'

McCann's face twitched. Ward smiled.

'Funny things happen when family are involved. Emotions run high. A man could get his wires crossed, come up with crazy ideas, think that the police are working with murder squads, targeting people, family members, brothers even.'

Ward shook his head. He reached into his pocket and took out one of the sympathy cards in its envelope. He held it on the table, tapping it nonchalantly.

'You disappoint me, Gerry. You see there was a time, you know, when someone wanted to kill you, they just told you to your face. Or else you never knew, until they were waiting for you and it was all over. Sympathy cards?' More shaking of the head. 'A bit childish, eh? It's not a bit of wonder the Northern Bank boys didn't invite you to the party.'

Ward stared at McCann, allowing his words to settle. After a while he stood up.

'Gone soft you reckon? Castrated? Well, if you want to put

134

that theory to the test, you know where to find me.'

Ward turned and started walking. O'Neill slid in behind. As they passed, Tierney made to get down from his stool. O'Neill moved quick, catching him off balance, pressing him against the bar.

The room went silent, heads turned.

O'Neill glared. 'Don't even think about.'

After a second he let go, Tierney slumping into his seat.

The two cops walked through the doors, out into the cold March morning.

On May Street Ward lowered himself behind the wheel of the Mondeo. O'Neill got in the passenger seat, realizing he'd been sweating. They drove back to Musgrave Street without speaking. As they pulled into the car park O'Neill broke the silence.

'So what was that?'

'I wanted you to hear it from me.'

'About McCann's brother?'

'Yeah.'

'Did Special Branch have him killed?'

Ward paused. 'No.'

'Did they have a file on him?'

'We had files on everyone.'

'Right,' O'Neill said. 'And what about the sympathy cards?'

'Nothing to worry about.'

O'Neill didn't buy it but let it go. He pulled the handle and stepped out of the car, Ward staying behind. The younger detective bent down.

'Food?'

'Give me ten minutes.'

O'Neill made to move off. 'Hey,' he said casually. 'You heard from the Public Prosecutor?'

'They're coming at three.'

'Who landed it?' O'Neill said casually.

'Ronnie MacPherson.'

He shrugged, one solicitor as bad as another.

'See you up there.'

O'Neill closed the car door, leaving Ward on his own, staring out at Musgrave Street car park.

Kearney and Larkin were in CID when O'Neill walked in. They pulled their feet from their desks and busied themselves.

'Flat out then,' he said.

O'Neill pulled a black notebook from his drawer. In the back was a list of phone numbers. He ran his finger down, searching, finding what he was looking for.

Kearney stood up from his desk. 'I'm away to drain the weasel.'

O'Neill watched him leave the room before picking up a case file and handing it to Larkin.

'Run this up to the Chief's office, would you?'

Larkin took the folder, asking what his last slave died of.

'Laziness,' he said, watching the detective leave the room.

O'Neill reached for the phone and dialled the number.

'Public Prosecutor's Office.'

'Ronnie MacPherson, please.'

'Can I ask who's calling?'

'DS O'Neill. Musgrave Street.'

The phone went silent for ten seconds before a middle-aged Scottish voice picked up. 'Detective,' MacPherson said. 'It couldn't wait until three o'clock?'

'I don't think so.'

The solicitor picked up the tone. 'Go on.'

'Not here. Meet me in Bewley's, ten minutes.'

136

O'Neill sat at a table watching pensioners slurp tea and gossip about their neighbours. It was almost two and lunch was tailing off as folk headed back to work. Bewley's was near Musgrave Street, but far enough so as not to be seen.

O'Neill watched as Ronnie MacPherson shuffled between tables. He was in his forties with wire-frame glass and a mop of dishevelled hair. MacPherson looked doddery but knew criminal law like no one else in the PPS. He slid into the chair, dumping the case file on the table.

'A busy man,' O'Neill said.

'In this game? You kidding? So what's with Bewley's and all the cloak and dagger?'

O'Neill looked at MacPherson, still only half sure. 'I'm going to help you dodge a bullet.'

It took five minutes to brief him on Tomb Street, to talk about Mullan, his previous, his motive for going after McCarthy. O'Neill spoke about the DNA, about the footage of the cloakroom, the jackets beside one another.

'You told Wilson?'

'Doesn't care. We'll have our charge and our clearance. It'll be your problem then.'

MacPherson sat back from the table. 'So it goes all the way to court only to be thrown out at the last minute. Doesn't make my boss look good. Doesn't make me look good.'

'What about stalling this afternoon?' O'Neill said. 'Say you want to look at the evidence, review the footage from the club, buy us some more time.'

MacPherson nodded. 'The Chief Inspector won't be happy.'

'He'll get over it.'

MacPherson thought for a second. 'Why you doing this?'

O'Neill smiled. 'Ours is not to reason why ...'

MacPherson laughed.

O'Neill looked at his watch. 'I need to get back. See you around.'

# SIXTEEN

Petesy dreamed he was holding Sinead Quinn's hand. They were lying on his bed, still in their clothes, for the moment anyway. His granny was out at the bingo and they'd the house to themselves. Petesy leaned forward and started kissing the girl. She arched her back, coming up to meet him. He ran his hand through her hair, cradling her head, feeling the curve of her neck. Sinead pulled away from him, putting her hands to her waist, pulling her top off before lying down and raising an eyebrow. Petesy leaned over, his hand on her stomach, moving upwards, working his way—

Downstairs a fist pounded on the door.

Petesy opened his eyes and looked round his room.

'Fuck sake,' he said, realizing he'd been asleep, that there was no Sinead Quinn, no top off, no raised eyebrow.

Bang, bang, bang – again, as if the house was on fire.

Petesy knelt on the bed, noticing the boner in his boxers. Below he could see Marty on the porch, hammering at the door. He had his hood up, and was looking up and down the street, like one of them meerkats.

Petesy came downstairs and turned the bolt.

'All right, calm do—'

Marty was in.

'What took you so long?' he snapped, pushing Petesy aside and snibbing the door. He marched into the living room and sidled up to the window. He looked through the net curtains, craning his neck to see both ends of the street.

Petesy screwed his face up.

'What's going ...'

Marty was past him, bounding up the stairs, two at a time.

'I've no classes this morning,' Petesy called. 'In case you're ... checking up.' His voice faded, realizing Marty wasn't listening.

Upstairs, he found his mate in the bathroom, stripped to the waist, head beneath the tap. Marty straightened and looked in the mirror. His eyes were two slits, like he hadn't slept. Petesy had climbed the stairs too fast and his knees were throbbing. He headed to his bedroom to sit, Marty following.

'What's going on then?'

Marty marched in and handed him a pair of brown envelopes.

'What's this?'

'Application forms.'

'For what?'

'Passports.'

Marty was up at the window, looking up and down the street before pulling the curtains closed. He went back to the bathroom, squinting at the alley that ran along the back. He moved frenetically, unable to stand still.

'Come on,' Marty said, marching back into the bedroom.

'Come on what?'

'Start writing.'

'Passport applications for who?'

'Me and you.'

'Where we going?'

'Enough of the Anne Robinson. Just fill them out.'

Petesy sighed, opened an envelope and pulled out a form. He grabbed his canvas bag from the floor and scrambled for a biro.

Marty seemed to slow when he saw his mate getting on with it. He looked out between the crack in the curtains again, before going to the bathroom and rechecking the back.

Petesy looked at the form, thinking about Marty back at school. When they were ten he'd pronounced reading and writing 'a load of shit' and threw a box of pencils at Miss Delaney so that she would send him to the headmaster's office. Petesy had never asked but he was sure his mate couldn't read.

'Middle name?'

'Francis.'

Petesy wanted to joke, but thought better.

'Date of birth?'

'Thirteenth of November 1988.'

'Address?'

'Use here.'

Petesy kept his head down and continued writing. His granny hated Marty and would do her nut if she found out. He figured he'd be able to get the post before she saw anything with 'Martin Toner' written across the front. As he worked his way down the page his mate unwound a bit, going from manic to just plain wired. Every thirty seconds he was up at the window, peering up and down the street.

Marty sat on the bed and lit a cigarette. Petesy's granny didn't allow smoking, but he didn't say anything, figuring he could take the bollocking when she got home. Petesy continued to fill in the form.

'So what's going on?'

Marty looked at the smouldering cigarette. 'You not heard?'

'Heard what?'

'Everyone knows.'

'I haven't been out the front door yet.'

Marty took a long drag, pulling smoke into his lungs and holding it. Finally he exhaled. 'Someone tried to do Tierney last night.'

'Tried?' Petesy said.

Marty shook his head. 'I fucked up.'

'How?'

'It wasn't my fault. The fucking gun ... piece of shit.'

'Jesus Christ,' Petesy whispered. 'What did you do?'

'You mean, what did I not do?' Marty paused, feeling like it was some sick joke.

'It was perfect. I'd sussed it all out, picked my spot. It was dark, quiet, I'd three getaway routes. I waited across from his house, his ma's place, where he always goes after a few pints. Two frigging hours, sitting there, getting pissed on. No one saw me. The whole time, just watching, waiting. I'd nicked this gun last year from some house off the Ravenhill. The guy was into military history. He had books and posters and old uniforms, a swastika even. Anyway, he had this Browning 9mm that looked pretty new.'

Marty offered the fag to Petesy who shook his head.

'Anyway, Tierney rocked up the back of one. Got dropped off, the car rolled out and I'm across the street, hood up, scarf round the face, everything. Then I'm six feet away, point blank, can't miss. He tried to say something and I just point the gun at him and pull the trigger. Fucking thing jams. Can you believe it? Anyway, he comes at me and I just bolted. Some guy at the top of the street tried to nab me, got the hood down, but I got away and took off through the Holy Lands.'

Petesy shook his head. 'What did I say to you? What did you think you were going to do like?'

Marty stared at him, eyes boring into his skull.

'Did you think getting Tierney was going to fix my knees?'

Petesy allowed his voice to trail off. He imagined Marty, giving himself a story, wanting to be the big lad, the hero, the great avenger. It was all bullshit.

'Did they see your face?'

'Yeah,' Marty said, before hesitating. 'No.' Another pause. 'Ach, I don't know.'

Petesy had never seen Marty this tight before.

'So what's the plan?' he asked.

'I'm outta here. Screw Belfast, screw Northern Ireland, screw everything.'

'Where you going?'

'I dunno. Ibiza maybe, or Thailand, or America.'

'You've really thought this through then.'

'Up yours, Petesy. In case you haven't noticed I been kinda busy.'

Petesy turned back to the forms on his desk. 'Look, have you had a think about it? Do you know which one you might go for?'

'No.'

'Well, America would be hardest, 11 September and all. They clamped down apparently. Micky Trainer's cousin was coaching football over there and got deported for not having the right visa.'

'I've got money. I don't need to coach anything,' Marty snapped.

'I'm just saying like.'

'Ibiza then. We'll drop some pills, party for a few months, then come back when it's all blown over.'

'You think it'll blow over? You think Tierney'll just forget? Let slide the fact that you tried to blow his head off?'

Marty sat for a moment. 'Whose side you on anyway?'

'Look, I'm just saying. Anyway, do you know if that guy really saw your face? 'Cause if he didn't ...'

'How am I supposed to know what he saw?'

'Well, your name's not out there for a start, is it?'

Marty nodded, reluctantly agreeing.

'It would do to lie low,' Marty said, stubbing the cigarette out on his trainer. 'What do you say, our Peter? You fancy a wee trip? Hit Ibiza. A few margaritas, a few *señoritas*?'

'Sure,' Petesy said, turning back to the form in an effort to hide his doubt.

'Good lad,' Marty said. 'Me and you, Petesy, Butch and Sundance.'

Petesy started writing, refusing to look up. Marty checked the windows, front and back, before hovering in the doorway to the bedroom.

'You eaten anything?' Petesy said.

'Nah.'

'Wait here.'

Petesy went downstairs and returned with a box of Rice Krispies and a carton of milk. 'Get fired in.'

Marty was on his third bowl by the time Petesy got to the final page of the form.

'Here, you know this takes six weeks?'

'What?'

'I'm telling you. It says here.'

Marty leaned forward and sighed. 'I'm done then. How you supposed to hide for six weeks?'

The room fell silent. Petesy was unsure whether to ask Marty to sign the declaration at the bottom of the form. He couldn't bring himself to tell his mate about needing a witness, someone to sign the form, to verify it was legit. Marty sat still, cradling the empty bowl. After a while he set it aside and stretched out on the bed.

Petesy noticed his friend's eyes slowly closing. He wondered had he slept at all the night before.

'Marty.'

Nothing.

The duvet was lying in a heap at the bottom of the bed. Petesy picked it up and laid it over his mate.

Marty gave a faint smile, eyes still closed. 'Don't be getting in here, you fruit.'

Petesy sat back at the desk and looked at the other form. Every few minutes he got up and looked out the window, just to be sure.

Marty slept for an hour, until the postman pushed the mail through the door and woke him. The clink of the letterbox jerked him awake. He was bolt upright before he realized where he was.

'Easy,' Petesy said from his lookout at the window.

Marty smiled and put his head back on the pillow. 'How the forms going?'

'Done.'

Marty forced a smile and closed his eyes, wondering what a margarita tasted like.

# SEVENTEEN

Ronnie MacPherson came into Musgrave Street and played it to a T. He was cautious, sceptical. He reminded them that DNA wasn't enough. Juries didn't like convicting on the forensics; they needed witnesses, probable cause, a story that made sense. MacPherson said he'd have to go to his boss, they'd need more evidence.

In the corner of the room Wilson fumed quietly. When MacPherson was gone, he glared at O'Neill.

'Lawyers,' the detective said, head shaking. 'What can you do?'

Wilson, eyes narrow, lips pursed.

'Lawyers,' he echoed, unconvinced. 'A clever guy that MacPherson, pretty well informed.' He paused, picturing the headlines, the calls from the *Telegraph*, the questions about the lack of progress on the case. He'd already rung the Chief Constable the night before, told him they were home and dry.

'Know something, O'Neill,' Wilson said. 'If I smell you within a hundred yards of this ... I will send you to the back of beyond. Aughnacloy, Lisnaskea, Cookstown. You take your pick, son. You'll be arresting sheep the rest of your career. Belfast will be a distant memory. You'll dream about the days when wee hoods from the Markets spat at you and called you an effing peeler.'

O'Neill offered an innocent shrug and walked out of the Chief Inspector's office.

When he returned to CID, Larkin was at his desk.

'What do seven-year-old girls like?' he said.

Larkin raised an eyebrow.

'Daughter's birthday.'

'Oh,' he said, robbed of his punchline. 'I dunno. Barbies and shit.'

'They still sell them?'

A shrug. 'There's a massive toy place at the Abbey Centre. Got everything. One of the wee girls there'll help you.'

O'Neill worked late, going over Tomb Street, back from the start. He looked at his mobile, thinking about Sam. He didn't want to hound her and knew she'd probably be rough after the knock on the head.

Uniform were on the street with Martin Toner's photograph and orders to lift him on sight. O'Neill read over McCarthy's bank statements and credit card bills, looking at lifestyle. They'd seized a laptop and the IT boys cracked the security on it. There were photos, emails, a search history devoted to Liverpool FC and semi-naked girls. There was work stuff too, business accounts for local companies, names like Speedy Wash, Paradise Tanning, a dozen others. O'Neill made a list and went to the map, looking for connections.

At dinnertime he went outside for a smoke. O'Neill stood in the car park, close to the wall. He thought about Ward in the George, squaring up to Gerry McCann. When he came back in, he went into police records and pulled the file on the murder of the solicitor, McCann's brother.

5 October 1991. 88 Osbourne Park, South Belfast. Michael McCann arrived home from work at 7.23 p.m. Two gunmen attacked him, firing a total of sixteen shots, all from close

range. The victim was struck twelve times – legs, torso, head. He died at the scene. A silver Ford Escort used in the attack was later found burnt out at the bottom of the Shankill Road.

O'Neill scanned the report, looking at the follow-up. Pat Kennedy had led the investigation with David Price providing backup. Ward was a peripheral figure. New to Special Branch. His name appeared on a few of the interviews but not much more. O'Neill remembered Wilson's warning about Special Branch and how they played by their own rules. He remembered Gerry McCann's face from the bar earlier, his unswerving belief that the police were involved in his brother's death.

O'Neill got back just after ten. He lay on the sofa, flicking channels, searching for anything that wasn't a cooking show or home improvement.

A knock at the door startled him awake. The TV was still on. He looked at his watch, almost twelve. He slid up to the window and peered out, keeping himself out of sight.

Sam Jennings stood outside, hands in pockets, rocking on her feet.

O'Neill moved quickly, clearing the coffee table of empty bottles and the remains of a chicken chow mein. He ran his hand through his hair and smelled his armpits, grabbing a can of deodorant and giving a quick blast before opening the door.

Sam looked up at him, her face pale, a small graze on her forehead. She looked tired and shaken, like she hadn't slept.

O'Neill stood aside and she stepped into the hall. He closed the door behind her thinking about what to say.

'You want coffee?'

She shook her head. They stood in the hall, both of them looking at one another. O'Neill was about to speak, ask how was she, what the doctor said …

Sam stepped forward and put her face against his. She kissed him, a sense of desperation, of hunger, of need. He put his hand to the back of her head. Sam pulled away, wincing.

'Stitches, remember.'

'Sorry.'

'Don't worry about it.' Sam sniffed. 'Chow mein?'

'Afraid so.'

Sam smiled, taking a step back and shedding her coat. It fell to the floor. She didn't pick it up but instead turned and walked towards the bedroom.


Afterwards, they lay together, their legs intertwined. At last Sam spoke.

'That was easier than I'd thought.'

'Were you expecting resistance?'

'Not really.'

She lay there, O'Neill behind, arms round her.

'So you gonna ask what happened?' she said.

'Last night?'

'No. I mean with us.'

O'Neill didn't speak.

'Like where I went? Why I never called you?'

'I figured you had your reasons.'

O'Neill could smell her hair, the cleanliness of her shampoo. It brought him back to her apartment, to a year ago and the few nights he'd stayed.

'And what about now?' Sam said. 'You want to know why I'm here?'

'I figure you have your reasons.'

O'Neill thought about Madrid Street, knowing it had rattled her. He wondered if that was the only reason she had come, or if there was more.

Sam unwrapped his arms and wriggled free, sliding out of bed.

'Is that it then?' he teased. 'Got what you wanted?'

'Yip,' she said, smiling. 'Kitchen. Water.'

O'Neill watched her walk out, her slender hips and square shoulders. From the kitchen came the sound of cupboards being opened, a tap running until the water was cold. She came back with a glass and offered him some.

'I'd sack the maid if I were you.'

'Too late. She walked out.'

Sam laughed and took the water back. 'So tell me, Detective, what have you been doing for twelve months?'

'You know me,' he said. 'Different bird every night.'

'Aye, you wish. Your divorce through?'

'Why? You about to propose?'

'Unlikely, sailor. She take half?'

'Pretty much. Still, half of nothing ...'

Sam lay back, breath held as her head touched the pillow. 'A divorced detective. Talk about a cliché. All you need is a drink problem.'

'I'm working on it.'

Silence fell.

After a while O'Neill spoke. 'What about you then?'

'What about me?

'Fellas?'

'Maybe. Why do you want to know?'

'I'm a detective. Can't help myself.'

Sam smiled, deciding whether to tell. 'A solicitor, a footballer and a barman.'

'Sounds like the start of a joke.'

'Aye, a bad one.'

They lay listening to the night outside. Taxis tooted horns, cars climbed the hill, drunk students on their way into town. Sam ran her hand across O'Neill's chest, lingering over the holy medal that hung round his neck.

'Who's this then?'

'St Michael.'

'You're a bit old to be an altar boy.'

O'Neill didn't speak.

'One of God's good soldiers,' she teased.

'If you say so.'

They lay for a while, each of them lost in their thoughts.

'Last night,' Sam said. 'It could have been really bad.'

She paused, remembering how close she'd been. The four on two, her partner going down, the distress call. After A & E she'd gone home and tried to sleep. She'd managed three hours, waking at eight with a migraine, unable to get off.

Lying there, Sam hesitated, unsure about telling him, about letting him in. She sniffed and felt a tear welling up, but forced it down.

'I was scared.'

'Nothing wrong with that.'

'I mean really scared. I though it was Game Over.'

O'Neill heard her sniff but didn't look at her.

'We had this talk,' she said, 'back at Police College, for female cops. Dawn Bradley was a Chief Inspector, ex RUC, shot by the Provos in the late eighties. I was expecting all sisterhood and solidarity, you know, the usual stuff. She

151

closes the door and stares us down. I don't care what it is, she says, I don't care what you're dealing with – a dead pensioner, a dead child, a dead baby – *you* do not cry. You hear me? YOU-DO-NOT-CRY. One of the lads cries, he gets a pat on the back. The big hero, what a heart, cares so much. If you cry, that's it. Your credibility's gone. For ever.'

Sam fell quiet, the story hanging over them. O'Neill felt like he should speak, that he should share something, open up, tell her about last night, about the panic he'd felt when he heard the distress call, the relief when he saw her, what he felt watching her in the back of the wagon. She needed to hear it, needed to hear something, needed more than just a friend, a colleague she could sleep with when the fancy took her. He paused for a second, searching.

'How's Brian Stout?' he said, the best he could do.

'Cuts and bruises. Nothing major.'

Sam closed her eyes and lay still. He thought she'd fallen asleep until her voice came out of the darkness.

'When did you know?' she said.

'Know what?'

'That you wanted to be a peeler?'

'Dunno,' he said, dodging it. 'You?'

'I was ten. We were living in this semi in Knockbreda. There was a family next door. The Morrisons. I used to play with their daughter, Carrie. Then suddenly my mother wouldn't let me. It was the da. You could feel him, looking at you, you know? No one in the street liked him, he might have been inside at one stage, I'm not sure. Anyway, he was fond of the bevvy and used to knock Carrie's mum about. One night my mum called the cops. They dragged him out, kicking and screaming. He threatened all sorts. There was this one peeler, a woman, she strode across the garden and helped wrestle him to the floor. When they finally got him in the wagon she came back to get her hat after it had been knocked off. I was at my bedroom window. I remember she pulled her hat down, real low, almost covering her eyes. She looked at me and nodded, like that was that, job done.'

O'Neill smiled. Sam adjusted her legs beneath the duvet.

'I wanted to be her. To do what she'd just done.'

O'Neill lay in the dark, not moving.

'Your turn,' she said, poking him with an elbow.

He paused for a second, moaning quietly, like he was drifting off.

'Did you hear any of that?' she said, playfully angry.

'Mmmmmm.'

'Honest to God.'

O'Neill kept his eyes closed. 'Hats ... gardens ... mmm.'

In the dark Sam slid further below the covers, nestling against him, allowing herself a quiet smile.


O'Neill was woken by a sound and looked up to see Sam getting dressed in the dark. He propped himself on one elbow, still groggy.

'What time is it?'

'Half five,' she said.

He allowed his head to collapse on to the pillow. 'You want a shower or something?'

'You joking. In that bathroom?'

Sam was dressed in two minutes. She grabbed the glass of water and drained it before leaning over and kissing him on the mouth.

He reached up for her but she'd pulled away and was moving towards the door.

'I'll see you later.'

O'Neill fought the urge to ask what her plan was, tomorrow, the next day, the weekend. Instead he lay still, smelling her hair on the pillow, listening as the front door opened and closed.

He stayed in bed among Sam's smell, the fragrance of her skin that lingered on the pillow beside him. An idea struck him and O'Neill swung out of bed and headed for the shower.

It was 6.42 a.m. when O'Neill thundered on Peter Craig's apartment door. He'd waited outside, catching the main door as another tenant was leaving.

Craig answered in his boxers and a T-shirt, still half asleep.

'Sorry, Peter,' he lied. 'Did I wake you?'

'Eh, yeah.'

'Listen, I was just passing and something popped into my head and I wanted to stop in. Do you have a minute?'

O'Neill walked into the flat, not waiting to be asked. Craig stepped aside, still in a daze, barely thinking. He waited while Craig went to the bedroom to put on a pair of jeans.

'Listen,' O'Neill shouted. 'This has been niggling away at me and I just wanted to clear it up before moving on.'

Craig came out, eyes bleary.

'Drugs.'

'Drugs?' the flatmate said, like it was a new concept.

'Look, you don't need to worry. These days everyone is doing something. A bit of blow, the odd E, a wee line of coke.'

Craig shook his head.

154

'Come on,' O'Neill joked. 'You're telling me you and Jonathan McCarthy have never been offered? A wee try. To see what it was like.'

Craig raised his eyebrows and shook his head. 'No, not us, just not into it.'

''Cause you know we're about to get the pathologist report back. You ever seen one of those?'

'No.'

'Amazing things. They can tell you what your last meal was. How much you had to drink. If there was anything else in your system ...'

He let the thought hang. Craig held firm, shaking his head.

'Me and Johnny, we just drank.'

'You guys were best mates right?'

'Aye.'

'Lived together.'

'Aye.'

'Went out a lot.'

'Aye.'

'So if he was doing anything you'd definitely know about it?'

'Yeah. But like I said, it was just drinking.'

O'Neill sighed, looking round the flat in mock confusion. 'You see, I've been in a lot of flats, guys in their twenties, young fellas. And I've never seen a place as tidy as this.'

'We liked it that way.'

'Really.'

'Yeah.'

'So it's not like you were tidying up, trying to hide anything when you knew we'd be coming round?'

'Why would I do that?'

O'Neill produced his mobile phone and started scrolling through his numbers.

'Tell me, Peter, you ever seen a police dog in action?'

Craig shook his head, less sure of himself.

'They're amazing. Even if there's been the tiniest amount of something, even if folk have cleaned, hoovered, wiped things down, disinfected, they'll still get it.'

O'Neill paused and looked up from his phone, giving Craig a chance to speak.

Silence.

He pretended to press the call button and put the handset to his ear.

'Paul. DS O'Neill here. Where are you at just now?'

A pause.

'The Ravenhill? Great. Listen I'm at Bell Towers, top of the Ormeau. I need you over here with Tommy?' O'Neill paused. 'Right. See you in a few minutes.'

He looked up at Craig, a serious expression on his face.

'You see, Peter. Lying to a police officer is a serious offence. So is obstructing an investigation. We're talking jail time.'

Craig looked pale, like he wasn't feeling well.

'You ever been to Maghaberry?'

Silence.

'Not a nice place. You can fight though, right?'

O'Neill paused.

'It's the stabbings you gotta watch out for. Them boys hunt in packs. One squares up to you, his mate's behind you ... tea-bagging they call it. 'Cause they put so many holes in you that's what you end up looking like.' O'Neill shook his head. 'Nice middle-class boy like you. In with all those hoods. Tigers Bay, Turf Lodge, the Shankill Road. All of them looking at you. You can feel the hatred – your money, your grammar school, your university degree … I wouldn't like to say they'd come after you, but you know, human nature and all.'

O'Neill's phone rang. Ward.

He lifted it to his ear and answered.

'You downstairs, Paul. Dog ready? I'll come down and let you in.'

'Listen,' Craig said, suddenly desperate. 'We might have done a wee bit.'

'A wee bit of what?'

'Just coke.' Craig fell silent and looked away.

'Keep talking,' O'Neill said.

'I don't know anything else.'

'Where did you get it?'

'I dunno. Johnny always got it.'

'Always?'

Craig realized his mistake. 'Just once or twice I mean. At the weekends.'

O'Neill stared at him, letting the silence do the work. The boy looked away, unable to take it.

'So why did you lie?'

'Because of his mum and dad. I didn't want them knowing. With Johnny being dead and all.'

'What else have you lied about?'

'Nothing, I swear.'

'Who did you score off?'

'I dunno.'

O'Neill glared.

'Honestly, I don't.'

'How long you been doing it?'

'Saturday was the second time.'

O'Neill didn't believe him. 'You have any gear in the flat now?'

Craig shook his head. 'No. We used it all Saturday.'

'You're going to need to make a statement. Come down to the station later.'

Craig nodded like the world was about to land on him. O'Neill turned and headed for the door.

'What about the dog then?' Craig said, suddenly remembering.

'Give him a biscuit when he gets here.'

# EIGHTEEN

It was two days and uniform hadn't seen Toner anywhere. O'Neill pulled the file from the computer, wondering how hard they'd been looking.

He read the kid's record, details coming back – the addresses, the convictions, the serial offending. He was a small-time dealer from the Markets. His mate had got his knees done the year before and O'Neill had picked him up as a possible witness. He'd pressed him about punishment beatings, dangling revenge, getting your own back, sticking it to those bastards. Toner looked at the bait, gave it a sniff and walked away. O'Neill didn't blame him. It was the smart play and, in his shoes, he'd have done the same.

On paper Marty Toner had the classic juvenile record. Shoplifting, theft, burglary. Consumerism and commerce. Possession of a class B, possession with intent, onwards and upwards. Next stop would be Hydebank, then Maghaberry where he'd be in with the big boys.

O'Neill read the list of convictions, pausing at the bottom. Nothing for 2005. The last twelve months.

He checked if a page was missing, or if Toner had been locked up. He hadn't. There were two possibilities – either he'd gone straight or he'd gone serious. O'Neill knew which he'd put his money on.

At the top of the file was an address. O'Neill wrote it down and grabbed his coat.

Outside a grey sky emptied itself on to grey buildings, while grey faces hustled in out of the rain. Brollies were up, heads pulled into collars.

On the drive over, O'Neill tried Catherine's mobile. He needed to find out about Sarah's birthday and check about the present. The call went through to answerphone but he hung up. He thought about calling Sam but it didn't feel right immediately after trying Catherine.

The bell was broken at Toner's house. O'Neill pounded on the door and, after a minute, a woman appeared. It was after eleven and she was in her bathrobe, her eyes black where her mascara had run while she slept.

'Mrs Toner?'

'Who's asking?'

'DS O'Neill. Musgrave Street.'

'Oh aye?'

'I'm looking for your son.'

'What's he done now?'

O'Neill could smell the drink-sweats off her. She looked rough, the shakes in the post.

'When was the last time you saw him?'

She shrugged, uninterested.

'Mrs Toner ...'

The woman glared at him, thinking about her bed. 'I've no idea where the wee shit is. Now if you don't mind ...'

She slammed the door, leaving O'Neill on the step. He pulled out a card and thought about putting it through the letterbox, before shaking his head.

In the car, O'Neill got out his mobile and started calling. He heard Ward – you're only as good as your informants. He tried mothers, daughters, girlfriends, everyone he had. They all had sons, boyfriends, brothers, all of them out there, all going buck mad. Sometimes he was the only person who knew where they were. After twenty minutes, he learned Marty was riding a 'wee slut' called Becky Walters who lived off the Ravenhill.

O'Neill ran the name and got an address. He had a Land Rover meet him at the location and sent two peelers round the back, in case he tried to bolt.

Becky Walters was sixteen, and answered the door holding a cigarette, trying to act casual. After a minute protesting he wasn't there, Martin Toner walked down the stairs and gently pushed her aside. O'Neill figured he'd checked the back and seen the uniforms in the entry. Toner looked older than he remembered, his eyes tired, his face weathered.

On the way to Musgrave Street the boy didn't speak. He stared out the car window, at the rain teeming down, the city streets rolling by.

At the station O'Neill put him in a cell and went to see Ward, explaining about the CCTV. The DI remembered Toner from Laganview. Both them agreed it was a shot in the dark, but figured what the hell.

Interview Room 2 was bare but for a wooden desk and three plastic chairs. O'Neill ignored the recording equipment and took a seat opposite Toner.

Across the table Marty slumped in his chair, already retreating inwards. O'Neill watched him act out the inconvenience, the mild disdain at having his day interrupted. He sat opposite and opened Toner's file, making a pretence of ignoring him. Ward hovered in the background, leaning against the wall.

Eventually, O'Neill looked up. 'Impressive,' he said, nodding to the paperwork. 'You've been busy.'

Toner didn't speak.

'Where were you Saturday night?'

Silence.

The boy stared at table, miles away.

'Do you not remember?'

Silence.

'Do you not want to talk to us?'

More silence.

'We need to know where you were.'

Nothing.

O'Neill spent ten minutes going round the houses, acting dumb, like he was trying to figure something out. It was a waste of time. Marty sat like a piece of stone, and a mildly bored one at that.

O'Neill produced a picture of Jonathan McCarthy. 'You know who this is?'

A glance, then back to the table.

O'Neill changed tack, talking about obstruction of justice, aiding and abetting, lying to the police. It was elevator music; Toner didn't blink. O'Neill spoke about Hydebank, about being in there, about constantly watching your back. They were proper nut jobs, those boys, made knives from toothbrushes, stabbed each other over nothing, arguments about fags, the TV, the pool table.

'We're here to help you, son,' O'Neill said. 'Don't go down for something you haven't done.'

Marty sat still, allowing it all to wash over.

Eventually, O'Neill sighed and sat back in his seat. 'Forget it then,' he said and busied himself, writing something in the file.

'How's Petesy anyway?' he said, casual, not looking up.

No reply.

'Still on the sticks?'

Nothing.

O'Neill laughed quietly to himself.

'Like that, eh? Not even a word. Sure you wouldn't want folk thinking you'd talked to the peelers, eh?'

Marty didn't speak.

'Spoke to your ma this morning.'

Marty looked up, eyes intent.

O'Neill gave a faint smile, like he was talking to himself.

'Gin,' he said, pausing. 'It was gin for my ma, always the gin. At least at the start anyway. After a while she took whatever she could get.'

O'Neill's mother didn't drink, she was teetotal, never touched a drop in her life.

'It's like they say,' he continued, 'if it's not one thing it's your mother.'

He offered the boy a wry smile.

'Bringing men home was the worst. Next morning, some guy in the kitchen, staring at you. My ma singing as she made him breakfast. They never stayed round long. But that didn't matter, sure there was always the bottle. Least you could count on that.'

O'Neill could tell the kid was listening.

'Grow up fast in a house like that. You learn things, like the only person you can trust is yourself. If you want something done, well, you do it—'

'You never got them,' Marty said.

O'Neill waited.

'Got who?'

163

'The guys that did Petesy.'

O'Neill hesitated.

'Aye, you're right. But then we only had one witness,' he said, nodding across the table, 'and he didn't exactly kill himself to help us.'

Marty shook his head, as if O'Neill hadn't a clue.

'I was looking at your file before we brought you in. I'll let you into a secret. Except for the name at the top – Martin Francis Toner – it could be any one of a thousand files. Wee hoods, yous are all the same, wanting to prove something, get a rep, carve out a name. Vandalism, shoplifting, theft. Possession, burglary, assault. The charges get bigger, the sentences longer. It's not original, you know.'

Marty was immune to the lecture.

'Look at the first one here. Vandalism at Roselawn Cemetery. I mean, how old were you then, eleven, twelve?'

'Ten,' Toner said, correcting him.

'Nineteen headstones, a sledgehammer ...'

'It wasn't me.'

'Oh aye? How do you figure? We caught you in the graveyard.'

'I only did one of them and I didn't use no sledgehammer.'

'Really?'

'Aye, just the one. Took lumps out of that fucker.'

'Which one was that then?'

'My da's.' Marty's eyes burned at O'Neill before dropping back to the table.

'You know the interesting thing here?' O'Neill said, holding up the file. 'Last year. Not a single arrest. I mean nothing. Now I'm thinking, either this guy has cleaned up his act or he has got serious and knows what he's doing.

But I'll let you into a wee secret, Marty. If you've got serious and you're thinking of playing with the big boys, well, you're going to need more than a street corner and a bit of backchat.'

Marty looked up, half listening.

'You might hear things out there, about touting, about talking to the peelers. But I'll tell you something for free – everybody touts. How do you think we got Jackie McLarnon. Or Dessie Smith? Or Ozzie Fusco?'

Marty knew the names, everyone did.

'McLarnon's doing eight years in Maghaberry, Smith got five, Fusco three. Everybody touts. They use us – to settle scores, to get revenge, to get rid of the competition. So if you want to play with the big boys, son, that's how it works.'

O'Neill looked across. He had Toner's attention, could see him thinking. It was enough for now. O'Neill tore a scrap of paper from the file and wrote his mobile number on it. He slid it across the table, Toner glancing, not moving.

'You should take it.'

Marty gave a faint smile but kept his hands in his pockets.

O'Neill stood and opened the door, gesturing him out.

Wilson called O'Neill into his office when he'd finished. McCarthy's father was threatening a press conference on his front lawn. It had been a week and they'd heard nothing from the police. O'Neill was to go up there, reassure them, smooth things over. They couldn't go to the press, it would hurt the force's reputation, not to mention the investigation.

O'Neill was in no doubt which mattered most to the Chief. He was glad he'd gone to MacPherson, glad Mullan had walked, glad Wilson had to wait. He shook his head, remembering the threat about Bally-go-backwards. And now he was supposed to bail Wilson out, keep his beloved station out of the press.

The rain was easing as O'Neill drove out of Belfast, down the M1, past Lisburn. He turned up the McCarthys' driveway and saw the father about to get into his Range Rover. He was suited and booted, briefcase in hand. As O'Neill stepped from the car, the man put up his hand, shooing him away like he was a Mormon.

'I know why you're here,' he said. 'I told Wilson. Five days and not a peep. We need a public appeal. I'm sticking up twenty grand, asking folk to come forward.'

O'Neill shrugged like he didn't care. It had started with Portugal, since that couple's little girl was abducted. People reckoned the police were incompetent, that media attention was what you needed, that it was all about posters, public appeals, keeping the spotlight on your case.

'Mr McCarthy—'

'Listen, you've had your chance. The money will bring people forward, fresh leads, new information. Folk don't give a crap about doing the right thing. The only thing they care about is money.'

'Solved a lot of murders have you?'

McCarthy shook his head, stepping up into the Range Rover. 'Listen, if yous did your job we wouldn't be in this mess. One way or another, I'm going to find out who killed my son.'

O'Neill hesitated, imagining Wilson's face as he watched the news and saw his beloved PSNI dragged through the dirt. He thought about Tomb Street, remembering Jonathan McCarthy lying there, curled in a ball, battered beyond recognition. He didn't blame the father. He wanted answers and was doing whatever he could to get them.

'Mr McCarthy this isn't about PR. You do that press conference, announce that reward, we're going to have five hundred calls by midnight. All of them will be bullshit, folk chancing their arm, all of them after the money. You know how long it'll take to wade through that? To sift them all? 'Cause that's what we'll have to do.' O'Neill shook his head. 'You think you'll be bringing us closer but all you'll be doing is putting more obstacles in our way.'

McCarthy started the vehicle. 'I've somewhere to be, Detective.'

O'Neill put his hand on the door. 'We're looking into drugs.'

'Our Jonathan?' McCarthy snapped, offended.

'If you hold this press conference the police'll respond, talk about the case, about lines of inquiry.'

'Are you blackmailing me, Detective?'

'I'm telling you how it works.'

O'Neill let go of the door and stepped back. McCarthy pulled it closed and slipped the wagon into drive. Gravel crunched between oversized wheels as the Range Rover slowly pulled away. O'Neill watched it go through the gates and turn towards Belfast. He looked at the house, deciding to go knocking.

A girl in her twenties answered, long black hair, fringe to her eyebrows. She looked like her mother.

'You must be Jonathan's sister?'

'Yes. Who are you?'

O'Neill produced his warrant card. The girl apologized saying they'd been getting phone calls to the house, journalists at the door.

'It's Karen right?'

A nod.

'Just back from London.'

'Until Monday. They gave me a week. That's finance for you.'

She invited O'Neill in, leading him to the kitchen.

'You know about your dad's press conference? The reward?'

She nodded.

'Mum's dead against it. Says we should let you do your job.'

'She's right, you know.'

'Yeah.'

'He's a force of nature your father.'

'Yeah. Pretty strong willed.'

'Must have been tough on yous growing up?'

'Worse for Jonathan, being the boy and all.'

'How do you mean?'

'Just the rugby thing, then the business doing well. My father didn't come from money, so he figured we had to prove ourselves, show that we could make it on our own.'

'Did him and your brother get on?'

'You know any families that get on?'

O'Neill smiled, conceding the point. He sat silently, waiting for the girl.

'Jonathan was doing all right. He did well at hockey, got his degree, had his traineeship. Then they bought that flat.'

'Your dad helped them right?'

She shook her head. 'No. It was all them. Him and his flatmate.'

O'Neill nodded, like he already knew. He thought about the bank statements and McCarthy's spending. The clothes, the car, Miami Beach, Las Vegas. The numbers didn't add up. There was no way they lived that life on trainee lawyer salaries.

He asked could he look in Jonathan's bedroom again. The girl showed him upstairs and hovered at the door. O'Neill looked through drawers, studying team photographs, the school first XI. He looked in the cupboard, pausing over a box of medals lying amongst discarded shoes.

'These his hockey medals? There's a lot of them.'

The girl sighed. 'They've always been in there. For my dad it was rugby or nothing.'

On the way back to Belfast, O'Neill remembered school and the only piece of poetry he'd ever liked. It was Philip Larkin – 'they fuck you up, your mum and dad, they may not mean to, but they do. They fill you with the faults they had and add some extra, just for you.'

He pulled on to the M2, turning on his wipers as the rain started to come down again.

# NINETEEN

Musgrave Street, CID. Two DCs, Larkin and Kearney.

'I'm telling you – big BMW it was, X5, forty grand's worth. Driver's this blonde thing, all teeth and tits. She goes, "Yous uns only stapped me 'cause you're jealous." Excuse me, I said to her. "'Cause you can't afford a car like this."'

Larkin shook his head.

'No, madam, I says to her. I stopped you because you mounted the kerb and almost mowed down two pedestrians. "Whatever," she says.'

'So what you give her?'

'The lot – 3 points, five hundred pound fine.'

'Nice.'

'I thought so,' Kearney said, shaking his head. 'Just jealous ...'

Ward came in, asking if they'd seen O'Neill. No. He headed back to his office, thinking about the Public Prosecutor, his reluctance to go after Ronan Mullan for Tomb Street. O'Neill had tipped him off, about the DNA and how it was most likely a transfer from when they'd put their coats in the cloakroom of the club. Ward approved, enjoying the two fingers to Wilson and his beloved clearance rate. O'Neill would be keeping a low profile, dodging the Chief Inspector, staying away from Musgrave Street. Ward agreed with him. Mullan was too easy, too obvious, too storybook.

He opened the top drawer and took out the sympathy cards. He felt better than he'd done in weeks. It was the visit to the George had done it, sitting across from McCann, looking him in the eye. At least now he wasn't wondering, wasn't trawling the memory banks, thinking about the hundreds out there, all of them with a reason to go after him. He'd slept better that night as well, managing seven hours, before getting up and taking the dog for a walk.

Ward's pocket trembled and he reached for his phone. 'DI Ward.'

'Jack. It's me.'

He recognized Hugh Rafferty's voice. They'd been at Tenant Street together, Rafferty an Inspector now, up the coast in Ballymena.

'Have you heard?'

'Heard what?'

'I thought I should phone you ...'

A reluctance in his voice.

'Speak.'

'It's Pat.'

Ward pictured Pat Kennedy, in the Stormont Hotel four days earlier, tucking into his chilli.

'There was a road traffic accident.' A pause. 'He's dead.'

Ward thought it was a joke, that Kennedy put Rafferty up to it, that he was outside the door, about to burst in, laughing at him. Rafferty didn't speak though.

'Where'd it happen?'

'South of Dunloy, towards Ballymoney.'

'What happened?'

'We don't know yet. Looks like he lost control. Car hit a tree.'

Ward's eyes narrowed. 'Pat Kennedy? Lost control?'

'Look, we don't know yet. The car must have been doing at least sixty.'

'Pat drove rally cars.' Ward annoyed.

'Look, don't start on me, Jack. This is a courtesy.'

'What about the other car?'

'There wasn't one.'

Ward paused, eyebrows creased. 'You been to the scene?'

'No. It only just came in.'

'So you're telling me Pat Kennedy lost control of his car and wrapped it round a tree?'

'Look, Jack, I'm phoning you out of respect. I didn't want you seeing the news and—'

'Into a tree,' Ward, angry now.

'Listen, there'll be an investigation. Our boys are out there at the minute. We're going to—'

'Who told Eileen?'

'We sent a car.'

Ward snorted. 'Twenty-five years' service and you sent a car?'

'Look, Jack, we—'

'What was the road again?'

'Listen, we don't need you up here—'

Ward hung up, cutting him off. He lifted his car keys and headed for the door; Dunloy was a small place.

Fifty minutes later, Ward saw the roadblock on the Ballaghy Road, four miles south of Ballymoney. There was a patrol car blocking the road, a bored traffic cop turning folk around.

Ward slowed, flicked the badge and was waved through.

The B road stretched in front of him, half a mile, then a sharp right. In the distance he could see Saab, up on the verge, wrapped round the tree. He parked three hundred metres away and walked. The RTA investigator was there, taking measurements, pausing to write on a clipboard.

Ward let out a sigh and turned his head to look up and down the road. He took in the dull green fields, the tattered hedgerows, the overhanging trees with their branches shorn by passing traffic. Overhead the sky was depressed and grey. Not winter, not quite spring. The road was quiet and eerily still. Somewhere in the distance a magpie let out a caw, looking for his mate.

Ward clicked into character, forgetting about Pat Kennedy, focusing on the facts. The road was wet from an earlier shower and the verge churned up beneath the Saab. The car round an old elm, a deathly embrace, machine and nature. Ward snorted. The car had crumpled, the tree barely flinched.

He started sifting possibilities. There was no frost. Someone could have rounded the bend, taken it wide, caused Pat to swerve. Or something happened with the Saab – accelerator stuck, brakes failed, steering problem. Ninety-nine times out of a hundred it was human error. That was what he didn't like. He looked at the road. Kennedy could have taken the corner at eighty and still come out fine. The guy had driven rally cars for frig sake. Ward wondered about a stroke, a heart attack. Folk had seizures, the body went into spasm. He imagined Pat, the sudden pain, stamping on the accelerator, unable to move.

The ambulance had gone by the time he'd arrived. On the ground lay the debris. The film backing from the paddles, the wrapping from the chest tube, the lid from the adrenaline. Ward felt cheated somehow, like they shouldn't have moved him until he got there, until he'd seen it with his own eyes. He looked at the car, feeling numb. It was the same when Maureen had died. The initial shock, like an asthma attack. Then the ebbing away and the emptiness, the suffering, the pain.

The traffic investigator was surveying the scene. In a high-vis, he moved slowly, trailing a giant measuring tape. He worked methodically, looking, writing, looking again. He took distances, looked at angles, drew diagrams. Every so often he would pause to take another photograph. He looked up as Ward approached.

'DI Ward. Musgrave Street.'

A suspicious nod. 'You're a long way from home, Detective.'

'He was an ex-colleague.'

'Yeah. I heard he was police.'

'Hugh Rafferty called me,' Ward said, leaving out the part about staying away.

'Right. Tom Morris,' he said, offering his hand.

'So what have we got?'

The traffic officer passed over the clipboard. Ward looked at the pro-forma documents, the same for every RTA. Morris had a neat hand and had taken his time. He probably figured a bunch of cops would be coming behind him.

Ward read off the measurements and the description of the road. 'No skid marks,' he said.

'No.'

'So he drove straight into a tree.'

'It happens. Suicides mostly.'

Ward shot a glance.

'They normally don't wear seat belts though.' Morris backtracking. 'No skid marks, might be brake failure. Or heart attack. Apparently it's like being stabbed. Folk press down, thinking they're on the brake. They're off the road before they know it and it's bang, lights out.'

Ward glared.

'Sorry.'

The DI stepped forward, keeping the clipboard. Morris watched him walk towards the Saab. Ward leaned into the car, smelling the Old Spice that Pat had worn ever since he'd known him. He noticed two teeth on the floor.

'What about the airbags?' Ward said, studying the car.

'Never went off. We'll look at it. Manufacturer's fault maybe.'

There was blood on the steering wheel from where Kennedy's head had impacted. He stood for a second, thinking about the state of Pat's heart. He'd never said anything. Still, he could have been on death's door and you wouldn't know. Ward wondered if he could have had a stroke. There one minute, gone the next. The post-mortem would tell.

He walked to the back of the car and looked at the bumper. There was a dent in the middle. Ward stopped and leaned down. How do you damage your rear bumper driving into a tree? He stood up and looked around. What was Kennedy doing here anyway? A rural B road, the middle of nowhere. His house was half an hour away. Ward pictured the Saab being followed. Kennedy spotting the car, pulling off the main road. He imagined someone hitting him from behind, forcing the Saab off the road.

Ward shook his head, handed the clipboard back and walked towards the Mondeo.

Half an hour later he was outside Pat Kennedy's house. Eileen's Renault Clio was in the drive, another car behind it, a Ford Focus. Ward looked at the Clio on his way past. It was spotless, immaculate, like Pat's Saab.

He rang the doorbell and waited, memories coming back

of the 'hat in hands' he'd done in his career. He remembered the names, the addresses, who it was that answered the door. Ward had known cops that would rather walk into a riot than door knock someone to tell them about their husband, their wife, one of their kids.

A shadow moved behind the door and it opened. Ward looked up, about to speak, but stopped.

Eileen Kennedy stood before him.

'Jack,' she said, her eyes filling as she tried to batten the hatches. A tear spilled out, then another. Her shoulders shook and her face crumpled as the woman buried herself into Ward's chest. He put his arms around her, feeling her shudder with each sob. Ward felt himself start to loosen, but twenty years of policing kicked in and he couldn't.

The woman gathered herself and stepped back. 'Would you look at the state of me? Our Pat would have a field day.'

'He wouldn't,' Ward said.

She invited him into the house, showing him to the kitchen where another woman was sitting over a cup of tea. She was in her sixties, short grey hair, combed to the side.

'This is my sister, Theresa. Theresa, this is Jack. Him and our Pat worked together.'

The woman nodded and smiled. She stood up and reached for her handbag.

'Listen, I need to get back and get his dinner on. You know what he's like ...' She smiled apologetically, said she'd call later and headed to the door.

Pat's widow turned to Ward. 'Tea?'

'You got any biscuits?'

The woman laughed. 'You're a desperate man, Jack Ward. Let me see what I can do.'

Eileen set about rinsing the pot and boiling the kettle. She took fresh mugs down from the cupboard, working on autopilot. Ward watched, waiting for her to pour before he spoke.

'Did Pat say we had lunch?'

'Aye. It was the best form I've seen him in in a long time.'

Ward smiled faintly.

'He was full of beans when he got back. I was waiting on him telling me he wanted to get back on the horse and come out of retirement.'

The DI was happy for her to make fun, glad that there were good memories there to salve the gaping wound that had just opened up in her life.

Eileen smiled ruefully. 'It doesn't feel real.'

Ward listened.

'He just walked out of here three hours ago.' She pointed to a box on the counter, a chicken pie. 'That's his dinner.'

Ward let his eyes fall. 'Will your sister come back?'

'Yeah. She only lives down the road.'

He took a breath. 'Do you know where he was going?'

'For a walk he said.'

'And was he feeling all right? You know, no chest pains, dizzy spells, anything like that?'

'Our Pat, no, he was fine. Sure you know him.'

'What did the police tell you?'

'Just that it was a car accident. Didn't look like there was anyone else involved. He hit a tree apparently. He said there'd be a full investigation but that it was too early to tell. They're doing the post-mortem tomorrow.' Her voiced drifted, eyes glancing towards the bin in the corner of the room.

'What is it?'

'Ach. It's nothing, I'm sure.'

Ward raised his eyebrows, insisting. The woman stood and walked to the plastic swing bin. She pushed the lid open and ducked down, her hand inside.

She came up holding torn-up pieces of card. They were pastel pink, covered in flowers.

Ward knew immediately.

'I found this in the bin last week. I kept it aside, asked him about it. Pat said it was nothing. Just some old Branch guys messing about.'

Ward took the shreds off her and held them in his hand. 'Was there any more?'

'Not that I saw.'

He thought about the Stormont Hotel, telling the story about the sympathy cards he'd been sent. Kennedy had listened, drinking it in, not letting on. Ward shook his head, angry but unsurprised.

'You mind if I take this?' he said.

'No. Work away.'

'Thanks. Listen, I'm going to get on. Belfast – you know what it's like.'

The woman smiled and walked him to the door.

On the drive back to the city, Ward found himself glancing at the torn card sitting on the passenger seat. As he passed Aldergrove the rain came back on. Below him, Belfast lay shrouded in a thick grey mist. It was after seven and he thought about heading home. At the last minute, he changed his mind, signalled off the motorway and headed for Musgrave Street.

# TWENTY

A car backfired and Marty's eyes snapped open. His first thought, Tierney. His second, run.

He looked round him at the bare floorboards, the dirty mattress, the boarded-up window. It was Stewart Street, the disused house. It was his third night in a row and he knew he was playing with fire. It was only a matter of time before someone saw him, before word got round and they came looking for him.

On the floor next to the mattress lay the Browning, a half-drunk can of Coke and the empty crisp packet from last night's dinner. He'd slept in his clothes and trainers, just in case. Marty groped his way through to the toilet and took a drink from the tap. At least they hadn't turned the water off.

Back in the bedroom, he checked the crisp packet for leftovers, but he was out of luck. He'd fourteen grand above his ma's bathroom and here he was, living like a tramp. It would be the *Big Issue* next.

Marty hadn't heard any more about Tierney. He knew they were looking for someone but he hadn't heard his name. It might not mean much. He thought about the peeler the day before, the detective. He remembered O'Neill from last year, when he'd tried to get him to tout about who did Petesy's knees. He was different to other peelers, to the knuckle draggers in uniform, the ones that got off harassing folk. The cop's words were still ringing in his ears – 'everybody touts ... that's how it works ... if you want to play with the big boys'.

Marty remembered his three rules – trust no one, don't do gear, don't be greedy. They'd worked so far. He'd fourteen grand, which was more than Locksey had, more than Anto. Still, the words went round in his head – 'everybody touts ...'

Marty was on his tod, totally alone. He didn't trust his crew. Locksey and Anto would sell him out, as soon as they got a better offer. He shook his head. He wanted to speak to someone, someone that could tell him how it worked, what the play was from here.

He picked up his hoody and gave it a sniff. It had been three days since he'd managed to wash and he felt greasy, like he was dirty and, if he didn't do something soon, he might never get himself clean. Marty rubbed his face, thinking about a shower, some new threads, then he'd decide what to do.

He pocketed the Browning and sidled up to the window. There was a slit of light where the plywood had been nailed to the brick. On the street were a couple of kids, six, maybe seven years old. One was on a bike, trying to pull wheelies.

'It's my turn,' the other one shouted.

His wee mate gave him the finger and pedalled off round the corner.

Marty watched the other one chase after him. He went downstairs to the front window, prising back the plywood and lowering himself into the paved garden. He listened for a second before looking up. Coast clear. He put his hood up and set off.

At number fourteen a shadow moved behind the net curtains. Marty had his head down and didn't notice. When he got to the corner he turned into Cromac Street and broke into a slow jog.

At JJB Sports he bought a grey tracksuit, identical to his old one. There were no colours, no logos, no distinguishing marks. He bought spare socks and underwear thinking of a place he could stash them for later. The security guard followed him round, eyeing him suspiciously. It was ten in the morning and any wee hood about at this hour was up to no good. Marty felt the eyes on him and wanted to nick something, just to stick it to him. He fought the urge and walked to the counter, pulling out the fifty quid that was left over from dealing on Monday night.

Afterwards he walked to the City Hall and got a bus along the Shore Road to the Grove Baths. No one knew him there and it was too early for any young ones to be up. The bus went along York Street, skirting the New Lodge before a mural announced they'd entered Loyalist Tigers Bay. Kerbstones were painted red, white and blue. There were Union Jacks from every second lamp post. At the back of the bus, Marty pulled his hood up and slid further into his seat.

At the Grove, he paid for a swim and made his way to the men's changing room. There was a father there, getting his wee boy changed. He was late twenties and had a Glasgow Rangers tattoo at the top of his arm. The kid looked to be two maybe three.

'Come on, stop messing.'

Every time the da tried to get his underpants on the kid pulled his legs back and laughed.

'Stop fucking about.'

'I want a snack.'

'Get dressed.'

'No. Snack.'

'Stevie, come on, stop messing.'

After a few minutes the da conceded and handed over the bag of Wotsits.

Marty went to the corner and started to undress. He wondered if his own da had ever brought him to the swimmers. He looked at the boy with his wet hair, legs not touching the floor, crisps everywhere.

'Fuck's sake,' the da moaned. 'Would you look at the state of you.'

Marty watched them leave, the father holding the door while the boy passed under his arm. An old boy came from the pool. He was in black Speedos, just finished his lengths. He looked at Marty.

'All right son?'

'Dead on.'

'Few lengths?'

'Aye,' Marty said, pretending he could swim.

He'd always had nightmares about drowning. He used to dream he was at the pool, only it was quiet, like he was the only one there. He'd look at the water, wanting to get in but too scared. Then a hand would push him in the back and he'd tumble in, arms flailing. He'd come up, gasping for air, then go under. He'd sink to the bottom, a look on his face of resignation, confirmation, like this was always coming. There was no one else in the dream, no one to reach for him, no one to notice, no one to give a shit.

Marty looked at the door to the pool and thought about

walking through it, about jumping in, allowing himself to sink. Apparently drowning wasn't too bad. The initial pain, the body giving up, you just drifted away. There'd be no more Tierney, no more peelers, no more looking over his shoulder. The corner of his mouth went up and Marty almost smiled.

'Enjoy it,' the old boy said, dressed now, heading for the door.

On his own, Marty looked again at the pool door.

'Stop being a fruit,' he whispered.

He made himself think about the TV programme a few months ago. People buying houses, young ones, not much older than him. He pictured having a place of his own. Petesy would come round and they'd play 'FIFA Soccer' on the PlayStation, just like the old days. He'd get a car. Something flash, blacked-out windows, so no one could see. They would drive about, him and Petesy, looking at things.

Marty stripped off and headed for the showers. The water was warm and he turned it as hot as he could stand. He pumped the soap dispenser, working the lather over his pale body. He stood there for twenty minutes, imagining the water stripping away the worry and fear from the last three days.

Marty thought about the house and the car. It was good. Something to look forward to, something to aim at.

He'd never thought of himself as a criminal. Dealing was what he did, like being a postie or a brickie or something. With this job you used your head. You'd a chance to make some real dough. He thought about the cops running round trying to arrest hoods. Or worse the Provies, baseball-batting people they caught selling dope. He wondered how come they never went after the customers? The students in Queen's who spent their whole lives skinning up and smoking their brains out. Or the Lisburn Road crowd, their Beemers and their BlackBerrys, snorting coke and talking shite till five in the morning. It was fucked up. Like folk had no idea what to do, so they just picked on the hoods, 'cause no one gave a shit about them, and you could arrest a few tracksuits, throw them in Hydebank and pretend you were doing something about it.

After the shower, he got dressed, allowing his imagination to run away – no more Holy Lands, no more freezing your balls off, no more being treated like you were a piece of shit. The Tierneys of this world – that was where it was at, that was where you wanted to be.

Marty pictured himself with a girl. She'd be older, in her twenties, not some wee slut that would let you ride her for a few tokes on a spliff. She'd be smart like Petesy. He could talk to her, tell her stuff. They'd make plans, go away somewhere, on a plane even, somewhere sunny. She'd know where the money came from but wouldn't care. She'd understand it was supply and demand, that he was playing the cards he'd been dealt.

Marty found himself getting dried and slowly smiling to himself.

He put his hood up as he walked out of the Grove leisure centre. The cold air bit his skin and it felt good, like he was on his feet again, another round in him.

He had his old clothes in plastic bag and stuffed them into the first bin he saw. Nearby a pensioner eyed him suspiciously while his dog pissed against a shopfront.

Marty waited at the bus stop, wondering whether Petesy had gone into the Tech that morning. He thought back to the night that he'd been done. The two men taking it in turns to smash his knees, Tierney watching, orchestrating things. Petesy had screamed, begged them to stop. Afterwards, he lay there crying, the tears and snot covering his face like a two-year-old.

Marty had got off the ground and gone over to him. 'It's OK, Petesy. I'm here.'

'Go away,' he'd moaned, crying.

'Nah. Listen, it'll be all right, the ambulance is coming.'

'Leave me alone.'

'Nah, wise up now.'

Petesy had turned away, his voice low. 'Just go away.'

Marty heard the sirens and saw the blue lights of the ambulance pulling on to the waste ground. There was a peeler wagon behind it so he ran to the fence and hid there. He'd watched them lift Petesy on to a stretcher and load him into the ambulance. He felt his nose start to run and then there were tears, running down his face.

Waiting at the bus stop, Marty sniffed and rubbed his sleeve under his nose. He looked up, saw a payphone across the street. The handset smelled like cigarette smoke and stale breath. He dropped a pound into the slot and dialled the number he'd memorized from the day before. It rang twice before it was picked up at the other end and a voice said, 'DS O'Neill.'

# TWENTY ONE

Ward walked into Musgrave Street feeling like he hadn't slept. After seeing Pat Kennedy's wife he'd come in and spent six hours trawling through everything they had on McCann. Criminal record, case files, interview notes. Hard work in lieu of honest emotion. He'd gone home at midnight, exhausted and bleary-eyed.

Doris was on the front desk, an overweight woman in her fifties. Her husband had been RUC, survived a gun attack by the Provos, only to die of cancer six months later. Doris was civilian support staff and she'd been at Musgrave Street longer than the furniture.

'Morning, Jack.'

'Doris.'

'You misbehaving again?'

'Why?'

'You've been summoned,' she said, pointing upwards, to the third floor, to the Chief Inspector.

Ward gave a wry smile. 'Must be doing something right.'

He made his way to CID, thinking the lecture could wait. Word would have gotten back, from the traffic cop to Hugh Rafferty to Wilson. It would be the usual bullshit – jurisdictions, procedures, protocols. Ward had heard it a million times. Now though it was about Pat Kennedy, which only made him less inclined to listen.

In his office, Ward put two spoons of coffee in a mug and

filled it from the kettle. He kept seeing Pat's car, the Saab, wrapped round the tree. He thought about Eileen's face, her bloodshot eyes, her head shaking in utter disbelief. Ward took the envelope she'd given him out of his pocket and poured the pieces of pink card on to his desk. He moved them round, rearranging them, like a child with a jigsaw. He was four bits short but when he'd finished it didn't matter. Ward opened the drawer and took out one of the cards he'd been sent and laid it alongside. The flowers, the message, the handwriting: they were all the same. He sipped his coffee, staring at the unfinished mosaic. He thought about the George and McCann, sitting there, all smug. *'How's Pat Kennedy? ... And Davy Price? ... Bet you miss it ...'*

Ward felt his chest tighten. He imagined himself with McCann, in an interview room, the door locked. It would be like the old days, seven days detention, no solicitors, no lawyers. These people didn't deserve due process. They murdered cops, shot them in their beds, at the dinner table, walking the dog. He pictured Pat Kennedy in the Saab, flying down country roads, seventy miles an hour. He saw the other car behind him, black ski masks, guns ready. Then the bump from behind, the bend in the road, the car up on the verge.

The telephone rang, snapping him back to the present. He recognized Wilson's extension. The Chief would have been watching the car park, would have seen him drive in.

'DI Ward.'

'In my office, Detective.'

'On my way.'

The third floor was quiet, free from the noise of the cop shop, prisoners swearing at police, police swearing back. It smelled less institutional, more polished, less disinfected. It could be any other civil service department, a procession of grey-haired suits, shuffling paperwork behind closed doors.

Ward approached Wilson's office. There were voices inside, the chumminess of the golf club. He knocked and waiting through the customary pause. After a few seconds a voice ushered him in.

Wilson was at his desk. To the side sat Arthur Johnson, the Chief Super of B Division. He was a big man, six foot two, sixteen stone. Johnson was fifty-nine, a career cop from Yorkshire, chasing the big bucks in the PSNI. He'd eyes to be the next Chief Constable and was busy shaking hands, making friends, greasing the wheel. Johnson was in uniform, all shined up, like the first day at school. Ward knew the game. Wilson would want to crack the whip, show the Super he ran a tight ship, that he'd be useful in the future.

'DI Ward, come in,' Wilson said. 'The Super was just passing and thought he'd drop in and say hello.'

My hole, Ward thought, taking a seat.

'Do you know why I wanted to see you, Detective?' Wilson, the headmaster.

'Promotion?' Ward said, face deadpan.

The other men laughed.

'Not quite, Jack. I got a call from Chief Inspector Hugh Rafferty up in Ballymena yesterday. He says you were up working the scene of a road traffic accident outside Dunloy. Last time I checked CID didn't do RTAs. And they didn't do them sixty miles away on the B roads of north Antrim. But maybe I'm mistaken ...'

Wilson let it hang.

'It was Pat Kennedy.'

188

'I know who it was.'

'I'm not sure you do,' he said, adding 'sir' as an after thought. Wilson knew Kennedy and Ward had been Branch men. Kennedy was a dinosaur, another one who liked to blur the lines, who didn't differentiate between enforcing the law and making it up as you went along.

'I know you worked together—'

'Pat Kennedy locked up half the Belfast Brigade: Joe Lynch, Peter Hughes, Tommy Costello.' Ward was heating up.

'I don't need a history lesson, Detective.'

'Are you sure? Because last time I checked—'

'That's enough, Jack,' the Super said, stepping in. 'Pat Kennedy was a hell of a peeler. No one's doubting that. The issue is you, acting like you own the place, like it's all about you, every crime scene, every job.'

Ward listened, his eyes on Wilson.

'We've got people on Kennedy's accident. Cars go off the road, they skid out, they hit trees. If you're stressed and want a break, just ask. Some time away, take yourself off, get your head showered.'

'Are you suspending me, sir?'

They would have had the conversation.

'No,' Johnson said. 'But you stay away from Kennedy's accident, you hear?'

Eventually, Ward nodded.

'There's one other thing, Jack,' Johnson said. 'How close are we on the McCarthy kid?'

'We're working it.'

'Good. Because the father's got profile. He's capable of making waves if we don't get a result. And we could do with all the good headlines we can get.'

'Sure,' Ward said, non-committally.

'What about that kid you were about to charge? Ronan Mullan. Prosecutor got cold feet. Wouldn't play ball.'

Ward sensed them fishing, looking for O'Neill, trying to catch him with his hand in the till.

'Evidence wasn't there,' he said, talking to Johnson, holding Wilson's gaze.

'Right,' the Super said, sounding convinced.

A silence fell.

'You can go, Detective,' Wilson said. 'And if you happen to find yourself in north Antrim, just know you'll be collecting your pension from the end of next week.'

Ward nodded and left the room.

He passed Kearney on his way back to CID.

'Message for you sir, David Price, said he was an old mate.'

Ward looked up. 'What did he say?'

'Europa Hotel, an hour. Said you'd know.'

At 11 a.m. Ward was sitting in the front bar of the hotel. The morning traffic crawled along Great Victoria Street. It had been raining all morning and pedestrians ran for cover, heads pulled into jackets, umbrellas at angles. Across the street an open-top bus stopped, disgorging a group of tourists for their obligatory Guinness at the Crown bar.

Ward was surprised at the phone call. Pat had said Davy Price was in Iraq, training the police. A bunch of guys had gone, working as consultants. There were threats from insurgents but it was £500 a day.

'Fermanagh to Fallujah,' he'd heard. 'Same shit, different weather.'

The Europa was empty apart from two guys at the bar. Both

were mid-forties, both on pints. They'd watched Ward enter, eyes tracking him as he crossed the room. Ward felt it and sat where he could see them.

Someone had left a *Belfast Telegraph* on the table and he picked it up, scanning for Tomb Street. The McCarthy story was front page on Monday, page four on Tuesday. Now it was gone, vanished, a distant memory.

Ward tossed the paper aside and thought about the first time he'd met Pat Kennedy. He was in his thirties and had just joined the Branch. Kennedy was a Sergeant and took him out in a car, a maroon Cortina. They'd stopped round the back of the Smithfield on some waste ground that had been turned into a car park.

'What do you see?' Kennedy asked.

'Bunch of cars. Not much happening. Folk coming back, driving off.' He wondered what he was supposed to be looking at.

'That it?'

Ward hesitated.

'You see our friends?' Kennedy said.

Ward peered out, not speaking.

'Behind,' Pat said.

He looked in the mirror. A blue Sierra with two men, long hair, beards. They were scoping the place, pretending they weren't.

'What are they doing?'

'Watching.'

'Watching what?'

'That building.'

'Why?'

Ward paused. 'I dunno,' he said, annoyed at himself.

'That's right. So what you thinking?'

Ward hesitated, 'Em ...'

Kennedy laughed.

'How about, do we know them? Could you ID them again? How are they acting? What time is it? How long they been here? What's the registration? Is the car stolen? Should we stop them? Should we follow them? Do we need backup?'

Ward looked at the two men. They looked like Provos, slouched in the car, lying low, waiting.

'Start the car,' Kennedy said. 'Pull up alongside.'

'You serious?'

Two cops had been shot the month before when they disturbed two Provos on an operation.

'Do it.'

Ward felt his pulse quicken as the engine spluttered and caught. Surely they needed backup?

Kennedy rolled his window down as they pulled up alongside.

'Right, girls?' he said.

'Evening, sir.' Both men looking straight ahead.

'This here's Jack Ward. He's new.' Kennedy nodded at the car. 'Davy Price and Phil Mulrine.'

The two men nodded; nothing more.

'Any joy?' Kennedy asked.

'Nah.'

'All right. Keep her lit.'

Kennedy flicked his finger and Ward drove on, breathing a sigh of relief.

'Ours then?' he asked.

'Yeah. It's a safe house.' Kennedy gestured towards a doorway. 'We think the Provos are using it for weapons.'

Back on the road, Ward relaxed.

'By the way,' Kennedy said. 'Your timing belt needs tightening.'

Sitting in the bar of the Europa, Ward felt himself smile at the memory. The last comment stuck in his head, about the car. It was Kennedy to a T – the detail, the attention.

He thought about the traffic cop the day before, remembering his comment about brake failure – '... more common than you'd think'.

He didn't buy it. It might happen to other folk, but not Pat Kennedy.

Ward clocked Davy Price crossing Great Victoria Street, weaving between cars. He was in his early sixties and still had the walk, all focus, like he'd locked in. Price was bald and looked like Marlon Brando at the end of *Apocalypse Now*, those same dark eyes, the kind that had seen things and not looked away.

He swept the room as he walked in, clocking the drinkers as he headed for Ward. They shook hands before sitting. Price momentarily ignored Ward, looking at the two men at the bar.

'Watch,' he said, voice quiet. 'Big man leans in, whispers something, mate looks over.'

Ward looked up as they did exactly what Price said.

'Mates of yours?'

'Put them in Maghaberry. Six years, eight years.' Price paused. 'Yeah, they know me.'

'Should we be worried?'

Price shook his head, still staring. 'Nah.'

He kept his eyes on the bar, letting them know he was there, that *they* could go somewhere else.

'How's Iraq?' Ward asked.

'Hot.'

'How long you home?'

'Few weeks.'

'You hear about Pat?'

'Got a call.'

All the while, Price's eyes on the bar. Ward waited.

'I spoke to Eileen this morning. She said you'd been up.'

Ward nodded.

'You go to the scene?'

'Yeah.'

'It was no accident.'

Ward kept his counsel, listening. Price looked at the bar.

'I mean, Pat? Seriously? Loosing control of a car?' He shook his head. 'As for something mechanical, the Saab was two years old.'

'It happens,' Ward said.

'Not to Pat Kennedy it doesn't. You don't think he'd checked every spark plug himself?'

Ward nodded, conceding.

'Was he getting sympathy cards?'

Ward looked at him.

'You too then,' Price said. 'I thought so. Pat didn't tell you though, right?'

'No. Eileen found one, gave it to me yesterday.'

Price turned to him. 'They have to be got you know.'

Ward waited.

'I don't mean investigated, arrested, charged. It needs to be biblical, Old Testament. There's no other way.'

Ward felt himself hesitate, reluctant to join a lynch mob. Eileen's face flashed before him. Did he owe it to her? To himself? He wondered where the questions came from. Was it retirement? The Troubles being over? The idea that that was the past, that they'd moved on? He remembered McCann's words in the George, about the good old days, when there were sides and you knew who the enemy was and tried to get them before they got you.

Price watched him.

'Don't have the stomach for it? Yeah, Pat told me. He rated you, Jack. Said you had it in spades, a natural born peeler.' Price smiled, remembering. 'The other thing he said – you didn't like sticking the knife in, not unless you had to.'

'We don't stick the knife in,' Ward said, as much for himself. 'That's for them uns out there. Not us.'

Price smiled. 'Listen to you. Like butter wouldn't melt. You forget I've been around, Jack, that I know a thing or two.'

Ward waited to see how far he would go.

'I'm only messing,' Price said. 'You seen what the government did to us. Pat was right. You hold the line for thirty years, watch your mates die, your family threatened. Every moment looking over your shoulder, waiting on some wee bastard coming at you out of the dark like a fucking rat. And then what? They sign a Peace Agreement and the government picks you up, wipes their arse with you and tosses you away.' Price snorted. 'Some country, eh? You couldn't make it up.'

Ward listened to his own doubts come back at him like threats.

'You won't catch who killed Pat. There'll be no investigation, no trial, no conviction.'

'We don't know he was killed yet.'

'Wise up, Jack.'

Ward looked out at Great Victoria Street. It was lashing now. Folk huddled in doorways, trying to stay dry, waiting for it to pass. It was normal life, after so many years, when getting soaked was the worst thing you had to worry about. He looked back, feeling Price staring at him.

'You know who it is, Jack.'

Ward stayed silent.

'Tell me?'

Ward stared, knowing if he spoke he'd be signing a death warrant. That wasn't what he wanted. It would be cheating, changing the rules, just because it was difficult, the rewards hard to come by. Price had always pushed the envelope, even by Branch standards. Ward thought about his cancer, wondering if it was back, if he'd nothing to lose.

'You sick again, Davy?'

'What if I am?'

Ward shrugged. Price forced a laugh.

'Look at me, would you? Fit as a fiddle. But this isn't about me, is it, Jack? It's about Pat.'

He stared at Ward, not letting up.

'It's one of three people. I know that much myself.' He spoke slowly, his eyes fixed on Ward. 'Peter Hughes ... Joe Fusco ... Gerry McCann.'

Ward looked back, eyes blank. After a few seconds he spoke.

'This isn't the Wild West. I'm not going to—'

Price stood up, cutting him off. 'Don't worry about it Jack. I've got what I came for.'

Price walked out of the bar past the two drinkers. It was slow, deliberate, letting them know they weren't forgotten, that their sins hadn't been forgiven, not by everyone.

# TWENTY TWO

Saturday morning, 10 a.m., Ormeau Park. The sky dark, the trees leafless, the ground wet. O'Neill was in jeans and jacket, a black hat pulled low, heading for the old Victorian bandstand. The rusted iron and flaking paint spoke of inevitable decline, of former glory, of a bygone era. It was cold out, the park deserted except for the occasional dog walker. Martin Toner had called on Friday and O'Neill had set up the meet.

He took a seat on a bench and looked at his watch. He would do this first, then he had Sarah's party in the afternoon. O'Neill took a bite from the sausage roll he'd picked up on the way. Near the bandstand a woman stood next to a buggy. She sipped from a polystyrene cup, while two young kids chased each other with sticks.

O'Neill saw Toner approach, recognizing the tracksuit and the familiar slow swagger. The kid looked over his shoulder, one way, the other, before slowing and sitting at the far end of the bench. O'Neill slid a brown paper bag towards him. Marty picked it up, inspecting the sausage.

'What, no sauce?'

O'Neill laughed quietly.

The two of them sat in silence, watching the kids sword-fighting on the bandstand. O'Neill nodded.

'Fiver says it ends in tears.'

'How come?'

'It always does.'

Marty gave a 'huh' and took a bite of his sausage roll. When he'd finished he took out a cigarette and lit up. He took a drag and exhaled, looking at the smouldering point of red ash.

'So how does it work?' he said. 'You want information. Stuff about stash houses, who's running what, when the gear's coming ...'

O'Neill shook his head.

'Nah. I've informants coming out my ears. You need to do better than that.'

'Like what?'

O'Neill shrugged. 'Tell me about Tomb Street. You recognized the photo, Jonathan McCarthy.'

Marty paused, deciding whether to jump.

'Tierney was looking for him. I saw him at the club, phoned it in.'

O'Neill felt his pulse quicken. He remembered Tierney in the George with Gerry McCann. He wondered how far Tomb Street went? Who it touched? Was McCann involved?

Tierney ran half the dope in South Belfast. The cops knew it, but could never get near him. He was cautious to the point of paranoid. Moved round a lot, never used a phone. O'Neill saw why Marty was scared. There were myths about Tierney, tales of disfigurement, stories about pliers, about fingers being broken, teeth taken out. He'd a pit bull he kept for special occasions.

'We need him on tape.'

'Who?'

'Tierney.'

Marty laughed, like it was a joke. He looked at O'Neill, saw he was serious.

'How do you want me to do that?'

O'Neill shrugged, downplaying it. 'Dunno, a wire or something.'

'Away to fuck.'

O'Neill made to stand up. 'No problem, son.'

'Here, hang on.'

O'Neill looked at him. 'You're wasting my time.'

'Look, it doesn't sound fair. It's all on me like, all the risk. I mean, what about yous?'

'Understand something, son. I go home at night. To my dinner, to my bed, to a couple of beers and some shit football on the telly. You're the one running the streets, you're the one dealing dope round the Holy Lands, you're the one shit scared of Johnny Tierney … Now, is it fair? No. But then life's not fair. So get over it.'

Marty squinted as he stared out across the park. 'Why a wire then?'

'Think about it. Tierney? McCann? If you want to get them it can't be no shitty possession charge. Six months in Maghaberry? Wise up. You need them to go down hard, a proper stretch, takes more than a tip-off. It's not easy. Most guys don't have the balls.'

Marty smiled, watching the cop bait the hook. He took another drag, thinking.

'Hey,' O'Neill said. 'You could always keep trying to pop him in the street.'

Marty didn't look up.

'That was you, wasn't it? Wednesday night. What happened? Gun jam? You bottle it last minute.'

O'Neill smiled at his own guesswork. The kid made to stand up and leave.

'Sure, you walk away, son. But keep walking, mind. Because when word gets to Tierney that it was you tried to do him ...'

Marty's eyes narrowed at the implicit threat. He stared hard at O'Neill.

'What?' the cop said. 'You wanted to play with the big boys, didn't you? Well, this is it. Welcome to the Premier League.'

Marty sat back, his face dark, his head shaking.

'Listen,' O'Neill said, trying to soften it. 'My bosses don't give a shit about the likes of Tierney. As far as they're concerned you're all that matters. We should be chasing after yous, locking yous up, sending yous to Hydebank. And uniform? They don't give a crap either. They never see the Tierneys of this world. You're all there is to them. And for most of them, none of yous even have a name. Why should they give a shit? Tomorrow'll be another shift and there'll be some other wee bastard telling them to shove it up their arse.'

Marty glanced. 'So what about you?'

O'Neill shrugged. 'Dunno. I'll tell you what I think though. I think some people deserve a beating. They make a balls-up, step outta line, break the rules. Fuck 'em, I say, if it's their fault. Guys like Tierney though, they don't play by the rules. Yous are out here taking all the risks, handling the gear, but they get all the reward. And when they don't like how you're doing it? Well, look at your mate Petesy.'

O'Neill stopped talking, letting the name hang between them, allowing the memory to come back. After a few seconds he spoke, pushing again.

'How is he by the way? You see him much?'

'He's out.'

'Really.'

'Yeah. Gone clean. Back at school.'

'No shit.'

Marty looked down, spitting between his legs. 'So what do you need?'

'You were at Tomb Street last Saturday.'

Marty didn't speak.

'What went down?'

'It was Tierney. I called him, told him the kid was there. McCarthy, or whatever his name was.'

'Why? What does Tierney care about him?'

Marty shrugged. 'He just told me to find him and make the call.'

'We need him on tape talking about it.'

Marty's eyes narrowed. 'The wire I'm wearing. It'll be like that shit on *CSI*?'

O'Neill thought about the clunky technology the PSNI used. 'Exactly.'

Marty watched the two kids on the bandstand. They were pushing each other now, the sword fight spilling over.

'Tonight,' he said. 'I'm seeing them tonight.'

O'Neill tensed. It was short notice. Not enough time to get sign off, to get the gear sorted. 'Too soon,' he said.

'Meet me halfway, fuck's sake?'

O'Neill knew he was right. There was a window here.

'OK,' he said. 'What time you seeing them?'

'After five. Haven't heard yet.'

'Right. I'll call this afternoon. Pick you up in town.'

Marty raised an eyebrow.

'It'll be an unmarked van.'

'All right then. This better work. You hear?'

On the bandstand the older boy had tripped the smaller one and twatted him round the head. The wee one was bawling his lamps out, his face red. O'Neill and Marty watched.

'You see. Always ends in tears.'

Marty stood and started to walk.

'You owe me a fiver,' O'Neill said.

'Put it on my tab,' he said, not looking back.

At Musgrave Street O'Neill caught himself scanning the car park, looking for Sam's red Honda. It wasn't there. He wondered where she was, what she was up to. He felt lifted by the meeting with Marty and thought about texting her, asking if she was around later. He wondered why it was different with her, easier, less defensive. Hang on, he thought. She was upset, needed a shoulder, you shouldn't get carried away. He closed the car door and headed upstairs to CID.

It took two hours of form filling and phone calls before he got the go-ahead. He'd pick up the van and equipment after four. O'Neill put the phone down; the bureaucratic annoyance had cancelled out the elation. He left a message for Ward and grabbed his car keys. Sarah's party was in ten minutes.

It was after two as he ran into the Toys R Us on the Shore Road. It was like an aircraft hangar and he made a beeline for the Barbies. He remembered Sarah's disappointment the previous Christmas after the shop assistant convinced him My Little Pony was all the rage. O'Neill shook his head at the choice before grabbing one in a pair of roller skates and heading for the checkout.

Three balloons – pink, green, blue – were tied to the gate at Tivoli Gardens. O'Neill pulled up and looked at his watch – 2.46 p.m. He'd meant to be early, or at least on time. He stepped out of the car, ready to stave off the looks from other parents, the silent accusations.

He looked at the cars, trying to spot any he knew. He saw Amanda and Tom's Lexus. She was Catherine's older sister, a primary school teacher whose husband worked for the Northern Bank. Catherine never liked her big sister, said she spoke to her like she was a child. It was all about skiing holidays, the Caribbean, the five-bedroom house they were building.

O'Neill heard the frenzy of seven-year-old girls as he approached the house. He was glad he'd arranged to take Sarah to the cinema tomorrow, to spend time with her, just the two of them. He took a breath and rang the bell.

Catherine answered. She looked like she wanted to say something but didn't want a scene in front of her mummy friends.

'Sorry I'm late. I—'

Sarah came charging, throwing herself into his arms. 'Daddeeeee!!!! I got Dora the Explorer from Gemma. It's amazing so it is. It talks to you and asks you questions and you help it solve the puzzles and find treasure and ...'

'OK, love, OK. I get it.'

The girl looked at the wrapped present he was carrying and raised her eyebrows. O'Neill handed it over.

'Ooooohhh,' Sarah moaned. 'Is it Bratz? I'll bet it's Bratz. Bratz are my favourite. Amanda in my class is always going on about Bratz and we are going to start up a club with her Bratz and my Bratz and they can all go on holiday together and have adventures and ...'

Her voice trailed off as she tore the paper free and saw the Barbie doll beneath. Sarah looked up, her disappointment obvious.

'What do you say, love?' Catherine commanded.

'Thank you, Daddy.'

She hugged him briefly before running back into the living room to join the high-pitched chaos.

Catherine looked at him. 'Come into the kitchen. Amanda's here.'

Catherine's sister was in a pastel twinset, leaning against the sink, the make-up perfect. She was good-looking, in an uptight, prim sort of way. Amanda saw O'Neill and her face fell, like he'd just mugged a pensioner.

'John.'

'Amanda.'

'How are you?'

'Fine. You?'

'I'm good.'

A pause.

'How's work?' she said.

'Good. Yours?'

'Fine.'

O'Neill felt the hatred behind the highly polished exterior. It was a silent judgement, a look that said 'you left my sister and I hope your balls drop off'. He wanted to tell her it was Catherine's idea, the whole 'on a break' thing, but it would be a waste of time. Amanda was one of those people who needed a good boot in the hole. Catherine's words, not his.

O'Neill felt his pocket tremble and took out his phone – Musgrave Street, Ward.

'Sorry, I've got to take this.'

Amanda rolled her eyes as he stepped into the hall.

'We on then?' Ward said.

'Yeah. About seven o'clock, tonight.'

'Get me at the nick. How'd you get him to go for this?'

'Luck I guess.'

Back in the kitchen, Catherine was preparing a tray of cocktail sausages and miniature buns.

'Let me guess,' she said, not looking up. 'You've got to go.'

'I was just going to ask if you wanted a hand.'

She stared at him, doubtful. 'Carry these then,' she said, passing a set of plastic plates.

In the living room, one of Catherine's friends was at the stereo, controlling the volume for Pass the Parcel. Ten seven-year-old girls sat in circle, tearing wrapping paper, their faces expectant. The parcel got smaller and eventually a miniature Bratz doll was revealed. A girl shrieked with delight, pulling the toy to her chest.

O'Neill sighed a 'fuck me', quietly to himself.

Catherine walked past. 'Apparently they're all the rage.'

She called the girls to the table and the swarm ran through him like he wasn't there. O'Neill stood and watched, Amanda joining him, along with the other mums who had stayed to help. He looked round, realizing he was the only man in the house.

'Where's your Tom?' he said.

'Golf. Did you know he just got into Royal Belfast?'

O'Neill nodded at the status update. Royal Belfast was all bankers, barristers and surgeons.

'No boys at this party?' he said.

'Chalk and cheese at this age.' Amanda said it like an

accusation, like he would know that if he hadn't taken off, hadn't walked out.

O'Neill looked round the room. The girls tucked into their food, talking with their mouths full. Catherine passed glasses of champagne to the mums.

'A wee treat, girls.'

O'Neill picked up on the furtive glances and stepped back from the table. He felt like an intruder, like an outsider, like he didn't belong. There was an awkwardness in the air, a reticence. He was sure he'd brought it with him. He watched Sarah, his reason for being there. He wanted her to look up and see him, to smile or stick out her tongue like they used to do. He stood there, waiting, willing her on. Without looking at him, she slid from her chair, announced she needed the loo and left the room.

O'Neill looked around at the faces of the other mothers. He wondered why he'd come, what he'd expected. He took in the room, the house, his ex-wife. It was all operating smoothly, without him, the fifth wheel. He suddenly felt like the relative no one likes, the one they invite for Christmas out of obligation and a sense of duty. He found himself looking at his watch, wondering about the time.

Two minutes later, Sarah came back and sat at the table. Again she never looked up. A hand flicked the lights out and the dining room went dark. Catherine edged in carrying a cake, her face lit by the glow of the candles.

'Hap-py Birth-day ...' she intoned, the rest of the room joining in.

Sarah beamed with the attention, her face illuminated as the cake was slid in front of her.

'Make a wish,' Catherine shouted, as the singing finished.

The girl inhaled and blew with everything she had. A cheer greeted the blowing out of the last candle. Someone flicked the lights on again and Catherine began to cut the cake. She was struck by something, a change in the room, the atmosphere different.

She looked up and saw that O'Neill was no longer there.

# TWENTY THREE

Saturday evening, Bridge Street. O'Neill and Ward, parked up in an undercover transit. The van was filthy, dust everywhere, the rust holding it together. They sat in silence, both of them pretending Toner wasn't twenty minutes late. Outside the Northern Whig two smokers were chatting about the football.

'They were shit.'

'Sure, so were we.'

O'Neill glared out at Saturday night, which was slowly gathering momentum. Groups of lads marched towards bars, shirts untucked, hair gelled. Underage girls in short skirts and high heels flirted with bouncers, trying to get in. O'Neill pictured Jonathan McCarthy setting out the week before. He didn't know he wouldn't be coming home. Then again, no one ever did.

O'Neill scanned the faces as they passed the van. Where was Marty Toner? Maybe he'd bottled it. He thought of McCarthy and Tierney, the junior lawyer and the junior gangster. How were they connected? Was McCarthy dealing? Supplying his yuppie mates with Tierney's coke? Or did Tierney have him on the hook, blackmailing him, threatening his da's good name?

In the van beside him Ward sneezed with the dust. He'd barely spoken since he got in, his mind elsewhere. O'Neill thought about the George, about McCann and what was really going on. How out there had Special Branch been?

He'd heard the whispers, knew the rumours. They'd traded on reputation, just like the Provos, all part of the game. Ward denied it, but he wondered if the DI had blood on his hands. McCann's brother, the solicitor. Was Ward involved? Had he known and turned a blind eye? Let events take their course.

A blonde girl stepped out of a taxi, her hair pulled back. O'Neill thought about Sam. He'd missed a call earlier. He wondered where she was, what she was doing. He went back to Tivoli Gardens, to the birthday party that afternoon.

'Fucking Barbie,' he muttered.

Catherine and Sarah were doing fine. They didn't need him, only the maintenance cheque. It was fatherhood by direct debit.

Ward sat in the passenger seat, watching the street life. He'd spent the afternoon looking for Davy Price at his old address, then at the usual bars in Bangor, Newtownards, Comber. He'd called at the Sea Dog, Paddy Murphy's, the Old Hotel. He saw Alec McAttackney, Peter McLean, but no Davy Price.

O'Neill glanced at his watch. The kid had lost his nerve. He sighed and reached for his cigarettes.

On Castle Place, Marty Toner stood in darkness of a doorway. He had his hood up, his face hidden, a fag in his mouth. He stared at the Transit van and the two cops, parked on Bridge Street. He shook his head; too busy. There were smokers, bouncers, the bus stop. A lot of people, a lot of eyes.

'Frigging peelers,' he whispered, 'trying to get me killed.' He sighed, tossed the fag and stepped into the early evening.

O'Neill saw the tracksuit and squinted. 'I think we're on here.'

The figure approached but didn't stop. It kept going, head down, flicking them the finger on the way past.

O'Neill smiled. 'It's him.'

Ward watched him pass. 'Where's he going then? Has he bottled it?'

'No.' O'Neill looked round. 'Shit. It's too busy. Or there's someone he knows.'

He pulled the van into the traffic, doing a U-turn at the end of Bridge Street. They followed the tracksuit down a side street where it was quieter, a through road, no shops or bars. O'Neill overtook him, drove twenty yards and pulled in. Marty checked over his shoulder before pulling the door and jumping into the back of the van.

'Right homos.'

O'Neill pressed the accelerator, causing him to fall against the back doors.

'Mind your head there,' he said, over his shoulder.

They parked near St Ann's Cathedral, beneath a hundred-foot Celtic cross, lit blue against the night sky. The Saturday night crowd was arriving in the Cathedral Quarter where overrated bars sold overpriced drinks to overdressed young ones.

O'Neill climbed into the back of the van where Marty had perched on a milk crate. The kid looked at the tattered headphones, the mess of leads, the broken dials.

'What's this shit? You said *CSI*.'

'Calm yourself.'

'Does this even work?'

''Course it works.' O'Neill pressed a button which lit a row of LEDs. 'You see.'

Marty looked round the van, unimpressed.

'Right,' O'Neill said. 'Lift your shirt.'

A snort. 'Bet you say that to all the boys.'

O'Neill shook his head.

Beneath the tracksuit he was pasty and skinny. You could count the ribs. O'Neill could see old scars, long healed, signs of beatings. He imagined a childhood on the run, dodging the belt, the stick, whatever was handy. Marty caught him looking.

'Pretty eh?' The voice flat.

O'Neill remembered what he'd said in the interview, about vandalizing the headstones, about how he only did his da's. Hoody off, O'Neill saw how young he was. He'd a mouth like a sailor, but beneath it all he was a seventeen-year-old kid. Kneeling there, skin exposed, he looked vulnerable. Easily damaged, easily hurt. O'Neill thought about calling it off. What if something happened? What if he lost his nerve? What if they sussed him? O'Neill knew it would be on him. Whatever happened, he'd have to wear it. He wondered if he could carry a seventeen-year-old, have him on his conscience, the rest of his career.

'Come on fuck sake,' Marty said. 'I'm ball frozen here.'

O'Neill used three pieces of tape to attach the wire and mic to his chest. He lifted the headphones and held them to his ear.

'Say something.'

'Your ma.'

O'Neill nodded. 'It works.'

He waited while Marty put his top on.

'Whatever you do don't get frisked.'

'No shit, Sherlock. 'Cause I hadn't thought of that.'

O'Neill could see he was bricking it, that the slabbering was a front. He looked at him, imagining the worst.

211

'Listen to me, son. If they figure it out, if you get made ... we're coming for you.'

Marty avoided his eyes, suddenly uncomfortable.

'Do you hear me?' O'Neill insisted.

The kid turned to him.

'Whatever it takes, we're coming. You hear?'

Marty hesitated, unsure. Finally he said, 'Right.'

From the front seat Ward's voice. 'McCann. We need McCann's name on the tape. Do you hear?'

Marty looked at him and nodded. 'Right then,' he said. 'Come on, Cagney and Lacey, let's go.'

Marty moved towards the back of the van, speaking over his shoulder. 'I'm meeting Tierney on Cooke Street off the Ormeau. There's a house we use to stash the gear. Number twenty-two. I'll walk up, be there in twenty minutes.'

He opened the door, stepped on to the wet cobblestones and disappeared into the night.

O'Neill and Ward were parked at the end of Cooke Street. On one side was waste ground, on the other a line of red-brick terraces. Overhead the night had closed in, the grey sky taking on a purple hue. The street lights were on, creating haloes of orange sodium amid the pervading darkness.

The van was silent.

'You think he'll do it?' Ward said.

'Don't know.'

'A wire at seventeen. He's some balls. I'll give him that.'

At 7.23 p.m. a grey tracksuit turned the corner and came down the street. Hood up, head down, Marty passed the Transit without breaking stride. O'Neill and Ward were in the back, headphones on.

'All right, ball bag?' Marty whispered into the mic.

O'Neill allowed himself a smile.

He watched Marty stop at the gate. He hesitated for a split second, like he wasn't sure.

'Go on,' O'Neill said, the words involuntary.

Marty pushed the handle and walked through. He didn't knock on the door, instead reached over and tapped the window with his lighter. They watched the curtain twitch and a shadow move inside the house. The door opened and a figure stepped out. O'Neill and Ward listened, pressing headphones to their ears.

'Right, Tierney,' Marty said, making the ID.

'Good lad,' O'Neill whispered.

They watched the man point at a car. 'Come on. We're going somewhere.'

The man stepped towards a Vauxhall Astra. Marty followed, without looking up.

'They're moving,' O'Neill said, suddenly thrown, things already out of control. He climbed into the front and started the engine, but left the lights off. Ward stayed in the back, listening, as the Vauxhall revved up and passed them on the driver's side. At the end of the street it turned left and headed up the Ormeau, away from town. O'Neill pulled to the end of Cooke Street where they'd to wait to join the traffic on the main road.

Eventually, he muscled his way out, accelerating hard.

'Come on for frig sake.'

'Easy now. Don't get him busted.'

O'Neill saw the Vauxhall in the distance and put his foot down. They were five hundred yards away. Ward listened to the voices start to crackle and fiddled with the radio.

'I'm losing them here. There's not much range.'

O'Neill switched lanes, overtaking three cars on the inside.

'What are they saying?' he shouted over his shoulder.

'Kid's asking where they're going,' Ward said. 'They've some kind of job to do. He's telling him to shut up and stop talking.'

O'Neill had a knot in his stomach. Marty had said nothing about going anywhere. He told himself to calm down, it was all right, the kid was fine.

At the top of the Ormeau Road the Vauxhall turned without signalling. It screeched into the underground car park at Forest Side shopping centre. O'Neill slowed and signalled as a white BMW came from nowhere and cut him up. Both vehicles braked hard and stopped. O'Neill went for the horn but stopped.

'Move, dick head,' he shouted.

The BMW accelerated, window down, flicking the finger as it went.

Ward listened to the headphones, hearing car doors open, others close.

'They've got out,' he said. O'Neill scanning the car park, looking for heads. Ward heard more doors, then an engine. 'They're switching cars.'

At the far end O'Neill saw a black Peugeot with tinted windows pull out of a space and accelerate up the exit ramp. He put the foot down, trying to catch up with them.

'What's the car, son?' he whispered to himself. 'You've got to tell us.'

He put his hand to the headphones.

'Another voice now, there's three of them.'

O'Neill drove up the exit ramp, one car separating him from the Peugeot.

'Come on, kid,' Ward encouraged. 'Give us something.'

Neither cop noticed the grey Ford Focus pull out behind them and follow them up the ramp. They didn't notice the driver, nor Tierney in the passenger seat, nor Marty in the back.

The Transit van turned left, following the Peugeot along the carriageway towards town. Behind them the Focus waited as an elderly woman pushed a trolley in front. The car signalled right, waited for a break in the traffic and pulling out slowly in the opposite direction.

Two hundred yards down the carriageway Ward announced he was losing the signal. O'Neill felt his chest tighten.

'Fuck it,' he said, accelerating alongside the black Peugeot. The driver was a young fella, twenty or so. In the passenger seat sat his mate who looked the same age. Neither of them was Johnny Tierney, neither of them Marty Toner.

'Fuck, fuck, fuck,' O'Neill shouted, bringing his hand down on the steering wheel.

He did a U-turn, mounting the kerb, almost causing an accident. He launched the van into the oncoming traffic, horns blaring, cars stamping on brakes.

Thirty seconds later, they were back at Forest Side. O'Neill jumped out of the Transit, running up and down the lines of cars. He wanted the Astra, wanted to see Marty. He was panicked, imagining the things they'd do to him.

After thirty seconds he found the car.

They were gone.

O'Neill banged his hands on the bonnet, the word 'fuck' echoing round the concrete car park. A pensioner looked over and shook his head. A woman shepherded her kid away, like O'Neill was some kind of lunatic.

Ward pulled up in the Transit. 'Let's go. There's nothing you can do.'

O'Neill opened the door slamming it behind him. He wound the window down, feeling sick.

'So what do we do now then?'

'We wait.'

'Wait for what?'

'Wait for him to call.'

'That's if he calls.'

The two men sat in silence as Ward drove towards Musgrave Street. After a while O'Neill spoke.

'You ever lose an informant?'

He watched Ward hesitate, like he wanted to speak but thought better of it.

'Give it two hours. If you haven't heard start calling hospitals.'

O'Neill put his head back and closed his eyes, picturing the worst.


Marty had felt his heart quicken as soon as Tierney stepped out of the house. He'd wanted to bolt when he pointed at the car but found himself shrugging and lowering himself in. They had never done this before. The gear was in the house, it always was. It was in and out, no problems.

He'd glanced at the back of the Transit van as they passed, wanting to call the whole thing off. At the end of Cooke Street the car slowed and he thought about jumping out and taking off. They'd make him for sure though so he stayed put and asked a few questions before being told to shut the fuck up.

As they drove up the Ormeau Road, Marty felt the transmitter dig into his side. He wanted to touch it, to rip it off and toss it out the window. The tape round his chest was tight, suffocating him. He tried to breathe slowly, pretending to be bored.

At Forest Side they pulled into the underground car park. He wanted to look over his shoulder to check whether the van was there but didn't dare.

The peeler had said they'd be there, that they'd be coming, first sign of trouble. Marty went over his three rules – don't do gear, don't be greedy, trust no one. He tried to ignore the voice in his head, asking what the fuck he was doing, wearing a wire for these peelers. He slid lower in his seat feigning further indifference.

Without indicating, Tierney pulled into a parking space and opened his door.

'Let's go.'

Marty saw Sean Molloy, another of McCann's boys, in another car. They were out and in, Tierney in front, Marty in back. Molloy looked at him in the rear-view mirror and allowed himself a smile.

Something inside Marty screamed 'RUN!' He reached for the door handle and was about to pull it when Molloy drove out of the space and they were off. He looked out and saw the Transit van in front of them. He knew it was wrong, that they'd missed the switch. The Transit signalled left and pulled out of the car park, heading back towards town. Molloy indicated right, waited for a break and pulled out.

Marty wanted to scream.

He dug his nails into his hands, using the pain as a distraction. He felt sick and wondered if he asked would they stop the car and let him out for a second. No, they knew what they were doing. It was Game Over. He slouched in the seat, like he didn't give a shit, like there was still nothing to worry about.

'Here,' he said, 'just so yous know, all this gallivanting's not good for business.'

He was right. Saturday evening was prime time. Folk wanting to score, to get themselves sorted.

'There's customers out there. Doesn't pay to keep them waiting.'

'Shut up,' Tierney said.

Marty looked out the car window, aware of how dark it was, how few people were about. The houses thinned out as suburbia gave way to country. He'd no idea where they were going.

After ten minutes they were in the back of beyond. Marty glanced over his shoulder looking for the Transit. There were no other headlights. O'Neill's words rung in his ears – *whatever it takes ... we're coming.*

He sighed, knowing he'd been stupid. He thought about the microphone, the wire, the transmitter. If you're going to go down, might as well go down swinging.

'Here, Tierney, that was some hiding you gave your man last week.'

Tierney glanced sideways at Molloy.

'Tomb Street like. Was he skimming or what?'

Marty bluffed, like McCarthy was another dealer. The two men ignored him.

As they turned a corner, Molloy shifted uneasily in his seat. He winced, reaching for his lower back.

'Still bad?' Tierney said.

'Fucked like.'

'Teach you to buck seventeen-year-olds.'

Molloy smiled. 'She'd some hole on her though.'

The two men laughed, falling back to silence.

After ten minutes, the car slowed and turned into a gap in the hedge. They were in a wide open space, a corrugated barn on one side, a field on the other.

Molloy stopped and pulled the handbrake. Marty's stomach lurched.

He thought about the stories he'd heard, about the things Tierney and Molloy had done to people. Guys disappeared – driven to the middle of nowhere, they never came back. He looked at the barn, wondering what was inside. He thought about being tortured. Did you just pass out? With the pain and all? Or would it be a bullet in the head? The loud noise, then lights out.

'Right, let's go,' Tierney said. They were out of the car, all three of them, Marty on autopilot. The door of the barn lay open, offering a three-foot gap into utter darkness. Tierney pointed at it.

'You first.'

Marty stepped in front of the two men, waiting for the sound, the sudden pain, the blackness swallowing him. This was it. He suddenly felt calm, like he'd always known it would end like this – alone, on his tod, just Marty. There was some comfort that at least something had worked out like he'd imagined.

He stepped into the darkness and closed his eyes.

The burring of an engine startled him. A generator kicked in and lights flicked on. Marty opened his eyes, smelling cow shit and diesel. He looked round. In the corner were hay bales, stacked five high, like giant Lego.

'Come on then,' Tierney said, walking over. 'The gear's in

here. The cripple here done his back, so it's me and you.'

Molloy looked on, smiling, pleased to get out of the lifting.

Marty began moving bales, suddenly ecstatic.

'Calm down,' Tierney said. 'They've got to go back, so don't throw them so far.'

After ten minutes they found a box, wrapped in a black plastic bag. Tierney and Marty lifted it out to the car before returning to build the stack again. Marty had to stop himself from laughing as he threw the hay bales on top of one another.

In the car on the way back, he sat quietly. As they pulled into Cooke Street Tierney turned to him.

'Now listen to me, you wee hood. You shift whatever gear we give you. Don't lecture me about what's bad for business. And as for that wee cunt on Tomb Street, you don't need to worry about him. He got what was coming to him.'

Marty listened, his eyes narrow, letting on he didn't care. Molloy went into the house and came out with his package for the night. It was after nine but there was still time for his round, still time to make a buck.

Marty thought about what Tierney said, about Tomb Street, about the dope. He had him by the balls. He'd all but confessed. Marty couldn't believe it and had to fight the urge to run down Cooke Street shouting at the top of his voice.

# TWENTY FOUR

Sunday morning, 8 a.m. Ward stared out at Castlehill Park, a suburban cul-de-sac in East Belfast. It was the worried wealthy, all two-car garages and holidays in the Dordogne. He shifted in his seat, watching number forty-six in the rear-view mirror, waiting for McCann.

The night before they'd had driven back to Musgrave Street. O'Neill was panicked, thinking they'd lost the kid, fearing the worst. Toner had phoned just after nine, bouncing off the walls, bragging about how well he'd done. O'Neill told him to lie low and arranged to meet the next day. He let the kid have his moment, not telling him they'd lost the signal, they'd no recording, that he'd have do it all over.

Ward looked out at the dull grey morning. The sky lay low, as if there was a sun up there, but no one was taking any bets. He watched an old man walk down the street, a Yorkshire terrier following behind. He came back in ten minutes with Sunday papers, a packet of soda bread and a pint of milk.

Ward glanced at the *Sunday Life* on the seat beside. He'd bought it, knowing Tomb Street wouldn't be there. He wasn't disappointed. This week's menu was political corruption and sexual jealousy. A local MP's wife had been caught cavorting with a nineteen-year-old. Ward pictured Castlehill Park tutting their disapproval over their jam and crumpets.

He closed the paper, allowing his thoughts to drift. He saw Pat again, thinking he would like this. The Sunday morning stake-out, the waiting game, the fishing trip. His funeral was the following Thursday. Ward figured it would be big. He imagined Eileen, embarrassed by the turnout, by all the old peelers and how well they knew her husband.

He thought about Davy Price, wondering where he was. His words from the Europa Hotel echoed round his head – *Old Testament … it needed to be biblical …*

Deep down Ward agreed. A few months' jail was nothing to these boys. It was a holiday camp, living with the lads, a break from the missus. But did it justify turning vigilante? Being judge, jury and executioner? Death penalties were what paramilitaries were about, not the police. Ward wondered if Pat would say the same. He pictured him smiling, shrugging his shoulders, telling him that the North was a unique place, where black was white, and everything was a shade of grey.

At 9.45 a.m. the door opened and Gerry McCann stepped into the morning. He was in dark jeans, a white shirt and a black jacket. He looked like a property investor or one of the folk you see lunching at The Merchant. A woman appeared in the door, wearing a black silk nightie. She was late twenties, curly blonde hair, young enough to be his daughter. She put her arms round him, giving him a long, lingering kiss. He turned and lowered himself into a black Mercedes parked in the drive. Ward shook his head.

'You're a long way from the Markets, Gerry.'

The car started up and purred out of the drive. Ward bent into the passenger footwell as it passed. The Mercedes turned right down the Newtownards Road, towards town. Ward started the car and set off after it, sliding behind an old couple on their way to church in their Sunday best.

McCann drove slowly, taking his time. He stopped at the Esso and came out with a newspaper and a packet of cigarettes. Ward watched him exchange 'Mornings' with a guy filling up his Range Rover.

'That's right, Gerry,' Ward whispered. 'Hanging with the locals.'

Back in the car, McCann headed for town.

His first stop was a tanning salon on Lower Ormeau. Three kids sat outside on bikes, leaning against a wall. They eyed the Mercedes as it pulled up, ready to say something. When they saw McCann get out they cycled off, knowing better.

The sign read TROPICAL TAN. Eight state-of-the-art tanning beds, 50p per minute. Ward watched McCann enter, noting the time. He exchanged words with the girl on the reception before disappearing into the back. The name of the shop caught in Ward's head but he couldn't place it. He wondered about earlier jobs, if there had been a robbery there, or someone was lifted coming out.

Ten minutes later, McCann came out with a sports bag and dropped it into the boot of the Merc. He got in the car and drove off. The same thing happened at PARADISE BRONZING on Cromac Street. In then out, bag in hand.

At eleven, McCann pulled into a manned car wash on the Ravenhill Road. Two young guys in waterproofs set about foaming and rinsing the Merc. Ward watched the speed and hustle. They weren't locals. McCann disappeared into the office and came out with a navy bag, the kind shops use for their lodgement.

After the car wash, he headed into town, turning down Victoria Street, passing the Albert clock before curling round to Laganside. At the back of Customs House, the car turned into a temporary car park next to a building site. A large billboard announced Obel Tower. There was an image – a hundred foot glass tower rising over the city's skyline. It was a new apartment complex – Belfast Quay – all waterfront views and state-of-the-art living.

Ward did a loop and came back, parking on Waring Street. He watched and waited. Forty-five minutes later, McCann emerged from a set of glass doors. Ward allowed him to pull out and drive off. When he was gone, Ward walked through the blue gates of the car park. He pushed the heavy glass door and entered the mocked-up apartment.

Ward picked up a brochure. Work was scheduled to start in April. Obel Tower would be '*The tallest building in Ireland*'. Size, it seemed, did matter. Twenty-eight floors of apartments, duplexes and penthouse villas. The picture looked like a shard of glass, stabbed into the ground and left for all to see.

Ward wandered round the open show home. It was minimalist luxury. Clean lines, egg-white walls, full-length windows. The lounge flowed into the dining room and on into the kitchen. He traced his fingers along the polished granite counters, heels clicking on the solid wooden floors.

A man in a dark suit appeared, offering his hand. 'Eric Carney. I'm the Sales Manager here at Obel.'

He was from the South somewhere, Dublin, maybe Wexford.

'Fred Wallace,' Ward said, playing along.

The previous week Obel had featured on the six o'clock news – an historic building, a landmark project, the dawn of a new era.

'Nice to meet you, Fred. Your first time down to the site?'

'Aye.'

'It's a lovely spot. We've been getting a lot of interest, local and foreign investors. You work in town?'

It was casual, undersold. Carney was fishing though, trying to qualify him.

Ward nodded.

'What line of work you in?'

'Business.'

Carney raised an eyebrow, Ward didn't bite.

The two men looked out over the show apartment. Carney told him he reckoned they'd sell all 182 apartments when they were released next week. People were buying off plan. Twenty years in property, he'd never seen folk as nonplussed about a price tag.

He handed Ward a brochure. 'How about I let you have a wander and I'll come find you, answer any questions?'

Ward walked out into the living room, glancing at the booklet. What was McCann up to?

The brochure had a series of glossy images – the shimmering glass tower, Belfast at night, the sun setting behind Black Mountain. There were blurbs, pull quotes, snappy phrases.

*A one-off event.*

*A residential landmark.*

*A phenomenal superstructure.*

In each picture the glass tower shone before a perfect blue sky. There wasn't a cloud to be seen. Ward looked out at the dull grey morning and smiled to himself.

Carney came up alongside him. 'There are a variety of opportunities here. Studio apartments, one bedroom, two, three. Was there anything in particular you were after?'

Ward stared at the photograph, the broad vista, out across

the city. It looked to the horizon, to the dark green hills surrounding Belfast. It looked beyond the maze of streets, the terrace houses, the red Belfast brick. The Markets, the Short Strand, the Lower Ormeau.

He smiled at Carney, said thanks and headed for the door.

Back in the car, he sat, staring down Waring Street. Ward thought about the TV report, McCann's donation to the boxing club. He thought about the businesses he'd visited that morning, about the Obel Tower. McCann was pulling up the rope, protecting himself with a wall of money. He'd have an accountant, a lawyer, a public profile. Soon he'd be gone, out of reach, totally untouchable.

Ward looked at his watch. Almost three. He thought about lunch but didn't feel like eating. He turned the ignition, put the car in gear and headed for Musgrave Street.

# TWENTY FIVE

Marty Toner stood on a patch of waste ground, kicking stones, smoking. He looked up, still no sign. It was Sunday morning, early doors, Belfast was still in its pit. He'd hardly slept. He kept replaying the car journey with Tierney and Molloy. The country lanes, the utter darkness. Dead one minute, alive the next.

A navy Mondeo turned into the street and pulled to the kerb. The peeler got out, the detective. He leaned against the car and lit a fag. Marty looked round, before slowly walking to the car. He looked at the cop's face, expecting a 'well done, that-a-boy', something at least. The detective looked pale, his face drawn.

'How do you like that then?' Marty said, ignoring the doom mongering. The cop forced a smile.

'I'm telling you. I should be in the movies or something. *The Bourne fucking Identity*, 007 James Bond. Bet you were worried when we got into the car? I was bricking it myself mind, wondering where we were going, if I was for the chop, if that was it ... *sayonara*, Marty son, nice knowing you, don't call us we'll call you.'

O'Neill put his hand up in an effort to slow him down.

'We've got him though. Hook, line and sinker.' Marty threw some fake punches. 'Ali versus Foreman – the jaw, the body, the jaw ... boom! Down he goes.'

'Calm down, son.'

Marty looked up, his face puzzled. 'Calm down?'

'That's what I said.'

'I just nailed Johnny Tierney. Nailed that son-of-a-bitch. Do you know what that—'

'You didn't nail anyone.'

Marty's face furrowed. 'He said it on the wire, we got him, admitting it, Tomb Street.'

O'Neill shook his head.

'He fucking did,' Marty said, his voice desperate.

'We lost you at Forest Side.'

'What?'

'We lost you.'

'So? I was on the wire and all. It doesn't matter where *yous* were.'

'You went out of range.'

'What?'

'There was no signal. We haven't got anything.'

Marty went ballistic, cursing his head off, ranting. He couldn't believe it. He could have been killed. Worse even. And they couldn't even follow a car.

O'Neill let him go, knowing he needed to vent. After thirty seconds he'd heard enough. 'Listen. Nobody said it would be easy.'

Marty shook his head.

'You're going to have to do it over.'

'Fuck away off.'

'I'm serious.'

'You're going to get me killed.'

'Last time I checked, you didn't have many options.'

Marty spat on the ground, thinking about the rules – trust no one; no exceptions. He'd looked at O'Neill, remembering him in Ormeau Park, about how he went home to his dinner every night, about how he said this was Marty's life, his choice, his decision.

'You're going to have to man up again. There's no other way.'

Marty thought for a moment before nodding his head. 'Sure,' he said, turning to walk away. 'I'll call you.'

He put his hood up. He'd been stupid and he'd been greedy; the peeler could go fuck himself.

Marty walked with his head down, not looking up.

Wee Anto walked out of the Spar clutching a bottle of Coke and a packet of fags. He was rough as guts, his head pounding from the two bottles of Buckfast the night before. Marty hadn't shown up with the gear so him and Locksey had gone and got wasted. Marty was a dick, especially after the lecture he'd given them about being professional and not messing about. They agreed to go on their own, to ditch Marty and talk to Tierney about getting their gear.

Anto stopped in his tracks. There was a cop, next to the waste ground, leaning against a navy Mondeo. The cop was plain clothes but since he was six Anto had been able to spot them. He stopped in the shop door. He took a drink of Coke, waiting for the policeman to move on.

Anto watched someone in a grey tracksuit approach the peeler. He shook his head.

'Fucking touts,' he whispered.

The guy stopped to talk, his back to Anto, a hundred yards away. Anto watched, thinking he knew the guy, recognizing the shaved head, the way he stood. After a minute the guy turned to walk away. Anto almost dropped his Coke.

'Holy shit,' he whispered, as Marty Toner put his head down and his hood up.

'What time's this film?' O'Neill asked.

'Two,' his daughter replied.

'Right. Waterworks then?'

'Yay,' she sang, skipping towards the car.

They drove down the Cave Hill Road, passing the back of Antrim Road police station. It had been O'Neill's first post, back in uniform. Sarah was jabbering in the back, talking somersaults and high bars, what Miss Cunningham said, who'd gave her what at the party. O'Neill almost turned into the station out of habit.

The Waterworks dated from the 1840s, when the reservoir held the Belfast water supply. It was a nature reserve now and on a good day there were greylag geese, mute swans and a few coots. O'Neill remembered doing laps with Sarah, pushing the buggy at seven in the morning. He never knew a baby could scream so much.

They parked and got out of the car. O'Neill saw a black Mercedes, S Class, parked on the Cave Hill Road. It was the same kind of car he'd seen parked outside the George, Gerry McCann's, two days earlier. O'Neill looked at the registration and pulled his mobile. He paused, telling himself to calm down, it was his day off, there were probably a thousand black Mercs in Belfast.

He called Sarah over and put his arm round her. They walked towards the playground, O'Neill staring at the road. The windows were tinted so he couldn't see inside. After a few seconds the engine started and the car drove off.

'Daddy, can we do a lap of the water?'

'Sure,' he said, his attention on the car as it headed towards the Limestone Road.

At the reservoir there was a lone fishermen, sipping at a can of Super Lager. Apparently there were trout, but O'Neill had never seen a fish pulled out in his life. As they walked, he glanced back towards the road.

He let Sarah rabbit on, trying to keep up with schoolyard politics, her new best friends, the gymnastics teacher. After a few hundred yards he started to relax.

'So how's your mum doing?' he said, interrupting.

'She's fine.'

'And who babysits you now?'

'Karen, from two doors up. She paints my nails and—'

'Was she babysitting last weekend?'

'Yes. Saturday. We watched the new—'

'Does she babysit a lot?'

'Em. Most weeks. Or weekends even. Mostly Saturdays. No wait. Some Fridays.'

'Right,' he said casually. 'And where does your mum go?'

Sarah paused, unsure. He tickled under her arm.

'Go on,' he said.

She squirmed, trying not to laugh. O'Neill kept tickling and she hopped forward, out of reach.

'What is it?'

'I'm not allowed to say.'

'I'm your dad.'

The girl squirmed. More tickling.

'Mummy's got a boyfriend.'

O'Neill stayed calm, putting on a panto voice.

'Oh no she hasn't.'

'Oh yes she has.'

231

He faked a laugh, Sarah joining in. A few yards more.

'You met him then?'

'Not yet.'

'What's his name?'

'Andrew.'

'How did she meet him?'

'I don't know,' Sarah said. 'I think he knows Aunty Amanda. Maybe he's a teacher.'

'Aunty Amanda, eh?' he said, jaw tense.

Sarah spied the swings and started running, cutting him off.

O'Neill sat on the bench and checked his phone, looking for a distraction. He looked at Sarah, watching her hang from the monkey bars.

'No hands. Look.'

'Very good, love.'

O'Neill forced a smile. It hadn't taken Catherine long to move on, not with her sister's help. He thought back to the party, the way Amanda floated about, like she knew something he didn't. He wondered if Catherine was seeing him that afternoon. Andrew the teacher. He imagined sweaters and sensible shoes. His grip tightened on his mobile.

O'Neill was about to suggest they made a move when he noticed the black Merc on the main road again. It sat there, engine idling. He stood up and started walking towards the gate. From the distance and angle he couldn't get the licence plate.

'Daddy,' Sarah called, 'where are you ...'

'Wait here, honey. I'll be two minutes.'

O'Neill quickened his pace as he left the park, walking, marching, jogging. The car sat still, its black windscreen egging him on. When he was a hundred yards away, the car sprung to life, pulling out and peeling off up the road.

He tried to tell himself it was a coincidence. That the kid hadn't done the dirt on him, hadn't tipped off McCann and Tierney, that last night's fiasco hadn't all been planned. He turned round and started heading back to the park.

When he got there Sarah was on the ground, wailing. She'd fallen off the monkey bars and hit her head. There were adults kneeling beside her, a man and a woman. They looked up, searching for him, reassuring Sarah he wouldn't be far. Their own kids were behind on the swings, silently spectating. O'Neill felt the woman's disgust as he approached. He stared at her, daring her to say something. She sensed his anger and sloped away, shaking her head. She whispered to her husband when they were out of earshot.

Sarah had fallen and knocked her head. It was shock more than anything and she calmed after a few minutes. O'Neill asked about hospital, but she knew it would mean no cinema.

An hour later, they had their tickets and were lined up at the sweet counter.

'You get popcorn,' Sarah said. 'I'll get ice cream?'

She was sure of herself, liked to be in charge, liked telling folk what to do. O'Neill went along for the ride, trying to forget about the Merc and the fall in the park.

Sarah chose the seats, two rows from the front. The place was busy and O'Neill sat in the dark, tuning out from the movie. Maybe Catherine had been right. Maybe he wasn't cut out for the whole father thing. She'd be better off with Sensible Shoes or whatever his name was. Least he'd be home at night. Not running off after every muppet that looked like he might cause trouble.

He sat in the dark, holding the popcorn, needing a cigarette. Sarah's fingers delved in and grabbed a handful and shovelled it towards her mouth. He smiled at how natural she was, how unselfconscious. The world was there to be grabbed, chewed up, enjoyed.

After ten minutes, O'Neill fell asleep. The soft chair, the dark room. He'd no chance.

He was woken by Sarah pulling at his arm. He jolted up, looking around at the cinema, empty now, the lights back on.

'The film's finished,' she said.

He was dazed for a second. He'd been dreaming about Tomb Street, the scene again, McCarthy's body, his head caved in. He looked at Sarah and pushed the images away.

'Any good then, the film?'

'It was OK.'

'Right,' he said. 'Let's get you home.'

# TWENTY SIX

Marty was woken by his mobile vibrating beneath the pillow. He was still in his clothes, curled up on the bare mattress in Stewart Street. The floor was strewn with Mars bar wrappers and crumpled fag packets. Outside it was morning, the grey light illuminating the edges of the boarded-up window.

Marty rubbed his eyes and looked at the phone. Petesy.

'Right, homo,' he said.

'Where are you?'

Petesy was outside, walking somewhere, panicked.

'Why? You about?'

'Just tell me where you are.'

'Chill out. I'm at Stewart Street, that place—'

'I'm outside it now. There are guys here, two cars, they're—'

Marty leapt to his feet and went to the window. He saw his mate go past the house. Petesy had his head down, stick in one hand, phone in the other. He moved slowly, not stopping, not looking up. Marty glanced down the street. There was a grey Astra parked near the corner. The front seats were occupied, two guys in baseball caps, their faces hidden. Petesy reached the other end of the street, still on the phone.

'The blue Focus,' he said. 'One guy.'

Marty grabbed the bag of gear from the ground next to the mattress. He wondered who it was. How did they know he was there? Was it the peelers? Some undercover thing? Had that detective done the dirt on him, fed him to Tierney?

He went to the window again, checking the cars, his heart racing.

'Shit, shit, shit.'

He ran to the back bedroom, looking down at the yards stretching the length of the entry. There were washing lines, wheelie bins, scrawled graffiti. A man in a tracksuit leaned against the wall, his hands in his pockets. He had a white scar on one cheek from where he'd been done with a Stanley knife.

'Christ,' Marty said.

He thought about running. He was quick and might make it to the main road. There were four of them though. What if they were carrying? He thought about the Browning but it hadn't been much good the last time. The images came back to him, the night they'd done Petesy. He remembered Tierney's boot, grinding his face into the tarmac. He remembered the beating they gave Petesy, the hurling sticks, the nails.

He shook his head, feeling like he was already dead. Had Tierney figured out he'd been skimming? Selling his own gear on top? Did he know about the peeler? He'd said nothing but it wouldn't matter. They would kill him, but they'd want to know everything first. He pictured pliers, a nail gun, an acetylene torch. He saw blood, heard screaming, smelt burnt flesh. He pictured himself blacking out, coming through, pleading with them to just do him. He went back and forth, his heart racing. Think, think. He grabbed his phone, scrolled to Eddie and hit Call. He heard it ringing.

'Come on, come on.'

'Martino. Another pick-up.' Eddie was jovial.

'I'm fucked here. Stewart Street. I'm pinned in, two cars.'

'Peelers?'

'Worse.'

236

Eddie knew. 'Cunts,' he said.

'You need to come get me.'

Eddie was a mad bastard but he still hesitated.

'It's worth a grand,' Marty said.

'Right. Ten minutes. I'll call when I'm close.'

Marty hung up and paced the floor, oscillating between the front and back window. He looked at his phone. What if they came before Eddie got there? He'd have to run for it, take his chances.

'Come on, come on.'

Marty gathered the gear and his money and tucked it into his sock. He looked at his phone, checked the windows. The back, the front, the back again.

'Come on,' he said.

It felt like an hour. Finally, the phone lit.

'Red Mazda. I'll come down the street slow. Back windows open.'

Marty went downstairs, into the living room. It was bare, except for brown seventies carpet and a two-bar fire that didn't work. He prised the board away from the window, climbing on to the sill, lowering himself down. In the front garden he crouched, ready to bolt. He peered over the wall. A red car tootled along the street at twenty mile an hour. In the driver's seat was Eddie, wearing some auld boy's flat cap.

The Mazda drew near and Marty crept out, staying low, between parked cars. He dived in the window and lay along the back seat. Eddie whistled to himself.

'What the fuck you wearing?'

'Disguise,' Eddie laughed. 'You like it? It was in the car.'

Marty shook his head and rolled on to his back, looking at the roof.

'Where did you get the hairdryer?'

'Don't panic, son. It's Japanese. Kamikazes and shit.'

The car edged towards the top of the street. Eddie looked straight ahead, ignoring the grey Astra and the driver who turned to watch as he passed. They rounded the corner, driving slowly. Marty listened carefully. Neither of the other cars moved. They were on the side street when Eddie spoke.

'What did I tell you, mate? It's the disguise.'

The Mazda had gone ten yards when the guy with the scar came out of the entry. He walked along the footpath, glancing into the Mazda. Marty looked up as the face moved past the window in slow motion. Their gaze met, eyes wide. The guy went for the door.

'He's here,' he screamed. 'He's fucking here.'

The guy reached in, trying to unlock the door of the Mazda. Marty kicked out, Eddie flooring it. Scarface spun away. Tyres peeled behind them. Eddie floored it, tearing through the gears, the engine screaming. Marty flew across the back seat.

'Get us outta here!'

'Yeeeeoooow!' Eddie, shouting. 'Come on, ya bastards.'

He'd a hand on the gear stick, one on the wheel, feet dancing the pedals. There was one road out of the estate. The Astra was behind. The other car was trying to cut them off. They passed Petesy on the kerb, who pushed a wheelie bin on to the road. The Astra smashed into it, knocking him over as well.

Eddie threw the Mazda round a corner, the tail sliding out, clipping a parked car. A woman ran out of a house. 'You wee bastards!'

Three kids kicked a football. They dived out of the way as the Mazda roared towards them.

Eddie watched the blue Focus skid to a stop at the top of the street, hemming them in.

'Hang on,' he shouted, flooring it.

The driver's eyes widened as he saw the Mazda come straight at him. At the last minute Eddie pulled the handbrake. The car slid sideways, shunting the Focus and making a gap. He grabbed first and mounted the kerb, missing a teenage girl and her buggy by six inches.

On Cromac Street, Eddie forced the car out between a bus and a Tesco lorry. Horns blasted. He pulled into oncoming traffic, a Volvo skidding as the driver winced and swerved. He cut through to the Ravenhill, doing sixty, weaving between traffic. Behind them, the Astra was struggling to keep up. The distance got further. They turned at Annandale, cutting up an Ulsterbus. When they got round the corner Eddie killed the speed. He blended in, tootling at thirty miles an hour, his eyes in the rear-view mirror.

'I told you,' he said. 'Always trust the Japs.'

They drove on for ten minutes, taking various turns, waiting at junctions, watching for the cars. They went along Stranmillis, past the Botanic Gardens, on to the Lisburn Road. On Tates Avenue they parked up.

'This do?' Eddie said.

'Aye.'

Marty had his hand on the door, Eddie got out too.

'Later, mate.'

'Dead on.'

They walked in opposite directions, both looking round, scanning for movement.

A minute later, they were gone.

# TWENTY SEVEN

Tomb Street was a week old and still they had nothing. Ward sat behind his desk, O'Neill facing him, the door closed.

'Newspapers have been quiet,' O'Neill said. 'Think McCarthy had a rethink on his press conference. I might have done the Chief Inspector a favour.'

'Don't make it a habit.' Ward tossed a file at him. 'The scene report, Pat Kennedy's RTA.'

O'Neill opened it. Diagrams, distances, descriptions. 'What they saying?'

'Inconclusive.'

'That old chestnut. What about his ticker?'

'Post-mortem came back fine. No heart attack, no stroke. Look at page four. Dents on the rear bumper. Low impact collision.'

'Low impact? They have him leaving the road at seventy.'

'Yeah, but if he was bumped from the behind, even at that speed, it would look like a nudge.'

'You said he drove rally cars. Think he was reliving the glory days?'

Ward shook his head.

O'Neill looked at the rest of the report. 'So they're saying there's no way to know with the bumper. He could have reversed into someone in Tesco.'

'Yes. I spoke to his wife. She didn't know anything about it. If there was a prang it must have happened that afternoon.'

Ward screwed his face. 'Reversing into someone in a car park? Driving into a tree? It doesn't fit. Not with Pat.'

'Yous were pretty tight,' O'Neill said, fishing.

'Pat Kennedy was my first Sergeant. I was twenty-nine when he plucked me out of uniform. He'd been watching, reckoned I could make it in the Branch.'

'And Davy Price?'

'He was the year before. Same deal. Hand-picked.'

'Where's he these days?'

Ward paused. 'Why do you care?'

O'Neill looked away. 'I looked at the file, the murdered solicitor, McCann's brother.'

Ward stared at him. O'Neill looked back.

'Question everything, believe nothing.' It was a Wardism.

'Fair play,' the DI said.

O'Neill sat forward. 'Yous worked Michael McCann's murder.'

'Mostly them. I'd just joined the Branch. I was at a few of the interviews, including Gerry McCann, but was moved on before the case got going.'

'You must have a theory?'

Ward watched O'Neill, not backing off, not afraid.

'Did someone have McCann's brother hit? Someone on our side?'

Ward didn't speak.

'Did we hand him to the UV? Set the dogs loose?'

'Michael McCann was scum. He defended murderers, guys who shot peelers, who gunned them down in front of their wives, in front of their kids. Do you want names? Archie Long, Bill McAteer, Tony Duggan, Lennie Smith ... tell me when to stop. They were good men, all of them, they didn't deserve—'

O'Neill held his hands up. 'We're not doubting that.'

'So what are we doubting then?'

'We're doubting everything. That's the job right.'

Ward took a breath, suddenly feeling old. 'It was a war, son.'

O'Neill nodded. 'Things happen.'

Ward paused, watching him, knowing what he was at. After a while the DI spoke. 'I asked Pat Kennedy about it last year. You know, what happened? Were we having people killed? Was it unofficial policy?'

'What did he say?'

'He said the Provies didn't have a policy. He said they didn't care who they hit – women, children, didn't matter. It was collateral damage. It was inevitable. He said in a war there were casualties. Michael McCann being dead saved lives; that was what mattered. He used the same word.' He nodded at the report. 'Inconclusive.'

Ward stood and walked to the window, stared out. He shook his head.

'The Troubles, the Provos, the whole shooting match. Twenty-five years, three thousand dead and for what?'

He paused, his back to O'Neill.

'We had to do something. You couldn't sit around, twiddling your thumbs, waiting for them to come. How do you reason with a murderer? There's a man standing over you with a gun to your head ... do you need to have a fucking policy? Pat Kennedy reckoned sometimes it was about knowing when to close your eyes, when to leave the room, when to look the other way. Sometimes, he said, the law wasn't enough.'

Ward turned, eyes distant. O'Neill looked at him.

'And what do you think?'

'I think he was a hell of a peeler.' Ward paused, staring into space. 'I think he was wrong.'

A silence fell between them. O'Neill opened the traffic report, allowing the DI his memories.

After a while, Ward spoke. 'So where's the kid now then? Marty Toner.'

'Gone to ground. I saw him yesterday, said he'd go again but he was bullshitting.'

'McCann's going to disappear you know. I followed him yesterday, watched him driving round in that Merc. He did a loop of his businesses, a lap of honour – Tropical Tan, Paradise Bronzing.' Ward shook his head. 'He went to Obel Tower after that, the showroom, looking at penthouse apartments. I'm telling you, in six weeks' time he'll be gone, hidden behind his money, behind his lawyers, behind his accountants. He'll not set foot in the George again, except for old times, to remind himself how far he's come. We'll be left with the Marty Toners of this world, locking them up for six months while Wilson pumps out the stats and smiles for the cameras ...' Ward's voice trailed off. O'Neill not listening. 'Detective?'

Nothing.

'Hey!'

O'Neill looked up. 'Gimme a minute,' he said, standing and leaving.

He was back in two, holding a manila folder. Inside were business accounts. He sat in front of Ward, pouring over them.

'Tropical Tan you said – 426 Ormeau Road.'

'That's right.'

O'Neill flicked the pages.

'Paradise Bronzing – 84 Cromac Street.'

'Yeah.'

'Then you did a car wash on the Ravenhill, a nail parlour on the Dublin Road ...'

Ward nodded. 'Pretty much.'

'These accounts were pulled off Jonathan McCarthy's laptop. The kid wasn't dealing coke. He was a front. He was helping McCann to go legit, helping him wash his money, turning him into a businessman.'

O'Neill pictured the McCarthy house in Lisburn: the long driveway, the stables out back, the Range Rover. It was a lot to live up to. He thought about the hockey medals in the bottom of the cupboard, about never being good enough, about needing to prove yourself. Jonathan McCarthy wasn't an innocent victim. He wasn't in the wrong place at the wrong time. He thought he could play with the big boys, show his da what he was made of.

'Why does he front for McCann?'

'Who knows? Maybe he wants to prove something?'

'To who?'

'Dunno. They fuck you up your mum and dad ...'

Ward squinted.

'He was paying him. Blackmailing him too. They might have sold him some coke, hooked him, reeled him in. He was either with them or against them. He did McCann's books or else they ruin him, go after his da and all, make a few headlines.'

'So how does he end up dead?'

'He makes a balls-up, or a mistake, or decides he wants out. McCann can't have that. He knows too much. Someone

244

should have a word. Only McCarthy doesn't want to listen, so they make their point more forcefully. We end up in Tomb Street.'

Ward sat in his chair, thinking.

O'Neill held the accounts up. 'This is our ticket. The kid pointed at Tierney, said it was him. We get Tierney, offer him a walk, he gives us McCann.'

'You think he'll roll over on Gerry McCann?'

'What would you give for fifteen years of your life?'

Ward shrugged.

O'Neill stood. 'I'll be next door.'

# TWENTY EIGHT

Petesy sat at his desk, trying Marty on his mobile. No answer.

It had been three hours since he'd watched him tear out of the Markets in a stolen car. Petesy had seen the two cars go after him, screaming through traffic, desperate to keep up.

He tried Marty again. Answerphone.

'Right, son,' his grandmother called up the stairs. 'That's me off to the bingo.'

She went Mondays and Thursdays, blotting out numbers, hoping her ship would come in.

Petesy looked at the envelope from the passport applications on his desk. He listened to his granny mumble her checklist – 'handbag, brolly, keys' – before stepping out and closing the door behind her. He moved to the bed, closing his eyes, wondering about Marty. He pictured the cars catching him, saw his mate tied to a chair, blindfolded and gagged. Petesy wondered what they'd do if they caught him. Would he just disappear? Would that be it? He remembered Marty's face the other Thursday, the look in his eye, the pure terror.

Petesy sighed when he heard a knock at the door. It was his grandmother, back for her glasses – 'Forget my head if it wasn't screwed on.'

He rolled out of bed and went down stairs, ready to tease her.

'How many times ...' he said, opening the door.

Petesy froze. Johnny Tierney stood staring at him. He smiled, like he was looking at his dinner.

Petesy closed the door. Tierney stood still.

'That's not very friendly now, is it? No "how you doing?" I mean, what's the world coming to?'

A holy picture looked down on Petesy: Jesus with his sad face, his chest open, his heart on fire.

Petesy turned and limped through the living room, heading for the back door. Forty-six ornaments watched him. Pink piggies, fishing frogs, miniature clowns. Behind him Tierney's voice. Quiet, insistent.

'Peter. I need to talk to you son.'

Petesy burst into the kitchen. The room was small, old-fashioned, immaculately clean. His grandmother was that generation. He'd his hand on the back door when a large shadow crystallized on the far side of the frosted glass. Petesy stood back and watched the handle come down. The shadow pressed against it, trying to get in. A face came up against the glass: Sean Molloy. Petesy wanted to be sick.

'Come out, come out, wherever you are.'

Petesy looked round the kitchen, not sure what he hoped to find. There was a small black knife on the breadboard. He shook his head. It would only make it worse. The police were his only chance. He picked up the house phone. An elbow smashed through the glass in the back door. Mobile, he thought, upstairs.

Petesy didn't see Molloy's large hand reach through and turn the lock. He was in the living room, then the hall, past the front door. Outside Tierney had stopped knocking. He stood there, waiting for the door to open.

Petesy scrambled upstairs, two at a time, knees screaming.

In his room he closed the door and wedged a chair beneath it. His grabbed his mobile, dialled 999.

There were sounds on the stairs, thud, thud, heavy feet. The door exploded inwards, smashing the chair.

'Hello. Emergency Services. Which service do you—'

Molloy took the mobile and hung up.

Petesy looked up as a punch knocked him to the floor.

He bent double, winded, suffocating. After a few seconds it passed. Petesy looked up at Molloy, wanting to shit. Memories flooded back. The waste ground, his face in the dirt, the hurling sticks with nails through them. He'd begged them – *wise up, stop, I'm sorry, I'm sorry ...*

Molloy nodded towards the stairs and pulled Petesy up. He'd no stick and put his hand on the bannister, his knees wobbling. He'd gone three stairs when he felt a boot in his back. He was flying. Molloy watched him free fall, landing in a heap at the bottom of the stairs.

He lifted him again and dragged him into the living room. Petesy groaned, semi-conscious. Molloy stepped out to unlock the front door. Tierney came in the house, looking at the crumpled teenager on the carpet.

Molloy shrugged. 'He's a cripple. He tripped.'

Tierney dragged Petesy off the floor and dumped him in an armchair. He bent down, leaning over, inspecting his injuries. There was a cut above his eyebrow, a line of blood running into the socket and down his cheek.

Petesy was unsure where he was. Everything looked pink. His head throbbed, like it had been hit with a hammer. His shoulder was killing him. He sensed a face close to his, a man bending over. There were sounds, voices, talking. A pair of hands gripped his head, rolling it, making sure it was still attached. It came back to Petesy – Tierney, Molloy. He felt his body tense and he tried to get up.

A hand grabbed hold of his hair. Molloy punched him in the face – one, two, three. Petesy rocked back, his world exploding.

'Calm yourself, son. No more chaseys, you hear?'

Petesy lay in the chair, moaning. After a few minutes, he reached up and put a hand to his head. He tried to open his eyes. Objects moved, everything blurred. Someone was opposite him, in his granny's chair. The other man walked round the living room, picking up objects, inspecting them. He went into the kitchen, before returning and heading for the hall. Petesy heard feet on the stairs.

Molloy got out of his granny's chair and leaned forward.

'Where is he?'

Petesy didn't answer. Molloy slapped him in the face and his lip split. Petesy tried to cower while Molloy waited.

'I'm going to ask you one more time. Where is he?'

A pause, two seconds, three seconds. Molloy slapped him again and his nose burst. A cascade of blood ran over his mouth and on to his T-shirt.

Molloy laughed, then shook his head. 'Look at the state of you. You need to understand, we can do this all day. Eventually, you'll tell us. And you know what you'll be thinking?' His voice went deep and dopey. *'I wish I'd told them two hours ago.'*

Molloy laughed at his own joke. He put his hand to his back, groaning as he stood up. Petesy was dazed, half aware, his head pounding. Molloy reached for a dining chair and placed it in front of him. He reached down and straightened Petesy's leg, putting his foot on the chair, exposing his knee.

Molloy looked round the room, trying to find something big, something heavy. He frowned and stepped into the kitchen, rummaging through drawers.

He returned with a rolling pin.

Molloy stood over Petesy's leg, looking at the knee, shaking his head.

'You know it's amazing what the surgeons can do these days.' He smiled, prodding the knee with the rolling pin. 'But you know, they can only do it once. Second time round's a different matter. Then you're talking wheelchairs.'

Molloy straightened, adjusting his grip, changing his stance. He made a series of practice strokes, trying to figure the best angle.

'And you need to remember something as well.' Molloy paused. 'You've got two knees, two ankles, two elbows. We can take our time. One way or the other though we're going to find out where he is.'

Petesy looked up, face stinging, eyes rolling in his head. There was a sound of footsteps on the stairs. Molloy stood up, rolling pin cocked. He breathed in.

'Hang fire,' Tierney said, coming through the doorway.

Molloy exhaled, his face dropping.

Tierney held up Petesy's mobile. 'Less mess.'

Molloy looked disappointed, like he'd been told Santa didn't exist. He crouched down, a few inches from the bloody pulp of Petesy's face.

'You're lucky, son. Do you hear me? Lucky.'

Petesy wasn't aware of them leaving. It was two hours before his grandmother came home and found him there, sitting in the armchair.

# TWENTY NINE

O'Neill had lost the feeling in his lower back. He'd been sitting in the cupboard at Musgrave Street looking at a bank of monitors for three hours. The room was musty and stale. Six screens and no windows, health and safety would have had a field day.

Marty Toner had gone to ground, which left him with a dead body, half a theory and a set of Gerry McCann's business accounts. The kid had fingered Tierney, but there were a million reasons to doubt him. O'Neill had spent the day reviewing the case file and was now going over the tapes from the club and the street cameras around Tomb Street. It was grainy footage, people turning off Victoria Street, heading for the club. Four hours later, they staggered back out like extras in a low-budget zombie flick.

O'Neill paused the tape as the McCarthy group arrived, checking the time against his notes. He watched the footage inside the club. People clutching drinks, skulling shots – sambuca, tequila, Jäger Bombs. There was no audio. Folk leaned in and shouted silently in each other's ears. McCarthy and Craig were in the corner with the girls, oscillating between the bar and their table. O'Neill tallied their drinks. McCarthy put away five Becks and three shots in two hours. His flatmate kept pace, so did the girls. He watched Marty Toner arrive at the club after twelve with two other lads. They stayed near the bar, checking out the birds, commenting as they passed. McCarthy sporadically looked at his phone, checking texts, like he was expecting something. O'Neill watched, reminded that they never found his mobile. At 1.25 a.m., McCarthy said something to his flatmate and left the club. The door camera showed him walk between the two bouncers, turn left and vanish out of shot.

O'Neill sighed. It was nothing he didn't know. After a smoke in the car park he settled into CID and pulled the paperwork. He reread everything – witness statements, autopsy report, interview transcripts. The parents, the flatmate, the friends. He went back to his notes from the scene, looking at the diagram, the position of the body, the distance from the club. In the folder was a list of the other businesses along Tomb Street – post office, electrical wholesaler, digital designers. Kearney had done the follow-up, getting their CCTV, sitting through hours of footage in the hope of seeing something. It was donkey work, box ticking, you did it anyway.

O'Neill stopped and looked at the evidence log. There was something missing. The Cole Agency, a digital design company. There was no record of their CCTV.

He called Kearney on his mobile. They'd tried them three times but got no reply. Kearney had visited the premises last Thursday, but there had been no answer. O'Neill looked up the number and tried again.

'Digital Design, Nick Cole.' The voice was English, northern, Geordie maybe.

O'Neill introduced himself, explained about the incident.

'We've been in Munich at an industry show.'

'No problem. Listen, I was just wondering if you had any CCTV on the premises?'

'No. We've a camera on our door entry system but that's about it.'

Half an hour later, O'Neill was in Tomb Street. He stood in the door of the design office, looking towards the entry where McCarthy had been found. There was a direct line of sight.

He pressed the intercom and was buzzed up. The offices were minimalist, all white furniture, clean desks and no wires. O'Neill thought about Musgrave Street, the mass of cables and the institutional Formica. The owner was late thirties, dressed in black with a ginger quiff. The man led him to an Apple Mac, where he pulled some high-resolution footage of the door.

'We do it all through the computer.'

'Impressive,' O'Neill said, thinking about the kit they had put on Marty Toner, suddenly embarrassed.

'You're saying two weekends ago?' Cole typed as he spoke.

'Yeah. Sunday morning, between 1 a.m. and 2.'

An image appeared on the screen – night-time, the doorway, a metre of footpath. You couldn't see the street, let alone the entry where they'd found McCarthy.

'You see,' Cole said. 'It's really only a door entry system. We've nothing here worth stealing.'

O'Neill sighed and offered his thanks.

'Hang on,' Cole said. They watched the footage suddenly come to life. A shape at the bottom of the shot began to move.

'What the—' Cole, cut himself short.

A figure had been lying in the doorway, a wino. He got up slowly, looked to be in pain, the bones aching. He stumbled, steadied himself against the wall and made off down the street.

'Dirty bastard. Sleeping in our doorway.'

O'Neill looked at the tramp – the straggly beard, the pockmarked skin, the filthy complexion. He felt himself smile. 'Hello, Henry.'

'You know him?' Cole said surprised.

'Everyone knows Henry.'

Henry was Arthur Devine. He got his nickname from Henry Joy McCracken, the Belfast man they hung in Corn Market after the '98 rebellion. Two hundred years later Arthur Devine had tried the same trick. He'd botched it. The police were called to Corn Market, to a homeless guy screaming his head off. The rope had snapped and he broke both ankles. Henry lay screaming for two hours. Folk ignored him, thinking he was one of the local crazies. There was no fixing Henry. Mental illness, alcohol addiction, substance abuse. Where would you even start?

O'Neill went back to Musgrave Street and pulled a file. Henry had a list of offences, mostly Public Order, the odd Criminal Damage. He was forty-two but looked sixty. He'd brown unkempt hair, a long ratted beard and clothes he'd pulled from a skip. He had the classic alkie face – burst blood vessels, swollen nose, scabby lips. In the mugshot his eyes stared out like there was nothing inside. He had been sleeping rough for over a decade and spent whatever money he got pouring Christ knows what down his throat.

Henry was a local celebrity. He'd get pissed and walk the Lisburn Road, abusing folk. Eventually the cops were called. Older officers would stand aside, let the rookies take charge. Henry was a right of passage. He'd stand there, calling them all the names of the day. Eventually they cuffed him. The bracelets would barely click when Henry would hold his breath and his face would turn red. Five seconds, ten seconds, then he'd stop and start smiling.

The smell would suddenly hit and the peelers would jump back.

'Dirty bastard's shit himself.'

Older cops stood laughing.

'Control your suspect, son.'

Later they'd sit over a beer, recounting stories of when they'd each been 'Henried'.

'Waited till he was in the back of the wagon on me.'

'Here. That's nothing. He put it on his hands with me. Started spreading it over the inside of the car. He tried to get me with it.'

From CID O'Neill did a ring round, calling the hostels to see if anyone had seen Henry. He came up blank but knew a list of spots where he might crash and decided to call it a night.

Seven in the morning, bottle in hand, O'Neill cut across the Botanic Gardens. He left solitary tracks in the early morning dew. To his left, the white ribs of the Victorian glasshouse. To his right, the stone edifice of the Ulster Museum. He'd jumped the wall into the deserted park. Bottles peeked from the top of bins – White Lightning, Merrydown, Buckfast. The Botanics were a favourite of winos and hoods, the undeserving and the unwanted, folk with nowhere to go. A place to count your coppers and commune with your poison in peace. For those with no hostel, the bushes towards the back offered some token cover. It was a place to kip, once the booze had done its job and won you a few hours of blissful annihilation.

O'Neill had a quarter-bottle of Black Bush in his pocket and headed for the back of the Botanics. In the corner, behind a rhododendron he hit the jackpot. He approached quietly, looking for a head among the dirty blankets and old newspapers.

'Hey, Henry.'

Nothing.

'Henry.'

Nothing.

O'Neill prodded the shape with his foot.

'Go fuck yourself,' it said, eyes closed.

The shape broke into a coughing fit, loose phlegm rattling.

'Police, Henry.'

Eyes still closed. 'Definitely go fuck yourself.'

O'Neill stopped prodding. He leaned over the heap, unscrewed the quarter bottle and poured a splash across the cracked lips. The nose twitched, the tongue flicked, a quiet moan.

O'Neill screwed the cap on and left the bottle. He stepped away and lit a cigarette. After a minute, there were a series of groans, then curses, as the shape righted itself. The screw top opened, he heard a slug being taken. There was no gasp, no release, no sense of the whiskey burning.

O'Neill came round and saw Henry slumped, tipping the bottle back. He was talking to himself, the words spilling out in semi-delirium.

'No surrender. *Sláinte*. Up the Rah.'

Henry laughed and a hacking cough cut into him like it might kill him. It lasted two minutes, leaving him breathless.

A dribble of phlegm hung from his mouth and he wiped it with his sleeve. O'Neill watched him relax as the whiskey did its work. He figured there was a ten-minute window. He was no use sober, too much craving. And he was no use steaming, too much nonsense. You needed him lightly oiled, the tongue loosened.

Henry tipped the bottle, taking a slug, the whiskey half gone.

'New interrogation technique? If I'd a known I'd a talked years ago. God bless the PSNI.'

O'Neill looked at him. 'Tomb Street.'

'No comment,' Henry, bursting into laughter.

O'Neill waited. 'Tomb Street.'

'Wasn't me.'

O'Neill stared.

'The butler did it.'

'Did what, Henry?'

The wino stared at the half-empty bottle. 'Only a quarter-bottle? You're a cheap bastard.'

O'Neill looked on, thinking he was wrong, there was nothing to be had here.

'Give us a feg there?' Henry said. 'You never know what might spark a man's memory.'

O'Neill produced the packet of cigarettes, making to free one. He took it himself and tossed the box.

'God bless you, guvnor—' the voice, twee Irish '—a scholar and a gentleman.' Cigarette in mouth. 'Got a light?'

O'Neill threw it. Henry lit the fag and pocketed the lighter with a sly wink.

'Tomb Street,' O'Neill insisted.

'Oh, no problem. Come out of the Botanics, take a right past Queen's, down Great Victoria Street ...' Henry laughed, manic, hysterical.

'Good breakfast,' he said, fag in one hand, drink in the other. 'All the food groups.'

O'Neill made to walk away, but turned, thinking one last go. 'Tomb Street. Couple of weekends ago. Two guys fighting.'

Henry sang to the quarter-bottle. 'Of all the stars that ever shone ...'

O'Neill sighed, stood up and started walking.

'One guy,' Henry said, quietly to himself.

O'Neill stopped. 'What?'

The wino laughed. 'Henry sees, Henry knows.'

'Enough of the Yoda. What did you see?'

'One guy fighting. The other guy standing there, impersonating a punchbag.' A drunken smile. 'Used to box too, you know. Holy Cross, Under Sixteens. Stick and move, stick and move. I could a been a contender, I could a been somebody ...' The voice trailed off into a bronchial cough.

'The guy could box?' O'Neill said.

'Debatable. He was no Barry McGuigan. Southpaw mind you.'

'What?'

'He was a lefty.'

O'Neill waited.

'A shit southpaw, big left hand, swung like a hammer.'

Henry looked back at the bottle, squinting at the inch in the bottom. 'Ah Danny Boy,' singing again. 'The pipes the pipes are calling ...'

O'Neill took out a twenty pound note and held it in front of the wino. 'Do you know who it was?'

The tramp smiled, looking at the twenty. 'Henry's not a tout.'

'No, he's not. But Henry's thirsty though.'

The tramp sighed. 'Everyone knows.'

O'Neill proffered the twenty, closer now. 'Who was it?'

The wino smiled, surrendering. 'Johnny Tierney.'

O'Neill handed him the money and stood up. He turned and trekked back through park, the pre-dawn sky starting to lighten.

# THIRTY

'You need to get me out of here.'

O'Neill hesitated, taking a second to figure out who was on the phone. He was back in Musgrave Street.

'They're gonna kill me.'

Marty was freaked.

'People are watching. My name's out. You said if anything happened ... *we're coming for you ... whatever it takes ....*'

'Slow down.'

'Listen, the shit hit the fan. They're looking for me.'

'Where are you?'

'I'm not telling you.'

'Not telling?'

'How do I know it wasn't you sold me to Tierney?'

'What are you talking about?'

'I'm talking about my name all over a wall. "TONER'S A TOUT", that's what it says.'

'Calm down.'

'No, you calm down. You can go home to your bed at night, have a few beers, watch the telly. I'll tell you what. I've got nowhere. I can't sit still for five minutes without waiting on the door getting kicked in.'

O'Neill heard traffic noises, the kid walking, talking between breaths. He pictured him jittery and afraid, a piece of prey waiting to get eaten.

'Look, take it easy. We can figure it out. There are options.'

'Like what?'

'We can hide you. We've got safe houses. Places across the water.'

The phone went silent.

'I need to sort things out.' O'Neill said. 'Make a few calls. Come into Musgrave Street. You'll be safe.'

'I've got to get my money.'

'Bad idea, son.'

The line went quiet. O'Neill hesitated. 'I need your help with something.'

'I heard that before.'

'Listen, we've almost got Tierney. We need to know where he lays his head.'

'I told yous,' he said, patronizing, 'he doesn't touch the gear.'

'That doesn't matter. Where does he sleep?'

'Nah. Get me sorted first, then I'll give you Tierney.'

'No,' O'Neill said, his heart hard.

'What happened to the big speech ... *we're coming for you ... whatever it takes* ... full of fucking shit so you are. You might as well be Tierney and McCann for all the difference it makes.'

O'Neill let him blow.

'Look, son, this is how it works. The sweets aren't free. We need Tierney.'

There was a pause at the end of the line. O'Neill heard a siren in the background, louder then fading. He waited. At least the kid hadn't hung up.

'Stewart Street, Cooke Street, Rutland Street.'

'He has three addresses?'

'Aye.'

'What numbers?'

'Thirty-seven, eighty-two, forty-six.'

O'Neill memorized the details.

'Listen, give me an hour. I'll make some calls. Lie low you hear, don't be—'

The line went dead.

O'Neill turned the computer on and began to type search warrants for each address. It was after seven and they wouldn't get approved until the morning. Ward was right about informants, having folk on the street, having eyes and ears. O'Neill focused on the task, making sure everything was right. The smallest detail wrong and it would be an illegal search and some smart-arse lawyer would blow you out of the water. He looked at his watch. He'd get these finished, then see about Toner and what favours he could call in.

Two miles away Marty Toner hid in an alley off Botanic Avenue. He needed to go home, get the sports bag, secure his dough. It was dangerous going back. Folk knew him, they'd recognize him, all it would take was a phone call. Nah, he'd wait until it was dark. In the meantime, some food.

He watched folk coming out of Julie's Kitchen carrying takeaways, boxes of chicken and chips. It was too risky, he'd have to wait, he might be seen. He watched a lone student walk out with long hair and a Nirvana T-shirt, carrying some food. Marty followed him down Cromwell Road, smelling salt and vinegar and chips.

'Here,' he said, when they'd gone a hundred yards.

The student turned, half stoned.

'Twenty quid for your dinner.'

The guy thought it was joke, that he was going to jump him, nick his food. 'Serious,' Marty said, sensing the distrust, holding out a banknote.

The student reached for the money before handing over his grub and heading back to the chippy.

In an entry off Cromwell Road, Marty found a backyard and climbed the wall. It was cold and starting to drizzle. He wolfed the box of chicken wings, then the chips, scraping the salt of the bottom with his fingers and licking them. It was two days since he'd eaten properly.

He tossed the box away and looked at his phone. It had been an hour. He tried O'Neill but there was no answer.

The rain came on again, heavier now. Marty huddled against the wall, pulling his hood up and a piece of cardboard round his legs. He started to shiver and wished he'd more clothes, his gloves maybe, his hat and all. It would be dark soon, safer, he'd make his move.

Marty gripped his mobile in one hand, his fingers blue with cold. After a while, he started to shake, teeth first, then his hands. His eyes felt heavy and he began to drift off.

The phone vibrated, jolting him awake.

It was a text. Petesy: *All sorted. Got a plan. Come get me.*

# THIRTY ONE

Earlier that day Ward had driven past Queen's University and up the Malone Road. As he climbed the hill the road got wider, the houses bigger, the trees leafier. He found himself in Osbourne Park, where the solicitor Michael McCann had lived. He pulled into the kerb and switched off the engine. It was mid-afternoon and a trickle of kids wandered home in grammar school uniforms.

Ward looked at number eighty-eight, at the driveway where Michael McCann's life had ended. He leaned his head back and closed his eyes.

It was 1992 again, the night of the shooting. RUC Land Rovers blocked the street. Officers were upbeat, busy at their work, enjoying the job. Word had got round – it was Michael McCann, the Provo lawyer. There was a sense of justice, of a late equalizer, of being back in the game. You could read people's thoughts – he was asking for it, deserved what he got, slap it up him.

Ward was thirty-five, in Special Branch a month. He bent down to look at the car, the door riddled, glass in a million pieces. He imagined putting it back together, an impossible jigsaw, one you'd never finish.

He'd driven from Tenant Street with Pat Kennedy. The Sarge didn't speak the whole way up. At the scene, Kennedy was disinterested, like he knew what had happened and didn't need to look. After a while, he drifted off. Ward saw him with Davy Price, away from the rest, sharing a quiet word.

Fourteen years later, Ward tried to remember whether he knew at the time. Had he chosen to look the other way? Did that make him as guilty as the rest? Sure he'd done things – the lying, the cheating folk, the beating of suspects. Twenty-five years in the dirt, no one came out clean. Ward heard the old lines, the justifications, the explanations – there was a war on, it was gloves off, what did folk expect.

There'd been a lot of talk, accusations, a lot bandied about – collusion, murder, state-sanctioned death. He thought back, but it was all blank, a brick wall, a dead end. He couldn't remember what he knew and what he didn't know, what he felt and what he didn't feel. One thing he was sure of. There were no altar boys, no innocents, not on any side.

Ward turned the key and started the car. He drove to the motorway, heading out the M1 towards Ballymena, the Bellaghy Road and Dunloy. It was almost dark when he stepped from the car, the last hue of light fading in the west. A low mist had settled on the fields, a silence upon the land. Ward walked slowly towards the tree that Pat Kennedy's car had been wrapped round four days earlier.

But for the fresh soil and the lacerated trunk you'd never know. There were no flowers, no messages, no fuss. Pat wouldn't have wanted any. Ward approached the tree, running his hand along the scars. He wondered how long it would take for the trunk to weather, to toughen under the elements and hide the wounds of four days ago.

He looked at the night, gathering round him. In the distance a cowshed echoed with a low communal groan.

The fields were barren, the mud damp, the ground waiting. Winter was on its way out, spring a while away. Ward thought about Eileen, Pat's widow. The funeral was next week. He should call to see her, seeing as he was up this far. What would he say though? What could he tell her? How did you get it all to make sense?

He got back in the car and turned towards Belfast.

That evening Ward did another round of the pubs, looking for Davy Price. He wasn't at the Sea Dog, wasn't at Paddy Murphy's. There were familiar faces, a succession of shrugged shoulders.

'Davy about? Didn't even know.'

'Thought he was in Iraq?'

'Fighting the Tali-whatsits.'

He drove past Price's house but the lights were off. He called at the neigbours, who were suspicious until he showed his warrant card. They hadn't seen him all week. He was back for a day then disappeared. They assumed he was off to the desert again, back to Afghanistan, was that it?

Ward needed to find him. He thought about the Europa Hotel, the look in his eye, like he'd nothing to lose. Maybe Price was right, there was only one thing McCann understood, one thing he deserved, one thing that made sense.

In the pitch black, driving the back roads to his house, he tried to unravel it. The dog barked as he pulled into the driveway and got out, still unsure where he stood.

# THIRTY TWO

It was after eight when O'Neill left Musgrave Street. He'd spent two hours on the warrants to search Tierney's three addresses. They'd go up the line first thing tomorrow. Any luck they'd be in business by ten.

He'd called witness protection and got Gary Smith. There was nothing he could do until tomorrow. The kid was O'Neill's problem until then.

He sighed and tried Toner on his mobile, but there was no answer. He hung up and dialled again, same result. O'Neill put the phone down. He'd done his part and would check in tomorrow morning, first thing.

At the flat in Stranmillis he'd just lifted the lid on a beef Chow Mein when his mobile vibrated.

It was a text from Sam: *You up?*

He sent a reply: *Sure.*

They split the food and afterwards went to bed and made love. Sam fell asleep straight away, leaving O'Neill lying there, staring at the damp on the ceiling. He must have drifted off because his mobile woke him, rattling quietly on the bedside table.

He looked at the screen – Catherine.

It was 2 a.m.

'What's wrong?' he said, receiver to his ear.

'You're what's wrong.' She'd had a glass of wine, maybe two.

He got out of bed so as not to wake Sam.

'Hang on,' he whispered, pulling his boxers on, padding to the living room, closing the door behind him.

'Is it Sarah? Is she OK?'

'Oh, so you care now?'

At least two glasses. She was angry, on edge, spoiling for a fight.

'What were you playing at?'

'What?'

'Don't "what" me.'

He knew where she was heading but wasn't going to help.

'Running off. Leaving her. She's seven. Do you know that? Or were you gone by that stage of "Happy Birthday".'

'I didn't run off.'

'Whatever.'

'I didn't. Did you ask Sarah?'

'Oh, she never said anything. Don't worry about that.'

O'Neill felt a flicker of pride at the girl's loyalty.

'A friend of Amanda's was in the park. She recognized Sarah, watched you go off somewhere while your daughter fell off the monkey bars.'

O'Neill bristled but held back.

'She was there for ten minutes, crying her eyes out—'

'It wasn't ten minutes.'

'Oh, so you remember now.'

'Catherine—'

'Don't "Catherine" me.'

'Look—'

'No, you look. If you can't take your daughter to the

park without running off after someone, then maybe you shouldn't take her at all.'

He told himself it was the wine talking.

'I'm going to see my solicitor tomorrow. See about getting the custody looked at. If you're not interested in acting like a father then we won't ask you to.'

'So what? You going to ask Sensible Shoes?'

'What?'

'Mr School Teacher. Andrew, Glen, whatever his name is.'

'He's none of your business, John. *I'm* none of your business. You gave up the right to have an opinion on me twelve months ago.'

'I gave up?' he said, voice raised. 'Think you'll find this was all you – you wanted it, you suggested it, you were the one who said, "Let's have a break." So don't start taking the moral high ground with me. Last time I checked you were the one in a three-bedroom house, going out on dates, swanning round the town with every Tom, Dick and Harry.'

He said it, baiting her.

'For your information ...' Catherine paused, about to defend herself but thinking better.

The phone went dead.

O'Neill sat on the sofa in the dark. Eventually, he got up and went back to the bedroom. Sam was in the same position, facing the wall, her back to him. He slid in, pulling the covers up, staring at the ceiling.

After a while she spoke. 'You want to talk about it?'

'No.'

She breathed quietly, listening to him beside her. 'Sure?'

'Just leave it,' he snapped.

'Be easier if you weren't yelling on a phone in the middle of the night.'

'Really? You think so?'

Sam sat up, riled. 'Excuse me?'

'I mean, what do you want here? A quick shag after a hard day? You're stressed out, job's too much. Help you sleep, then up in the morning and out.'

She was up and out of bed, pulling her jeans on.

'Fuck you, John.'

'You already did that remember.'

'You are an arsehole, you know that? I don't know what I want. But I'll tell you what I don't want. Some guy who thinks he's the only one in the world who knows anything, the only person who has feelings, the only person who gives a shit.'

She pulled her jumper on, put her feet into her trainers and walked out. O'Neill heard the front door slam. After a few seconds, the house sunk back into a dark pervading silence.

# THIRTY THREE

Marty walked towards Petesy's granny's. He'd told himself he should have known better. His mate would have the answer, he was the only one who cared, he would figure it out. He pictured them down south somewhere, in Dublin or Cork or Wexford. They'd have Marty's money, get themselves passports, get shot of Ireland altogether.

He walked along Ormeau Avenue, down Cromac Street, turning towards the Markets. He said a silent goodbye to the Spar, to the offy, to the Maxol garage. Belfast could go swing. He walked to the Albert Bridge, for a last look at Lagan Weir, lit up beneath the night sky. The river flowed below him, black and pitiless on its way out to the sea. Marty looked up, thinking about what was out there, the places he would go, the stuff he would see. A small plane buzzed by, on its way into George Best Airport. The cranes stood still over the Titanic Quarter, the city holding its breath.

'So long river,' he whispered to himself. 'So long Tierney, so long Molloy, so long McCann.' Marty paused for a second. 'So long Ma, so long Holy Lands, so long Waterfront Hall. So long to the lot of you. Don't miss me too much.'

He turned and headed off the bridge, off to see Petesy and his new life, a million miles from this place and all the things it had never given him.

\*\*\*

Marty walked carefully through the Markets, watching cars, listening for voices. The police had done this to him, made him afraid, made him feel hunted. He'd had enough. No more.

At the end of the street he saw the light in Petesy's bedroom. He had an urge to run, like it couldn't happen fast enough. He hoped Petesy was packed, his bag at the door, ready to go. Marty jogged along the road, rounding the gate and approached the house.

He didn't want to face Petesy's granny so he started pinging stones at the upstair's window. A car turned the corner at the end of the street and stopped in the middle of the road. Marty saw it and pinged a little faster.

'Come on, Petesy.'

A car turned the other corner and also stopped, its headlights illuminating the street.

Marty watched the doors open, two figures get out. He snapped his head round. The same at the other car: two men on the street, waiting. Even in the dark, at this distance, he could make out the silhouettes of Tierney and Molloy.

They began to walk towards him, strolling casually.

Marty knew he should run. He wanted to hide, to curl in a ball, to make it go away. His heart weighed a ton.

He watched Tierney approach. He had a gun in his hand, a black pistol, by his side.

Tierney stopped ten feet away, nodded a greeting.

Marty found himself nodding back.

The man said two words.

'Let's go.'

They were on a motorway, speeding into the dark. Marty was in the back, sandwiched between two men he didn't know.

Molloy was driving, Tierney in the passenger seat. There was no talking. It felt rehearsed, decided, preordained.

Marty watched as exit signs rolled past – Lisburn, Hillsborough, Waringstown. All of them sounded good, like they had street lights, buildings, signs of life.

More exits – Dromore, Banbridge, Loughbrickland.

Marty wanted to get out. The men sat beside him like he had some disease, like they were afraid they might catch it.

Eventually, the car turned off the motorway. They made a right, drove for twenty minutes into the back of beyond. There was darkness all round, pitch black. Marty could feel his bowels loosen and he held on, determined not to shit himself.

The car kept driving, past isolated farmhouses, derelict buildings, far from civilization. Far from eyes that would see, ears that would hear. Far from any kind of voice, someone to speak up, to say, *Hang on, he's only a wee lad, seventeen for fuck's sake.*

Marty remembered the text message from Petesy. How did they get his phone? Was he OK? He wanted to ask but kept quiet, not wanting to mention him.

The car slowed and turned through a gap in the hedge. The headlights swung round and there were pine trees, thirty foot tall, as far as the eye could see.

Molloy killed the engine and the lights died.

It was Tierney who spoke. 'Out.'

The doors opened and Marty felt the pressure on either side lessen as the two men stepped out. A hand reached in and grabbed him by jersey, dragging him out. He was on his feet outside the car. He felt the grip loosen and, on instinct, without thought, he took off.

A hand grabbed him, but he slipped it and was away.

'You wee bastard.' A voice behind him.

Marty felt the sharp pine branches tearing his face, jagging his clothes, trying to slow him. He ducked and kept going.

Tierney: 'You useless fuckers.'

There was the sound of a car boot slamming. He could see torches, four white beams, dancing through the trees. He ran then hunkered behind a tree. Do you hide? Do you climb? No, he thought, you run.

He darted out, a light on him, a gunshot. The air parted, a whisping sound near his head. Marty ducked and kept going, running at an angle, tree to tree.

Voices echoed behind. Cursing, swearing.

His chest burned and he slid behind a tree, crouching down, trying to get his bearings. The lights were still dancing, a hundred yards away, maybe more.

There was a weight in his pocket, his mobile. He took it out and saw the missed call. There was a number, no name. The peeler, he thought, and pressed Call.

Forty miles away, O'Neill's mobile vibrated silently on the sofa. It was 3.06 a.m. He was in bed, stewing. He thought it would be Catherine, back for round two. Or else Sam, wanting to unload. He rolled over, turned his back to the door and closed his eyes.

Marty listened as the call went to answerphone. He had no time to hang up and stepped forward, leaving the tree, and picked his way across pine straw.

He looked back – there were no voices now, no torches. He wondered if they had given up. He looked round and saw he was in the open, five feet from the nearest tree.

A torch came on, hitting his eyes, blinding him.

There was a shot, Marty was on the ground, clutching his stomach. It burned so that he couldn't breathe, couldn't speak, couldn't think. There was only pain. White hot, radiating outwards.

A figure stepped forward out of the dark. Marty's eyes bulged, his mouth opened, gasping for air. He could see feet, ankles, shins and felt something metallic being pressed against his temple.

O'Neill woke at 6.30 a.m. and walked through to the living room. His phone was on the sofa and he remembered Catherine's call, the argument, then Sam and the front door slamming. He picked up his mobile and saw the missed call, the answerphone message.

It had been Marty Toner, three in the morning.

O'Neill held the phone to his ear. There were no words, only breathing, someone running. He heard the gun shot.

'No,' he said.

There was the sound of falling, a choked squirm, a winded moan.

O'Neill wanted to be sick. He had to sit down, his mouth open, eyes large. He listened to the second shot, to someone picking up the phone, the call being terminated.

The automated voice interrupted – 'If you would like to listen to the message again ...'

O'Neill sat for five minutes, maybe more.

Eventually, he got dressed and set off for work, not knowing what else to do. It was raining outside and all he could think about was Marty Toner, lying dead in a field somewhere, slowly getting soaked. He pictured a farmer in his tractor, rumbling over the hill, slowing coming to a stop.

A thought wrapped itself round his brain: *It's my fault*. Over and over, not letting go.

Behind him, a horn sounded furiously. O'Neill looked up as the traffic lights turned from green to red. The driver was incensed. O'Neill stayed in the car, unsure about what he might do if he got out.

At the station, Doris was on reception. O'Neill floated past, ghostlike.

In CID, Kearney and Larkin were arguing about football. O'Neill went to his desk and printed the warrants for Tierney's addresses. He felt guilty, looking at the pages, so gave them to Kearney to take upstairs and get them signed.

He looked round at the files, the mugshots, the pieces of paper. He didn't want to touch any of it, afraid of what might happen, who'd be next.

A voice behind him, Ward. 'DS O'Neill. My office.'

He followed the DI through, walking on autopilot.

Doris had called him.

O'Neill explained what happened – the addresses, the warrants, the answerphone.

Ward listened like he was hearing a confession for which there was no penance. There was no advice, nothing he could say, nothing he could do. O'Neill would have to carry it himself, to ride it out, to make peace with it in his own time. Ward told him the only thing that he knew would help – keep working.

# THIRTY FOUR

Ten o'clock, Musgrave Street, briefing room. O'Neill and Ward, Kearney and Larkin. It was grey outside, the rain easing to a drizzle. O'Neill looked ill, his face drained, bags under both eyes. He stood slowly.

'Should you be in, sir?' Kearney. 'No offence, but you look rough.'

O'Neill ignored it and circulated a photograph of Tierney. He looked at Ward. The DI stood up.

'You'll recognize the face: Johnny Tierney, one of Gerry McCann's boys. We've got a body in Tomb Street beaten to death, Jonathan McCarthy, a young man living well beyond his means. Initially, we thought he was on Daddy's dollar but from the daughter it turns out no. He's driving a nice car, buying property left, right and centre, and jetting off to Las Vegas when the fancy takes him. The boy's getting his money from somewhere. We seized a laptop computer from McCarthy's flat with copies of business accounts. These match up with various small enterprises that we think Gerry McCann is using to launder his drug money. This is all circumstantial though. We've no hard evidence. An informant fingered Tierney as the person who killed McCarthy. That informant is ...' Ward paused. '...no longer working with us. We suspect he was abducted and murdered by Tierney. Again, we've nothing concrete. At Tomb Street there were no witnesses except for some wino who, through a haze of turps, reckons he saw a southpaw taking McCarthy to the cleaners. Johnny Tierney was an amateur boxer back in the mid-nineties, Golden Gloves at the U-16 All Irelands.'

'So let's arrest him,' Larkin said.

'No,' Ward said. 'He's only part of this. It's McCann we want. He's the real target. The dirt might be on Tierney but it's there because of McCann. We need to watch Tierney, connect him to McCann, then try to roll him up.'

'You think he'll roll on Gerry McCann?' Kearney, doubtful.

Ward stared him down. 'Here are the addresses ...'

They spent the morning watching houses – Stewart Street, Cooke Street, Rutland Street; Kearney, Larkin, O'Neill. Ward sat at Musgrave Street with his notebooks, reading the pages on Michael McCann's murder.

The radio crackled.

'Bastard's having a lie-in,' Kearney said.

Larkin. 'Probably had a big night.'

In the Mondeo on Cooke Street, O'Neill turned down the volume. He stared at the address, trying not to think about the Tower.

Twenty minutes later, Kearney spoke. 'Yous owe me a fiver. He just walked out.'

'All right,' O'Neill said. 'Stay on him'

'10-4.'

Tierney headed for town, driving, parking in Blackstaff Square. O'Neill and Kearney ditched their cars, tag-tailing him on foot. It had been raining all morning and the drains were starting to backup. Folk jumped back from kerbs as passing buses sprayed water at them.

A mile away, Ward left Musgrave Street with three Land Rovers, ready to take the doors. O'Neill would call once they had Tierney and they'd hit all three addresses at the same time.

Tierney walked purposefully carrying a sports bag. Every so often he would sweep the street and look back over his shoulder. He passed City Hall, its manicured lawns beginning to flood with the rain. Tierney stopped at the Northern Bank on the corner of Howard Street. He looked round, holding the door for a pensioner before disappearing inside.

Kearney was across the street, fifty yards away, hanging back. O'Neill moved to the edge of window and peered through the thick, tinted glass. Tierney was in line, waiting for a teller. The bank was quiet, only three girls on, sitting on stools behind bulletproof glass. After a minute, he walked forward and produced a navy lodgement bag. He passed it through the slot. The teller was a young girl in her twenties. Blonde hair, ponytail, make-up. She emptied the bag out and passed it back. O'Neill watched her put a wad of notes in an automatic counter, then key something into the computer. She smiled and handed over a receipt.

O'Neill slipped into a doorway as Tierney walked out of the bank. He watched him look round him before heading off up May Street. He nodded at Kearney to follow and pushed open the heavy glass door of the bank.

Inside he looked round, weighing up his options. The teller would be tough – too young, too scared of the rules. The counter was pretty public and there'd be folk within earshot. He watched a woman in black suit, wearing an employee name badge, cross the foyer. She was confident, late forties, no wedding ring. O'Neill caught her eye and smiled. She returned the gesture before disappearing into an office off the foyer. The door stayed open and he followed, knocking gently.

She looked up. 'Can I help?'

O'Neill produced his warrant card and introduced himself. 'Do you have a second?'

'Sure. Have a seat. But I have to tell you, if it's about the robbery, I was in another branch when all that was going on.'

'No, it's nothing to do with that. It's actually a bit … delicate. A guy just came in and made a deposit.'

'That against the law?' she said, joking.

O'Neill smiled. 'Not last time I checked. Anyway—' he looked behind him, pretending to check '—I shouldn't tell you this, but we think he's dodgy.'

'I can't give out any information about our customers. It's bank policy.'

'I know,' O'Neill said, lowering his voice. 'Do you know what trafficking is?'

She hesitated. 'Sex trafficking?'

'Yeah. They bring in girls. Romania, Bulgaria, Moldova. Force them to work as prostitutes.'

The smile dropped from her face.

O'Neill leaned in, lowering his voice. 'These girls are eighteen, nineteen. Half of them don't speak English. They think they're coming here to work, learn the language, send money home. They're raped when they get here. They tell them they'll kill their families if they don't do what they're told. They say they'll let them go after six months, then they put them to work. Twelve-hour shifts. Think about it, drugged and raped, eight times a day, more even. Some of

280

them have kids back home. They're told they'll never see them again.'

The woman swallowed, her face sickened.

'He was served by the blonde teller. Depositing money, probably under the guise of a legitimate business or something. I need the account details, who it's registered to, if there are other businesses under the same name.'

She hesitated.

'You could make a real difference.'

'The blonde teller?'

'That's right.'

'Wait here.'

The woman stood up and straightened her jacket before striding out the door. She crossed the foyer, entered a number and went through a security door. A few seconds later, she appeared next to the tellers. She said something and the blonde girl stood up and walked out of sight. The manager lifted the transaction slips from her tray and flicked through them casually. She put them back and returned to her office.

Sitting behind the computer, she logged on. O'Neill remained silent, not wanting to interrupt her. The manager punched the keys in front of her.

'OK. The account is part of a larger set of business accounts. It says this one's a car wash. I can show you the companies that are registered.'

'That would help.'

'There you go. Paradise Bronzing. Looks like a tanning salon. And there's two more, plus another car wash by the look of it.'

O'Neill felt his pulse quicken. They were the same accounts they'd found on McCarthy's laptop. They had McCann, Tierney and McCarthy.

'What about funds? How much is going in?'

'Couple of times a week. Ten grand, sometimes twelve.'

'In each account.'

'Yeah.'

O'Neill did the sums. It was way too many suntans, way too much spray wash.

'Is there a name on the account?'

The woman scrolled down the page, typed at the keyboard. 'Hang on a minute ...'

He wanted McCann. More than anything he wanted her to say 'Gerry McCann'.

'Here it is ... a Mr John Tierney.'

O'Neill sighed, his face falling. He thanked the woman and stood up. On his way out of the bank, he lifted the radio to his mouth.

'Where are you?'

'Far side of the City Hall,' Kearney said. 'He's in a café, eating a bacon and egg soda.'

'We're lifting him. Wait for me.'

O'Neill was crossing the road, when the radio crackled.

'He's made me. Shit. He's moving.'

O'Neill heard running, then Kearney's voice. 'City Hall gardens. He's cutting through.'

O'Neill took off, climbing a bench and landing in a two-inch puddle on the lawn. 'Shit,' he said, feet soaked.

The grass was like a water-logged football pitch, huge puddles dotted across the surface. He saw Tierney marching away from Kearney. O'Neill took off running.

'Oi,' he shouted, head down, charging. Tierney looked up and raised his hands, like he was giving himself up. O'Neill didn't stop, tackling him into a huge puddle.

Tierney was on his side, O'Neill over him, a fistful of hair. He punched him in the head. Again and again and again. It was for Tomb Street, for McCarthy, for Marty Toner. It was for getting away with it, for the bullying, for the arrogance. It was for Gerry McCann, it was for sitting in the pub, it was for thinking you could threaten a peeler.

He pressed Tierney's face into the puddle. You could drown a man in two inches of water. He pressed harder, leaning with all his weight, forcing him into the earth. It was what Tierney dished out to others, what he understood, what he deserved. O'Neill pressed again.

'I got you, sir,' Kearney shouted, running into the puddle and taking the weight out from under O'Neill. Tierney's eyes bulged. He coughed up water, gasping in lungfuls of air.

O'Neill got to his feet and staggered backwards. After a minute, he made his way out of the puddle, utterly drenched.

Kearney had the cuffs on him.

'Radio Ward,' O'Neill said, getting his breath back. 'Tell him to take the doors.'

# THIRTY FIVE

Tierney sat in a holding cell while sniffer dogs and search teams ripped the three addresses to bits. Floorboards were pulled, furniture torn, mattresses split. There was nothing. The kid had been right. Tierney knew the game and the value of healthy distance. They'd seized the clothing in the hope they might get a trace of McCarthy's DNA. No one was holding their breath.

Ward spent the afternoon looking for McCann. He went to the George, the house, did a circuit of the businesses. There was no sign. He wanted to lift him before he heard about Tierney's arrest. There was a good chance he'd do a runner, go down south, or head to Spain.

Ward decided the house was the best bet and just before nine pulled into Castlehill Park. At the far end was McCann's place, the lights off, the driveway empty. Ward thought about Davy Price, wondered where he was, whether he'd jacked it in and gone back to Iraq. Two streets away a pair of Land Rovers sat in a cul-de-sac, waiting for the go.

Two hours later, the street was quiet. Folk were in their pyjamas, tucked up in bed, reading books, drinking hot cocoa. A cat prowled along the garden walls, moving silently, looking for a snack. It paused at the Mondeo and cast a cold eye on Ward inside.

The DI heard a car engine behind him and slid down in his seat. A set of headlights swung across the Mondeo. He glanced as it passed, expecting the Mercedes and McCann. It drove past, revealing a Volvo badge. Ward breathed again.

Halfway down the street the Volvo pulled into a space and killed its engine. Ward watched, waiting for the door to open.

Nothing.

The driver stayed put.

Ward looked at his watch, measuring the time. Thirty seconds, a minute. Still no movement.

Could it be Davy Price? Ward imagined a phone call to an old mate, someone still in the force – 'I need a favour ... an address?' It wouldn't have been hard.

Ward lifted the radio, called in the licence plate.

Control came back: 'Vehicle reported stolen. Earlier this evening. Address in Glengormley.'

Clever, Ward thought. You don't use your own car, why risk it, someone seeing you, getting the licence. He pictured Price in the driver's seat, service weapon at his feet, cleaned that afternoon.

Ward was halfway to the door handle when he stopped. He looked at McCann's house, at the Volvo, at the house again. He could turn a blind eye, go back to Musgrave Street, send the Land Rovers away. It would be his contribution, his part in settling the score for Pat Kennedy. No one would know. Not McCann, not O'Neill, not the rest of the force. It would guarantee a result. Tierney had lawyered up as soon as they lifted him. Chances were he'd say he didn't know McCann, let alone roll over. If that happened it would come down to the evidence and at best they were 50–50.

Ward took a breath, wanting a cigarette, knowing he couldn't. He thought about Pat Kennedy, wondering what he'd say, whether McCann's head would be enough to right the wrong. If he walked away and let Price kill him, it would mean Wilson was right. That he was a dinosaur, that he was still locked in the past, still fighting the old fight. Was it Wilson who'd said that or McCann? Ward wasn't sure. Either way it grated and he didn't like it.

He reached for the ignition, his hand pausing. In his head, he heard Eileen Kennedy, he watched her again, breaking down on her doorstep.

Would she be happy with 50–50? Somehow, Ward doubted it.

Gerry McCann steered the Mercedes out of the Cathedral Quarter, past the Albert clock and across the Lagan. He was still in love with the car – the new leather smell, the engine (barely audible) and the way it moved, like a luxury liner cruising the town.

It was a week night and getting late so the roads were quiet. In the passenger seat, Natalie sat with her eyes closed, the last glass of Moët tipping her over the edge. McCann looked at her, admiring her legs in the short red dress he'd told her to wear. There were looks as they walked into the restaurant, other men, eyeing her, pretending they weren't.

McCann remembered the strip bar in Glasgow a year earlier. He'd paid for her all night then took her back to his hotel. She was Ukrainian, Natalia something. He couldn't pronounce it but she didn't seem to mind. Next morning, they drove to Stranraer and the ferry to Belfast.

'What about my things?' she'd said.

He'd tossed her a wad of notes.

'Knock yourself out, love.'

They'd set up in a flat at the start, kept it quiet. The wife was used to him working late, staying out all night, not coming home. Six months later, he had Castlehill Park and Natalia was Natalie.

In the car next to him, the girl groaned, rubbing her hand over her slender stomach.

'You make me fat?' she said, her eyes still closed.

'Don't worry, love. You can work it off when we get home.'

McCann reached over and ran his hand over her breast. The girl smiled and made the appropriate noises.

Outside, the lights at the Knock carriageway were red. McCann slowed, enjoying the grab of the disc brakes. He tapped the top of the steering wheel, eager to get home, get inside, get her upstairs.

He indicated and turned into Castlehill Park. He was struck by how suburban it was, how middle class, how peaceful. These people didn't have a clue, he thought. Despite himself, he liked it. There were no hoods on the corner, no graffiti, no broken glass. He steered the Mercedes through the dark, slipping between the gatepost and the hedge that fronted the house.

McCann didn't see the door of the Volvo open, a hundred yards behind him. He didn't see the figure, keeping low, gun at his side. He didn't see him sidle up to the hedge, leaning back, listening.

McCann turned off the engine, the girl stirring, still drowsy. He got out, went round and opened the passenger door.

'Come on you.'

'I fall asleep,' she said, the voice playful.

On the footpath, the shadow reached down and cocked the gun.

McCann heard the noise, threw the girl aside and dived in front of the Merc.

Down the street, a diesel engine roared round the corner. There were headlights, the figure at the hedge frozen in the full beam.

Davy Price heard the Land Rover and knew it was the police. He tossed the gun under a parked car and put his hands up.

Uniform peelers swarmed the street. Two squared up to Price, levelling their weapons. Two ran past, into the drive. McCann was on the ground, the girlfriend trying to figure out how she'd ended up in a bush.

As the cops lifted her, she kicked out. 'Get you hands off me.'

McCann stood silent, palms against brick, allowing events to unfold.

On the footpath, one of the uniforms patted Price down. 'He's clean.'

'Check the garden and under those cars. He threw something.'

The younger of the two cops walked round the hedge, pulling his torch and scanning the lawn. Two minutes later, he was, on all fours, looking beneath the cars.

'Bingo,' he announced, reaching into the darkness, coming out with a Glock.

'Cuff him,' the older peeler instructed.

'Hang on,' someone said, stepping from the dark. 'He's mine.'

Price recognized Ward's voice.

'But, sir ...' the uniform began, proffering the gun.

'You deaf, son?' Ward said, taking the weapon. 'He's with me.'

Ward frogmarched Price away. He waited until they were out of earshot. 'Where's your car?'

'Three streets away.'

'Get in it, drive away and don't come back.'

'So what? You're playing by the rules now? McCann gets his day in court, gets to walk again, laughing at us.'

'You're looking at Attempted Murder here so save me the lecture about rules.'

Ward marched down the street, feeling uniform watching. 'You're getting a second chance. Next time, it won't be me. And, even if it is, I won't be doing this.'

'A true believer, Jack. Playing it straight, the brand-new day.'

Ward stopped walking and handed Price his gun. 'No more talking.'

The other man nodded, taking gun. He turned and started to walk. 'See you, Jack.'

Ward paused. 'Hopefully not.'

When Price turned the corner, he turned back to the house. McCann was being cuffed and walked towards one of the wagons. Ward put his head down, heading back to the scene and the rest of the night's work.

# THIRTY SIX

Thursday morning, just gone nine, Musgrave Street was quiet.

Kearney and Larkin were in CID, shuffling paperwork, resisting the first bite. In Ward's office, the DI sat with O'Neill and Ronnie MacPherson, the Public Prosecutor.

'So you were right about Mullan then,' MacPherson said. 'Wrong place, wrong time.'

'Looks that way,' O'Neill said.

'Well, thanks for the heads up. You stopped me looking stupid.'

O'Neill smiled, playing dumb. 'Not sure what you're talking about.'

MacPherson turned to Ward. 'He's coming on, Jack. Might make it this one.'

'We'll see.'

In custody, Tierney and McCann were in their cells. The younger man paced back and forth, unable to touch the breakfast that had been slid through the hatch half an hour earlier. McCann sat still, his plate clean, looking forward to his chat with Ward.

Just before ten, the front desk called up. The lawyer had arrived and was talking to his clients.

Ward asked who it was, listening to the answer before hanging up the phone. MacPherson looked at him.

'Tom Clarke?'

'You got it.'

MacPherson smiled knowingly. Ward looked at O'Neill.

'Clarke used to work with McCann's brother. They were partners before he was killed. He's a piece of work.'

Ward stood. 'Right then, let's go talk to some criminals.'

Phil Kerr was the Custody Sergeant on duty. When the three men walked in he was booking a fourteen-year old hood. He'd been caught shoplifting and stood in his tracksuit, flanked by two peelers.

'It wasn't me,' he squawked.

The Custody Sergeant looked up. 'Come again.'

'I said it wasn't fucking me.'

The Custody Sergeant caught Ward's eye. 'You hear this, Jack.'

Ward paused.

'The *wasn't fucking me* defence.'

Ward shook his head.

'A classic in its time.'

Ward put his arm round the kid. 'Listen, son, it's *no comment*. That's what you say.'

The hood looked back, unsure what was going on.

'Honestly,' Ward said, looking at the Sergeant. 'I don't know what they're teaching them these days.'

He led O'Neill and MacPherson to Interview Room B. As they approached, the door opened and Tom Clarke slithered out. He was in his fifties, receding hairline, expensive suit.

'Detective Inspector Jack Ward,' he said, like they were old friends. 'I hope you three weren't eavesdropping there. You know that's a violation of my client's human rights.'

Ward stared at him, unimpressed and unamused.

Clarke smiled. 'That's what I thought.' He nodded at

MacPherson before turning to O'Neill. 'Detective Sergeant O'Neill? How's the shoulder these days? I heard it took a while to heal.'

Clarke had defended Ivan Puslawski, the Polish bouncer who'd put O'Neill in hospital the year before. Clarke smiled, enjoying his audience, feeding off their hate.

'Yeah, you laugh, Tom,' Ward said. 'We've got your meal ticket in there. How you going to pay the bills when your goose gets ten years, when the golden eggs stop coming?'

'Please, Detective. My client's innocent. And besides, this is Belfast. You think there's only one goose in town?'

Ward stared.

'Now, if you'll excuse me. I need to have a word with Mr Tierney before we sit down for the interviews.'

The solicitor strutted down the corridor, high on self-importance. He opened the door to Interview Room D and stepped inside, closing it behind him. Ward remembered the old joke: *You've got Hitler, Stalin and a lawyer, and a gun with two bullets. What do you do? Answer – you shoot the lawyer twice, just to make sure.*

He sidled up to the door and looked through the slit at Gerry McCann. He sat at the table facing an empty plastic chair. McCann looked relaxed, like it was all working out. He glanced up at the door and saw Ward's eyes. McCann tilted his head and nodded.

In Interview Room D Clarke sat opposite Tierney.

'What took you so long?'

Clarke didn't answer.

'I called yesterday and—'

'Shut up.'

Tierney bristled, like he might throw a punch. 'What the fu—'

'I said shut up.'

Tierney stood down, realizing he wasn't on the street, that this was McCann's solicitor too.

'Have you said anything?' Clarke demanded.

A shake of the head.

'To anyone?'

Clarke was patronizing, like he was talking to an idiot.

'I'm not some wee hood you know. I know how it works.'

'I'm going to tell you how it works.'

Tierney waited.

'You're going to eat this.'

'What?'

'I said you're going to eat this. Tomb Street, McCarthy, the money. You're going to eat it all.'

Tierney's face fell. 'Where's McCann? I want to talk to him.'

'Where the fuck do you think I've just been?'

Clarke paused, allowing what he said to hit home.

'None of this touches McCann. You did it on your own. It was a bar fight that got out of hand. We plead manslaughter, you get seven, out in four. Job done.'

Tierney swallowed. 'Easy for you to say.'

'No,' Clarke said. 'What's easy for me to say is for you to go your own way, talk to the peelers, throw some names around. You'll need some legal aid mind, 'cause I won't be within a hundred miles of you. And if you try to give them McCann you better get a plane ticket, 'cause you'll be out on the street with every man and his dog knowing that Johnny Tierney's a tout. Let's see how bad four years look then?'

Tierney stared at the lawyer.

'The cops are going to make you an offer. Drop all charges in return for McCann. I just want to know one thing.' He leaned forward. 'Am I talking to a dead man?'

He watched, making sure Tierney heard. The other man shook his head.

'Good. I didn't think so. These peelers don't give a shit about you, son. Just remember that.'

He stood, about to leave.

Tierney looked sullen. There was nothing to be said, no play to be made, no angle to be worked. He would eat it, all of it, end of story.

'And about the other thing? That wee hood. Did you do it properly?'

Tierney nodded.

'I hope so. For your sake.'

Clarke looked at him, unable to understand the hesitation, the disbelief that this was how the game was played.

Tierney retreated into himself, allowing his face to harden, to settle into the scowl that he'd wear for four years, through the questioning, the trial, the conviction and every day as he walked the corridors of Maghaberry.

O'Neill and Ward spent the day beating their heads against a brick wall. Locked in a room – the two detectives, the two lawyers, Johnny Tierney. Tierney blanked them, the script already written, his thoughts elsewhere.

'You're looking at fifteen years,' O'Neill threatened.

Tierney shrugged.

'Fifteen.'

Nothing.

'In Maghaberry.'

Silence.

'You'll be forty-two when you get out.'

Nothing.

Clarke did his talking for him.

'My client will admit to the manslaughter of Jonathan McCarthy on Tomb Street. It was a drunken brawl, an incident that got out of hand and something my client deeply regrets.'

O'Neill looked across the table, doubting Tierney could spell 'regret'.

'What about the money?'

'Those are legitimate funds from bona fide local businesses. My client has nothing to say about them.'

Some time around four, they stepped out of the room, leaving Tierney with his lawyer. They stood in the car park over a cigarette, MacPherson philosophical.

'He'll do seven for manslaughter. It's not bad.'

'It's not McCann.' O'Neill said.

'It's all we're going to get.'

'What about the money? What about conspiracy? What about murder? Fuck sake, Ronnie, man up will you?'

MacPherson took the heat, then he looked at Ward. 'Tell him, would you?'

Ward was distant. An hour into the interview, he'd stopped listening. He saw how it would play out and knew they'd lost. He turned to O'Neill, watching him fight on.

'He's right.'

O'Neill shook his head. It was Marty Toner. He'd carried him for days, imagining the grey tracksuit, the skinny body, in a field somewhere. He pictured the cows standing over

295

him, before turning away and slowly walking off.

'What about the kid? Toner? Who answers for him?'

Ward wanted to say something but could only think in clichés – stuff about living to fight, about other days, about files still open. He cut himself off, not wanting to be that person.

'What about McCann?' O'Neill said, still going. 'He has Pat Kennedy killed and he gets a walk?'

'We don't know that.'

'Come on. He doesn't even get court, doesn't get accused, doesn't answer a single question.'

'That's right,' Ward said, the words bitter. 'It stinks. The whole thing. Stinks to high heaven. McCarthy's involvement, Tierney's indifference, McCann's arrogance. I get it all right. Don't think I don't get it.' The voice loud, angry now. 'Pat Kennedy was like a brother, like family. You think I don't want to walk in there, put McCann against the wall and blow his fucking brains out?'

Ward was shouting now. At the far side of the car park heads turned, folk wondering, then minding their own business. MacPherson was flustered, knowing he shouldn't be there. He excused himself and went back inside.

Ward stared across the car park at the row of white Land Rovers. He lowered his voice. 'It's fucked,' he said. 'The whole thing. The job, the city, the force.'

O'Neill let the silence settle. After a while he spoke. 'So that's it then.'

'Yeah,' Ward said, stubbing out his cigarette, heading back inside.

On his own, O'Neill leaned against the wall. He looked up at the sky, at the dark clouds gathering over the rooftops of the city centre. He sighed, thinking about Tivoli Gardens, about Catherine and Sarah. He was on his way out there too, sidelined, soon to be in the stands. Catherine had moved on, found someone who would treat her better, who would show up on time, bring her flowers. He didn't begrudge her, she deserved it. And Sarah? It was a slow pain, a gradual emptying, like a ship leaving shore. He'd messed up with Sam and all. She'd wanted someone to laugh with, to cry with, to share things. Why not him? When it came to it he couldn't do it. He'd nothing to tell her, except stuff from the job, the weird stories and the things that happened. O'Neill wondered if that was all he had now: a series of anecdotes that didn't add up to anything.

Ward was right. And in the back of his head he'd always known it.

The job was fucked.

O'Neill took a deep drag, stubbed his cigarette out and headed back inside.

# THIRTY SEVEN

9:30 a.m., Musgrave Street, Press Room. Chief Inspector Charles Wilson, surrounded by microphones. Wilson was extra well-groomed, the hair brushed, shoulder boards shining. Cameras and all, you wanted to look your best.

'Last night we charged a man with manslaughter in connection with the death of Jonathan McCarthy two weeks ago in Tomb Street.' Wilson spoke slowly, the voice solemn. You didn't showboat, not in public. 'Of course, this charge can do nothing to bring back the McCarthys' son and our thoughts, as always, are with the family. Our only hope is that they find some solace knowing that the police have done all they can in bringing the suspect to justice.'

'Chief Inspector, do you think ...'

At the back of the room, away from the huddle, Ward and O'Neill. The DI grunted and leaned off the wall.

'I've heard enough.'

'What time's Pat Kennedy's funeral?' O'Neill asked.

'Service is at ten, then up to Roselawn Cemetery.'

O'Neill nodded, undecided about going. Regardless, he had a house call to make in the Markets.

'See you later,' Ward said, leaving the room.

O'Neill rubbed his face, feeling the fog of half a dozen beers from the night before. He'd sat for two hours, flicking channels, drinking himself numb.

Wilson continued with the clichés: '... the integrity of the force … the future of the North … a safe place for everyone …'

O'Neill rolled his eyes – integrity, future. He wondered what it meant. What it really meant? He felt in his pocket, checking for car keys. Wilson didn't look up as he left the room. His was mid-flow and didn't skip a beat.

Petesy was in bed when he heard the front door. His instinct was to run, through the bathroom and out the window. Then he remembered his legs. He reached a hand to his face. His nose was still sore. He hadn't left the house for days, since Tierney and Molloy had forced their way in and beaten him to a pulp.

The knocking continued.

He got up and peered through a crack in the curtain.

It was a peeler, plain clothes. On the street, two kids stopped riding their bikes and stared. Even at ten years old they could tell.

Petesy pulled the duvet over his head. More knocking. He rolled out of bed and hobbled down the stairs, leaning on the bannister. When he opened the door, the peeler was back at his car. O'Neill turned when he heard the door and walked back. Petesy's eyes narrowed, recognizing the face.

'You remember me?'

'Hospital last year, when I got my knees done.'

O'Neill nodded.

Petesy stared. The cop looked ill, like he hadn't slept, like he was about to keel over.

'You know why I'm here?'

Petesy hesitated, not wanting to say it.

'Marty.'

Another nod. Petesy's face fell, like he'd been expecting it.

'He's gone.'

'Where to?'

O'Neill shook his head. 'Just gone.'

Petesy sniffed and looked away. 'Yous get Tierney?'

'Yeah.'

Petesy nodded, unconsoled.

'Marty talked about his money. Said it was yours, said you'd know what he meant.'

Petesy didn't speak. O'Neill turned and walked towards the car, feeling the fuck-you stare from the ten-year-olds. He didn't have the energy to glare back.

An hour later, Petesy watched Marty's ma come out the front door of her house. She was in high heels and leopard-print leggings, wobbling as she made her towards the Spar. She looked half-cut and was almost run over crossing the road. A car blasted its horn. She gave it the finger without looking up.

She passed Petesy on her way into the shop, doing a double take, then stopping.

'Here, you're our Martin's wee mate, aren't you?'

'Aye.'

'He always liked you so he did, Sean.'

'It's Peter.'

'Right, right, that's what I meant.'

She leaned in, lowering her voice. 'Here, Peter. Lend a girl a fiver, would you? I'm expecting my rent cheque any day.'

Petesy looked at her, the hunger in her eyes, the drink with its hand round her throat. He reached into his pocket and pulled out three quid. 'It's all I've got.'

She took it, forcing a smile. 'Such a gentleman,' she said, leaning over and kissing him on the cheek.

Petsey wiped away the residue of lipstick as she tottered off.

'Thanks, Sean,' she called back. 'I'll tell our Martin I saw you.'

Petsey watched her go, watched heads turn in cars as they drove past. When she'd gone, he headed round the back, to the entry and the yard, where she kept the spare key.

Inside, the place was a mess. The TV sat in the corner, a blanket on the sofa from where, Petsey guessed, Marty's ma passed out most nights. On the floor was an empty bottle of vodka and a glass that had been spilled but not cleaned up. On the arm of the sofa a pyramid of cigarette butts pointed up out of an ashtray. The place smelled musty and damp, in need of a good clean.

Petsey looked about, trying to guess where Marty would hide it. He checked the cupboards in the kitchen, before standing up and shaking his head. It had to be somewhere his ma never looked, like under a floorboard or something. He checked the carpet in the corners of the rooms, looking for signs it had been lifted. There was nothing. Upstairs he went into Marty's old bedroom. He remembered the two of them playing 'FIFA Soccer' on the PlayStation. Brazil versus France, always the same. A smile crept across his face thinking about Marty and his favourite saying – 'Ronaldo, you're shite.'

Petsey turned and walked on to the landing, looking for the trapdoor to the attic. He saw it was in the bathroom and climbed up on the side of the bath, groaning at the sudden jolt of pain in his knee. The panel lifted easily and he felt around with his hand, his eyes widening when he touched leather and pulled a bag down.

It felt heavy as Petesy lowered the Head bag and set it on the ground. He pulled the zip back and opened it. Bundles of money, forty, maybe fifty. They were in tight rolls, elastic bands keeping them together. Petesy took one out and looked at it. It was made up of tenners, at least five hundred quid.

He shook his head.

'Marty, you mad bastard.'

Petesy suddenly remembered where he was and what he was looking at.

He zipped the bag and stood up, putting it over his shoulder. Downstairs, he locked the back door behind him and replaced the key under the pot.

Sam Jennings turned the shower on in her bathroom, stripping off her running gear while the water heated up. She'd got up early and done ten miles, along the towpath, past Shaw's Bridge. Her legs felt tired, her head clear. She would jump in the shower and head to work. They were on security for a funeral that morning, some ex Branch guy. They were expecting a big turn out.

In the shower she thought about O'Neill and the fight a few nights before. She'd been wrong. There was no changing him. He'd drop you in a heartbeat. All it would take would be a call from Musgrave Street. Maybe that's all he had in him any more. It wasn't his fault. Sam could see it – the damp flat, the daughter he rarely saw, the ex-wife moving on. The job was the only thing that made sense, the only thing he could rely on, the only sure thing. There'd always be an assault, a spate of thefts, a gang of hoods. There'd always be the city, telling you to go fuck yourself. It was the only thing that would make sense, that you could count on.

In the shower, Sam heard her mother's words – 'You're not getting any younger you know. That clock's ticking. There's more to life than that uniform.'

She dressed in jeans and a sweatshirt and went down to the kitchen. She poured a bowl of muesli and made tea. The application forms were still on the table – APPLICATION FOR THE DETECTIVE EXAM.

Sam sat down and lifted the biro, pausing for a second before writing her name in the first blank space. She thought about her mother and her 'more than the uniform' speech. Sam gave a short laugh.

'You know something, Mum, you might just be right.'

Ward arrived late and sat at the back of the church. The place was packed, men in their sixties, short haircuts, weathered faces. There was a huge police presence. Land Rovers closed the street in case someone might try something. Ward scanned the room, ticking off the faces, the ex-Branch men, the former detectives, folk from Tenant Street. He looked for Davy Price, sure he'd be there, hiding somewhere.

The cortege had outriders the whole way to Roselawn. They stopped the traffic and crossed red lights, winding their way up the slope of the Castlereagh hills. At the gates there were cops directing cars. Ward recognized Sam Jennings. She was in her high-vis jacket, her hat pulled low. He lifted a finger from the top of the steering wheel and received a curt nod.

It had started to drizzle as they arrived. Guys got out of cars, looking upwards, God confirming what they already knew. At the graveside Eileen looked tiny, dwarfed by rows of men, standing motionless in dark clothes. She held her sister's hand, squeezing it like she might fall over at any moment.

Ward hung back, leaning on his car, watching from a distance. The minister said some things that he couldn't make out. He watched the crowd at the grave, the ritual of it all, the solemnity and importance. They'd turned up, as if to say 'Pat Kennedy mattered ... what he did mattered ... what we all did mattered.' You could see it in people's faces, in their eyes; the sense that they'd seen things and done things they'd take with them to their graves. They'd been hunted, stalked, gunned down. They'd arrested men, locked them in rooms, rolled up their sleeves. And when all was said and done they'd been retired, moved aside, paid off. They'd lived on words like duty, honour, respect. And now it was all gone. History had moved on and they were no longer needed.

Ward scanned the horizon, making out Davy Price leaning on a gravestone at the far end of the cemetery. He was smoking, watching events from afar. Ward wondered what he made of it all. How it all added up, were the scores even, had one side lost and the other won? He pictured Gerry McCann, sitting in the George, sipping a pint, making plans. Ward pushed the image away. He'd had enough for one day.

O'Neill walked around the car and leaned on the bonnet next to the DI.

'Sir.'

Ward nodded.

'Big turnout.'

'Yeah.'

O'Neill offered a cigarette and the two of them smoked in silence.

Through the sea of bodies they watched as the coffin was lowered. Men came forward, taking turns with the shovel, each emptying some dirt into the rectangular hole in the ground. Gradually, people turned away and headed back towards their cars.

'Is there a wake?' O'Neill said.

'Aye.'

'You going?'

Ward paused. 'No. I'll give it a miss.' He opened the driver's door. 'You need a lift back?'

'I'm OK.'

O'Neill watched Ward pull out, joining the line of cars as they filed out of the car park.

He pulled his collar up and walked out on to the grass between the rows of headstones. Roselawn was huge, gravestones stretching as far as you could see.

When he got there, O'Neill stopped and stared. It was the first time he'd been back since the funeral.

*In Loving Memory of Brendan Eugene O'Neill*
*1948–2005*
*Loving Husband, Devoted Father*
*May He Rest in Peace*

O'Neill stood for a moment, trying to feel something. He thought about Jonathan McCarthy and all the medals, hidden in a box in his bedroom. He thought about the hall in the house and its shrine to the father and everything he had achieved on the rugby pitch. He wondered how many guys spent their lives chasing after something, hunting a bit of approval, just a quiet word – *Well done, son*.

He stared at his father's gravestone, wanting an answer, not sure what the question was. After a minute, he gave up

305

and started walking towards the office, a small Portakabin next to the entrance. The door opened to a small room and a counter separating the public from a pair of desks. On the wall was a map with lettered rows and numbered plots.

An old man stood up and approached the counter. O'Neill pulled his warrant card and CID-ed him.

'There was some vandalism here a couple of years ago.'

The man snorted a sigh, 'There's vandalism here all the time. Hoods playing dominoes. See how many they can knock over.'

'I'm talking about a sledgehammer. Headstones cracked. About three, four years ago.'

The man nodded. He pointed to the map. 'Far corner. It's probably row K you're talking about. Twenty stones broken by some wee bastard. Used a sledgehammer, taken out of the sheds here. Mind you, police got the wee frigger.' The man leaned in, lowered his voice. 'I'd have done what them Muslims do. Cut his hands off. '

O'Neill headed up through the graveyard, retracing the path he'd walked a few minutes earlier. His father was 2005 and the dates worked back from there, the '04s, the '03s. He turned down row K, coming on the cracked ones. Dunlop, Turner, O'Hare ...They'd been split in half, some cemented back together, others still waiting to be replaced. He walked on, looking at the cracks, reading the names – Quinn, Boyd, Thompson, Bell, Toner ...

O'Neill stopped. It was Marty's father. *Michael Toner 1969– 2002.* Thirty-three when he died. That was about right. He stepped closer, crouched down, ran his hand over the headstone. You could see the marks, the chips, where the hammer had been taken to it. There were ten, twenty bites. It never cracked though. Not like the rest.

This one hadn't been a sledgehammer; it had been smaller.

He pictured Marty, thirteen years old, swinging at it, cursing, spitting. He couldn't break it, no matter what he did.

Marty had been right. The police had done him for them all. Chasing the stats, getting the clearance.

He'd only done one though, just the one, just his da's. O'Neill stood up, patting the headstone, pushing it back and forth. It gave a little. He pushed harder, a thought occurring to him: *Tip the fucking thing.* He felt a pair of eyes on him and turned. Five hundred yards away, at the office door, the man was watching him under the pretence of a cigarette.

O'Neill looked down at the gravestone, cocking his head.

At the office door, the old man sucked on his cigarette, watching O'Neill walk back towards him. As he neared the car park, the drizzle turned to rain, harder, heavier, more intense. O'Neill put his head down, running the last few yards to the car.

From inside, he looked out across Roselawn, across the rows of headstones, at the corner, his da, Marty's da.

Finally, he turned the ignition, put the car in gear and headed back toward Musgrave Street.